Likely Suspects

An Alexis Parker novel

G.K. Parks

Copyright © 2017 G.K. Parks

A Modus Operandi imprint

All rights reserved.

ISBN: 0989195805
ISBN-13: 978-0-9891958-0-5

For Rosie, you inspired my love of books and gave me the means to follow my dream. I am eternally grateful.

BOOKS IN THE LIV DEMARCO SERIES

Dangerous Stakes
Operation Stakeout
Unforeseen Danger
Deadly Dealings

BOOKS IN THE ALEXIS PARKER SERIES:

Outcomes and Perspective
Likely Suspects
The Warhol Incident
Mimicry of Banshees
Suspicion of Murder
Racing Through Darkness
Camels and Corpses
Lack of Jurisdiction
Dying for a Fix
Intended Target
Muffled Echoes
Crisis of Conscience
Misplaced Trust
Whitewashed Lies
On Tilt
Purview of Flashbulbs
The Long Game

BOOKS IN THE JULIAN MERCER SERIES:

Condemned
Betrayal
Subversion
Reparation
Retaliation

ONE

"Yes, I'm Alexis Parker. Pleased to meet you." I extended my hand and watched my reflection in the mirror. To say I was nervous for my interview was an understatement. After turning in my letter of resignation to the Office of International Operations, I hadn't been able to get so much as a call back from anywhere else, despite the dozens of applications I submitted. I wasn't ready to admit my leaving the OIO was a bad idea; the job required too much bureaucracy and red-tape for my liking.

I had spent four years of my life working investigations, chasing art thieves and smugglers, and I had nothing to show for it except a fairly sparse résumé and a meritorious service award. I sighed and continued to get ready, straightening my long brown hair and putting on the proper amount of makeup to look professional and serious without being over the top. I didn't want the guys at the Martin Technologies security office to confuse me with either a clown or a call girl.

I'm twenty-nine, single, and unemployed. *Who wouldn't want to hire me*, I thought bitterly, *especially when I'm such a great catch?* The truth of the matter is I always had what one would have considered a bright future. I'm fairly intelligent, well-educated, and decent enough looking. The problem is I lost my focus and drive to stick with one thing, which would probably explain my current lack of employment.

Before I could continue farther down the path of figuring out how my life had gotten so derailed and my internal thought processes could reach the combustible point, my cell phone vibrated across the vanity. I flipped off the flat iron and looked at the caller ID. Taking a deep breath, I hit answer, fearing my scheduled interview had been a clerical error.

"Hello?" I said, fumbling with the now unplugged flat iron I was trying to wrestle into the bathroom cabinet.

"Ms. Parker, please," the woman on the other end sounded annoyed.

"This is Alexis Parker." Two could play at this game.

"Ms. Parker, I am calling on behalf of the Board of Supervisors at Martin Technologies regarding your nine a.m. interview. Mr. Martin would like to be privy to the interviewing process, and he requests we move your interview to," the voice paused, as if rereading a memo to make sure the details were accurate, "10:15 today."

"That's fine." I was relieved my interview had only been rescheduled and not canceled.

"Okay. I will update the security office in the lobby to be prepared for your arrival at 10:15 instead of nine. Do be prompt. Mr. Martin does not like to be kept waiting." And with that, she hung up.

"Nice talking to you, too." I hit end call, wishing this was a landline so I could have slammed the receiver down. I took another breath and looked in the mirror. I was an experienced and capable investigator. I should be able to handle some security consulting work for a corporation, I tried to reassure myself.

At 9:30, I walked out my front door with my résumé and copies of my degrees in hand. What else would Mr. Martin of Martin Technologies need in order to properly assess my qualifications for the job? A certified copy of my birth certificate, a blood sample, and maybe my last will and testament? Perhaps these were just details the woman who called this morning had failed to mention during our brief conversation.

During the drive, I thought about how I had come to apply for the job at Martin Technologies in the first place. Mark Jablonsky had put in a good word with Mr. Martin, the company's founder and CEO. Mark had been my training officer at the OIO and insisted this potential opportunity would fit my personality and interests like a glove.

Mark and Mr. Martin were friends or colleagues of some sort. The actual connection was still a mystery, but Mark assured me I would at least get a chance to interview based on his recommendation alone. Initially, I resisted, thinking this was just another sign of quasi-nepotism, or at the least favoritism, running rampant in the workplace. However, after several weeks and no other job offers, I figured what the hell. It was at least worth looking into.

I pulled into the parking garage and checked my reflection once more in the rearview mirror. My nerves were getting the best of me. It was amusing to think I had been less anxious chasing armed thugs through the streets than I was going into an interview. There was something a little off inside my brain, and I suspected I was never properly socialized.

"Here goes nothing." I tried to bolster my confidence as I hurried to the MT building and pulled on the monogrammed brass door handle.

Entering the lobby, I was amazed at how open and airy the room felt. Light was filtering in from all sides. The security office was a circular desk, set about twenty feet away from the front doors. There were a few couches throughout and a row of elevators at the back of the building. It looked like a classy hotel, but as I approached the security station, I noticed numerous surveillance cameras, keypads, and other protocols in place.

"Can I assist you, ma'am?" one of the security guards asked from behind the desk.

"Miss Parker," I corrected automatically. I hated being called ma'am. That one word triggered too many bad memories. "I'm here to interview for the consulting position with Mr. Martin."

The security guard smiled and asked to see my driver's license, so I pulled out my wallet and handed it to him.

"Right this way, please."

He went to a filing cabinet, pulled out a visitor's pass, handed it to me, and led the way to the elevator banks. He swiped his security badge through a card reader and pressed the elevator call button. The elevator dinged, and the doors whooshed open. We stepped inside. He pushed seventeen, and up we went.

We exited into a hallway lined with lavish offices and conference rooms. The guard escorted me to conference room three and gestured inside. "Please wait here." Before I could say a word, he was gone.

"Friendly group of people," I muttered, taking a seat in one of the rolling office chairs surrounding the large rectangular table. I opened my bag, pulled out my documents, and placed them neatly on the table. I was fidgeting with the corner of the stack of papers when I heard footsteps.

"Hello," a woman's voice greeted. I spun around in my chair. "I'm Mrs. Griffin. I believe we spoke earlier on the telephone. You're here for the consulting position, correct?" I nodded and bit my tongue, ignoring the urge to mention her rude hang up from earlier. "I see you arrived with no issues. That's a good sign." She appeared to be speaking to herself, so I continued to nod, unsure how to respond to her odd comments. "Mr. Martin shall be in momentarily. Can I get you anything while you wait? Tea? Coffee? Water?"

"No, thank you. I'm fine." I couldn't get an accurate read on the woman, and before I could, she walked swiftly out of the room and closed the door behind her. I took a deep breath. The Martin Tech employees must be trying to perfect their disappearing acts.

Before I could muse much further, the door opened again. This time, a man in a three-piece Armani suit and Rolex walked through the door. If given the opportunity, I would have bet his shoes were Italian leather. His dark brown hair was cut short and expertly styled. He had the lean athletic build of a runner, probably in his mid-thirties, and his green eyes sparkled, indicating the wheels were already turning inside his head.

"James Martin." He extended his hand.

"Alexis Parker," I responded. "Pleased to meet you."

He frowned slightly. "To be perfectly honest, Miss Parker, I expected you to be male." I looked at him, unclear if this was an insult or flattery, but instead, it just seemed to be a comment. "My assistant wrote this appointment down as Alex Parker."

"Well, I don't plan to have any gender reassignment surgeries in the near future, but feel free to call me Alex. Most people do."

He smirked slightly but remained professional. I was quickly beginning to feel like a child sitting in the principal's office. "Miss Parker, you come highly recommended by Agent Jablonsky. He was your supervisor at the OIO, correct?"

"That's right." I sat up a little straighter. Despite the fact I had only stayed at the Office of International Operations for four years, I had spent the first two being trained by Mark and the second two running operations for him.

"Jablonsky claims you were one of the best and brightest agents he's ever seen, but you only stayed at that job a few years. Why is that?"

"Well," I honestly didn't know how to verbalize the answer succinctly, "I wanted to make more of a difference, and with an endless string of crime, things started to feel hopeless. The work became monotonous." I struggled to find the proper terminology to explain my feelings.

"So, you don't like structure or rules?" He stood and began to pace, clasping his hands behind his back.

"I'm okay with rules and following orders. To be perfectly honest, I'm not too fond of the red-tape, especially when I continued to see the same injustices day in and day out and knew my hands were tied. It made it difficult to accept the small wins in regards to the bigger picture."

"So you want to be a superhero out to save the world? A vigilante?"

"No." Was this a trial instead of an interview? "I want to step back and do something more impactful." The voice in my head screamed kiss this job good-bye, working for a company isn't what really counts, and Mr. Armani Suit should realize it by now.

However, to my surprise, Martin clapped his hands together. "Exactly." He was actually excited by my response, and I wondered if he had multiple personalities or suffered from an extreme mood swing disorder. He gave the briefest smile, or at least I thought he did because it appeared and disappeared so quickly I couldn't be sure. He looked down at his watch. "It's almost eleven. I have some business to attend to, but if you can have the assistant copy your documents," he glanced at my pile of papers, "I'll be in touch." He left the room and disappeared down the hall.

I sat there absolutely stunned. What just happened? I had the urge to pinch myself to see if I was dreaming, but before I could implement such actions, Mrs. Griffin appeared in the doorway.

"Follow me this way." She proceeded back into the corridor, and I hurried after her. Her office was situated next to the conference room, and inside, she copied my résumé and walked me to the elevator. "Someone from Martin Technologies will be in touch with you shortly."

"Thanks," I said, still somewhat dazed by the whirlwind interview.

The door to the elevator opened, and the security guard from earlier was waiting inside. We rode the elevator back to the lobby in silence, but as the doors whooshed open, he turned to me. "Badge, please," he said politely, and I handed him the visitor's pass. "I hope your interview went well."

"Thank you."

Once I got in my car, I pulled my cell phone from my purse and dialed Mark's home number. I knew he'd be at work right now, so I left a message on his answering machine. "What have you gotten me into this time?"

TWO

What a strange day, I thought as I rifled through the freezer looking for something to make for dinner. I had gotten home so incredibly baffled by the interview at Martin Technologies that I had put on my sweats and gone for a nice long run to clear my head, followed by a second shower for the day, and a nap. When in doubt, nap. This had become my philosophy as of late and continued to work fairly well. Perhaps I should write a book on the art of napping since I didn't see why anyone at Martin Technologies would actually want to hire me. Not to mention, I wasn't even sure if I wanted to work for someone who seemed to have a few screws loose.

"Ah ha!" I exclaimed, pulling out a microwavable dinner which had been buried under a pint of chocolate ice cream and a bag of peas. "Dinner is served."

I scanned the carton for an expiration date and cooking directions and checked the time. It was almost eight. Napping had a habit of making the day fly by; maybe that should be the title of my first chapter. Just as I popped holes in the plastic wrap, the phone rang.

"Hello?"

"Get dressed," a male voice I didn't recognize responded.

"Excuse me?"

"Semi-formal for dinner. There is a car downstairs to pick you up."

I pulled the receiver away from my ear to check the caller ID, but it only listed 'private' as the source of the call.

"All part of the interviewing process, Alex."

"Mr. Martin?"

"Of course." He paused. "Why? Are you interviewing elsewhere?"

"Can you ask the driver to wait? I'll be ready in ten minutes, or I can drive myself if you tell me where to meet you." I ignored his other question since jobs were like dates. I didn't want to appear too eager or too available, but at the same time, I didn't want to seem overly aloof or uninterested.

"Nonsense, why waste a perfectly good, chauffeured town car? The driver will wait until you are ready. No rush."

I tossed the frozen dinner into the trashcan and headed for the bedroom. Who uses a surprise dinner as an interviewing technique? I pondered this while rummaging through my closet, trying to find something semi-formal to wear. Settling on a black skirt, lavender blouse, and a black blazer, I put my hair in a ponytail and slipped on some open-toed pumps. *This better suffice*, I thought as I quickly put on some eyeliner and lip gloss, grabbed my purse, and headed for the door.

As I exited my apartment building, I spotted a black town car parked in the fire zone. James Martin was leaning against the back door with his arms crossed, chatting with the driver.

"Stunning." Martin smiled, and I blushed, despite my better judgment. He glanced at his watch. "And accurate too. It's only been eleven minutes."

"I try to be punctual." The driver opened the rear door, and I got into the car. "I didn't realize you were waiting outside my apartment, Mr. Martin," I said, implying the creepy nature of his sudden appearance, but he didn't seem to catch on.

"Please, it's no longer office hours, so it's James."

"Okay, James. Pardon me for being so blunt, but why the surprise dinner? If you wanted to continue the interview, you could have said so this morning or had your assistant notify me." Before I could continue explaining how his actions could seem a little stalker-like, he interjected.

"I like to see how potential employees react under surprise conditions. Based on your previous employment with ol' Jabber, I know you can handle stressful, volatile situations, so I wanted to see how you handle yourself during overly civilized functions." He grimaced slightly at the overly civilized.

"I see," I said, even though I didn't. "How am I doing so far?"

"So far, so good, but the night is still young." He might have winked, or it was just a trick of the lights.

For the rest of the drive to the restaurant, he asked questions about my background and experiences with ol' Jabber, which was his nickname for Mark. I answered easily and wished my morning interview had been this simplistic, without the interrogation. The driver pulled to a stop at an expensive looking French restaurant I had never heard of. The valet opened my door, and I stepped out. Mr. Martin, or James as I was supposed to call him this evening, came around to my side of the car and offered his arm.

"Shall we?" he asked politely.

This high-class scenario was probably to see how well his potential new security consultant could blend in with the hoity-toity aspects of his life, so I tentatively looped my hand through his arm.

"I guess so." The familiar nervous pang resonated in the pit of my stomach, and arm in arm, we entered the building.

The interior was decorated extensively in crystal and glass fixtures. The dining room was comprised of less than two dozen tables situated in concentric half circles with a waterfall cascading behind the back of the bar. The bar stood against the far wall, completing the space the half circle of tables had left bare. To say the décor was exquisite would be an understatement. The maitre d' greeted us immediately.

"Mr. Martin, it's so nice to see you again. Would you care for your usual table?" she asked, her expression and body language indicating she'd seen him without his clothes on in the not too distant past.

"If it's not any trouble," he replied, oblivious to her smile. "But we will need another chair. There is a third party joining us this evening."

I looked at him quizzically as we were escorted to a table near the back of the restaurant where we could gaze directly at the waterfall fixture and watch the bartender mix drinks. Once seated and situated with our beverage orders and menus, I turned to Martin.

"Is another executive joining us for dinner?" I wanted to know what other obstacles I might be facing tonight.

"No. I just thought Jablonsky could meet us here and praise you in person instead of in these nicely written form letters I keep getting."

I studied my menu to avoid further conversation. I hated interviews; although, if I were being honest, I'd say I wasn't a fan of intimate dinners either. Looks like a lose-lose tonight, Parker.

"Well, if it isn't Marty trying to scoop up the best and brightest yet again," Mark Jablonsky teased as he approached our table and extended his hand to Martin. "How the hell are you, you old son-of-a-gun?"

I looked at my former boss and my potential new employer. Since when did we transport back to the 1950s when people used phrases like old son-of-a-gun? The terminology didn't faze Martin. He merely stood and shook Mark's hand. The same look of mutual respect reflected on both of their faces despite how incredibly different they seemed.

Mark was older, in his early fifties, with graying light brown hair and a mustache. He had put on a bit of a gut from too many late nights in the surveillance van eating Philly cheese steaks and potato chips, and his suit, regardless of price, always looked as if he slept in it.

The two men sat down, and Mark beamed at me. "You look like a million bucks."

Before I could respond, Martin chimed in. "That goes

without saying, but the better question is does she look like she could protect a million bucks."

"Alexis Parker is one of the most capable people I know. I wouldn't have recommended her otherwise. I know what you need, and she can handle it." Mark picked up his menu to read. "I always tell you if you need proof, test your hypothesis, just like your workers do in the lab."

"Just so we're clear," I piped up; being silent was never my strong suit, "what exactly does this job even entail because security consultant is a vague term?"

Martin turned to me. "Martin Technologies is responsible for the development of many different things from cooking utensils to airplane parts. I personally try to provide more economical and eco-friendly alternatives worldwide, and therefore, I've made quite a few enemies." He paused briefly and picked up his glass. "Recently, there have been death threats, a kidnapping attempt, some manufacturing sabotage, and corporate espionage. I need a new face I can trust to keep an eye on things at work. Not to mention, the Board thinks it might be a good idea to update my personal security, seeing as how I have majority control of the company." He took a sip before continuing with what seemed to be a level of melodrama. "If something happens to me, there could be a coup, stocks could plummet, and the world could explode. You know, things of that sort." Although he attempted to joke, his eyes were as serious as I'd ever seen. Was the great James Martin actually afraid, or was that something else I saw flicker behind his eyes? Anger, perhaps?

Before anything else could be said, the waitress returned to take our orders. I requested a steak with Portobello mushrooms in a cream sauce, as did Mark, while Martin ordered the Chateaubriand. As she walked away, I glanced around the dining room. Most of the tables were empty, which seemed odd since this was an upscale restaurant, and it was early in the evening.

"If you need someone who can do all that, you've found your girl," Mark said, lauding my capabilities.

Martin considered it as he lifted his scotch and slowly swirled the golden brown liquid around the glass. "Perhaps you're right. You've been right so far."

I was about to ask for more job details and what the actual relationship between these two men was when I heard glass shatter. It was a much louder sound than if a waitress had dropped a tray of glasses. This sounded as though a wall of mirrors had simultaneously broken. Turning to the cause of the cacophony, I saw a group of masked gunmen enter the restaurant. The maitre d' was cowering on the floor next to her podium, and the entire glass façade in the foyer was shattered.

"Ladies and gentlemen, if we may have your attention, please," the masked leader bellowed. An older woman sitting on the other side of the restaurant gasped as the men invaded the dining room. "We shall make this as brief and painless as possible. Do not call the cops, and do not use your cell phones. Stay seated and place your valuables in the center of the table. This is a robbery."

Martin carefully set his glass on the table and whispered in my ear, "Congratulations, you're hired. Now do something."

THREE

I glanced at Mark to see what he was thinking. More than likely, he had his service piece and a backup with him. I didn't know him to go anywhere without a weapon, OIO policy, but he shook his head. I hadn't been planning to knock over any convenience stores on my way home, so I was also weaponless. Scanning the room, I counted four gunmen. Three entered the main dining hall, and one remained near the entrance. A couple more could be outside, but there was no way to tell for sure.

"I see four," Mark whispered.

I surveyed the rest of the room. Out of the dozen tables, only four were occupied. Two tables of four and two tables with two. Another three patrons sat at the bar, and I spotted a waitress, the bartender, and the maitre d'.

"What are you going to do?" Martin asked. He didn't understand the concept of mortal danger, or maybe after years of running a company he just expected answers and results with the snap of his fingers.

I glared at him. "Stay quiet. Do as they say. And do not draw attention to yourself."

The armed men moved away from the first table and headed around the semicircle. A woman at the next table screamed in horror, and one of the men backhanded her across the cheek, knocking her from the chair.

"Things could get ugly. I think our best bet is to do as

they say and hope they get what they want and go," Mark stated in a hushed tone. I concurred with his assessment, my eyes never leaving the gunmen.

As if on cue, sirens blared in the distance. So much for easy. The gunmen turned to the door, and I grabbed my steak knife off the table and slipped it up my sleeve. Mark did the same. A knife in a gun battle is basically pointless, but it was the only weapon available. It had to be better than nothing.

"What's the layout?" I hurriedly whispered to Martin. "Other exits, bathrooms, windows, the kitchen, anything useful to know?"

"The bathrooms are on the other side of the bar. So is the kitchen. I don't know what's in it since I've never been in there. The bathrooms have barred windows."

I bit my bottom lip and looked to Mark for ideas. Normally, he'd have a solution, but he was useless tonight. He simply shrugged.

The gunmen were getting antsy with the wailing sirens. The one who remained in the foyer yelled orders to the others. "We gotta go. Hurry it up."

The other three seemed distracted, to say the least. They split up, and each headed for one of the remaining tables. The flash of police lights reflected off the shattered glass pebbles on the floor.

"Shit," the head gunman cursed and bolted out the door, abandoning his comrades.

Gunfire erupted, followed by the sound of a bullhorn. "This is the police. The building is surrounded. Drop your weapons, and exit with your hands in the air."

The gunman farthest from our table fired out the front door. "Stay back," he bellowed.

Mark and I exchanged a quick glance. The situation would turn bloody any second, and we no longer had the luxury to wait it out.

"You take two o'clock. I'll get four." I indicated which of the remaining gunmen he should target. It wasn't a great plan, but their backs were to us. In the commotion, it was our best bet.

The third gunman, who had fired at the police, would be

a wildcard, but we would deal with him later. Mark held up his hand, preparing to begin the countdown. We had done this many times before. We knew what to do.

I leaned over next to Martin, practically pressing my lips against his ear. "When we move, get behind the bar, stay low, and don't leave that spot."

Mark silently counted down to three, and we sprang to action. I got behind my gunman. He held the automatic rifle loosely in one arm with his finger resting near the trigger but not on it. He seemed to be a professional or at least had some general gun safety lessons during the course of his lifetime. I came up behind him, knocking his wrist down with my right fist and simultaneously placing the knife against his jugular. His gun clattered loudly to the floor.

"Don't move." I yanked his right arm behind him to control his movements and used his body as a shield. Mark managed to get a similar hold on his gunman, but the third was now facing us with his rifle raised and his finger resting on the trigger.

"What are you?" he asked in a thick Boston-sounding accent. "Cops?" His trigger finger twitched slightly.

By this time, Mark had wrestled his gunman onto the ground and was completely unprotected without a human shield to use as cover. My acuity was skewed as time moved in slow motion. I shoved my gunman hard to the right, toward the foyer, dropped down to his weapon, grabbed it, and fired at the third gunman. I double-tapped the man center mass, and he went down. I turned back just in time to see my discarded human shield running out the door. Mark had his guy face down and was kneeling on his back.

I glanced around the room, making sure there were no other attackers. My adrenaline surged, and I wanted to be certain it was safe before I risked letting my guard down. Slowly, I stepped toward the man I shot when applause erupted from behind the bar. I spun around, gun still poised, to find Martin clapping his hands together.

"Bravo, Miss Parker," he cheered.

"You idiot. I could have shot you."

My nerves were raw. I was completely on edge, and Martin was making himself an easy target. Mark took the rifle from my hands. Why hadn't he gone to the downed man to check to see if he was alive or taken his weapon? Something was wrong. Why weren't the cops rushing in? Protocol required them to breach once shots were fired.

"Don't be mad," Mark said. He went to the downed gunman and offered him a hand. The man took it and stood up. I stared at them, completely bewildered. "They were just blanks," he explained, patting the guy on the chest. "See, he's okay. It was all..."

"A set-up," I finished his sentence and spun around to face Martin. "You set me up. In your screwed up mind, you just see this as another test, don't you?"

Martin, who was pouring himself a drink, spilled it as my volume increased. He decided it was best to ignore me and instead addressed everyone else in the room.

"Good job, everybody," he announced to the restaurant employees, patrons, and gunmen alike. "Thanks for your incredibly convincing performances. Your bonuses will be included in your next paycheck. Have a nice night."

The twenty remaining people in the room all stood, congratulated one another, and walked out the destroyed entryway. The gunman I had fired upon smiled and nodded to indicate no hard feelings, but I ignored him. He took his mask off, and I realized it was the security guard from Martin Technologies. Suddenly, I felt bad for anyone employed by this psychopath. It seemed absurd they were forced to play along in his little make-believe fantasies. I definitely didn't want to be one of those people. I clenched my fists, hoping to stop my hands from shaking. The joys of anger and adrenaline.

"Please, Alex, don't be so dramatic," Martin chided, coming around the bar and sitting on one of the stools. "I like to battle test my employees, and you passed with flying colors."

Mark touched my shoulder. "It's just like training. You've been through worse with my tests."

I looked at Mark. How could he deceive me for the likes of this Armani-clad douchebag? "You son of a bitch," I snarled and walked toward the destroyed front door. Behind me, Martin and Mark tried to determine who I had referred to as the son of a bitch.

As I approached the broken glass at the front of the restaurant, I realized it was an intricately designed front. The shattered glass was comprised of safety glass, which explained the loud shattering noise and the rounded glass pellets. As I carefully walked through the glass pebbles and out into the cool night air, I noticed a few Martin Tech employees packing up a sound system and some lights. The police presence outside had been another ruse elaborately staged by some former AV geeks. They paid no attention to me as they grabbed their equipment and headed for a van with the MT logo painted on the side.

"Dammit," I quietly cursed. It just now dawned on me I had no way of leaving this place, and to make matters even worse, I had no idea exactly where we were, anyway. If I had my car, I'd drive around until I found something familiar; instead, I was out in the middle of who knows where with no way to leave. Perhaps hitchhiking wouldn't be a bad idea. I could always go back inside and demand that Mark take me home, but I didn't want to see his face or hear his rationalizations right now, nor did I want to deal with James Martin at the moment either. My anger needed to seethe a little longer.

The group of Martin Tech employees quickly vacated the premises, and I watched the AV guys drive away. The only vehicles left were the town car and an old beat-up sedan. I was debating if I should ask the driver of the car to take me home when I heard a voice from behind.

"Hey, I am really sorry about this." I expected those words to come from Mark or even Martin, which is what I settled on calling him with or without a few adjectives and expletives surrounding his name; however, the voice didn't belong to either. It was the security guard/gunman. The Boston-like accent was gone, replaced with his normal speech pattern. "Mr. Martin has had us re-enact this scenario four times. So far, you're the only one who shot me." He grinned. Apparently being fake shot was an exciting prospect.

"Sorry about that," I said noncommittally, noticing my hands were still shaking from the leftover adrenaline.

"Want to sit down?" He perched on top of a low-lying retaining wall, and I took a seat next to him. "I'm Jeffrey, by the way. Jeffrey Myers."

"Alexis," I offered lamely. We sat in an uncomfortable silence for a few moments.

"So," we both began at once, and he laughed.

"Ladies first."

"I was going to apologize for coming off like a complete bitch, especially in there. It's just... I'm applying for this job, and your boss is a lunatic. How can you stand to work for him? The interview this morning was strange enough and now this elaborate fake robbery or hostage situation or whatever it was supposed to be. I don't get it, and I'm stuck here with no way to leave." I trailed off, my mind reeling. I knew I needed to shut up, but it was nice getting to talk to someone who might understand.

Jeffrey smiled. "I know what you mean. Mr. Martin can be a handful sometimes. He's a bit eccentric, but it might be because he's just so freaking smart. His brain is moving too fast for most of us to catch on, and once we do, he's five steps ahead again. I think he means well, though. And he really does need an upgrade on his security. He's been getting a lot of serious threats lately, and things within the company aren't going so well. I don't think he would have gone through all this," he gestured to the building behind us, "if he didn't seriously want to test your skills to see how well you could handle things."

I looked at him suspiciously. "How much extra are you getting paid to feed me the company line?"

"An extra fifty for trying. A hundred if it works."

"At least you're honest. I'll give you that much." I stood and looked back at the front entrance. Mark was standing near the door looking sheepish. "Jeffrey, your acting isn't completely convincing, and the accent definitely needs work. But perhaps you should still consider quitting your day job." I began to walk away.

"Perhaps you should consider signing on to my day job. Where else can you have this much fun?"

I turned and gave him my best 'you've got to be kidding' look before continuing to Mark. I stood in front of him, my hands on my hips. I felt like a petulant five-year-old who was upset by a practical joke, but the practical joke could have been life or death. He should know better than to do something this stupid.

"I knew you could handle it," he said in an almost reverent tone.

"What would have happened if I cut that guy's throat? Or thrown the knife at Jeffrey? Stabbed someone in the femoral artery?" My volume remained low, but I was still rather irate.

"That's not you. That's not how you work, and that's not the way I trained you," he said, as if this were explanation enough, but he spoke the truth. I didn't like lethal force unless it was absolutely necessary. Taking a life was not something I wanted to do if it could be avoided.

"Next time, I'll just stab you with the knife and let the attackers deal with your howls of pain while I escape out the back," I retorted.

"At least you've already come up with a plan for next time." He grinned, but the serious demeanor quickly returned. "Does that mean there's going to be a next time? Are you taking this job?" I looked him directly in the eyes. "James needs you on this. Honestly, I don't know if he'll make it without you. I'm moonlighting as much as I can, but you know how it goes."

I gritted my teeth, doing my best to stop any response from coming out of my mouth because I didn't want to say yes, but I wasn't sure I could say no to Mark. I owed him a lot. Despite all the shit he just put me through, he was always on the level when it counted.

"What is he to you?" I asked.

Mark got a far off look in his eye, as if he were seeing somewhere else entirely. "Let's just say I owe him my ass. When I needed an escape route, he provided one, even when our own guys couldn't." He swallowed uneasily. That was not the answer I was looking for, but now wasn't the right time to press the matter. If James Martin had Mark's back, it would have to be enough for me.

Over Mark's shoulder, I caught sight of Martin approaching the entrance. "We'll see about the job," I said, locking eyes with Martin.

FOUR

Martin slowly approached us. I would like to believe he was afraid I'd attack him. Realistically, he was probably trying to make sure he didn't trip on the glass pebbles scattered about. In his left hand, he held a drink, and in his right, he carried my purse. In all the commotion, I completely forgot about it. Clearly, I'm not the girly girl type.

"I thought you could use this," he said, stepping out the front door. I reached for my purse, but he put the drink in my hand. I looked at him confused. "The drink, not the bag. Although, I guess you'd probably like to have this back too." I took my purse and then the offered drink, downed it in one gulp, and handed him the empty glass. "Nice," he said appreciatively. He looked at Mark. "Are we all settled here?"

I interrupted. "First, I would like an apology. Second, I hope this never happens again because frankly, given your problems, you can't afford to be the boy who cried wolf." It was his turn to interrupt.

"Fair enough. I'm sorry for the charade, Alex. But honestly, how could I have seen your actual field reaction if you had known what was going to happen? Think of it as a pop quiz. I believe you got an A." He attempted a charming smile, but I remained impassive. He looked to Mark for help, but Mark kept his mouth shut. "Fine. What can I do to fix this? You want a raise? We haven't even discussed your salary yet, so that might be a bit premature. You don't even know how much you're making, anyway."

"I never agreed to take the job, Mr. Martin."

"Please, it's James." The damn smile appeared again.

"Mr. Martin," I emphasized, "I would appreciate some honesty. I need to know exactly what it is you expect, and what it is you need. Mark is going to help you explain it." I looked at Mark; obviously, he was wrong to think he was in the clear. "Then afterward, we can discuss if I'd be willing to help you with said problems." I paused, looking sternly at both men, but before I could continue, my stomach growled audibly.

"How about we get some actual dinner and then discuss things?" Martin's grin was gone, replaced by something real. He was no longer the smooth-talking businessman or the perpetual showman but an actual person dealing with a crisis.

"Okay. We'll try this again, but this is it. Everything better be on the level from here on out. I'm not doing this anymore." I gestured to the destroyed building.

"You got it," he promised, waving for the driver to bring the car around.

*   *   *

On our way to Martin's compound, we stopped at a drive-thru for cheeseburgers, fries, and colas. Despite Martin's affluence, he seemed very down to earth devouring his fast food directly from the brown paper bag. I was in no position to criticize; I licked the sauce off the wrapper when I finished eating. Shooting fake gunmen definitely increased my appetite. Hopefully, this wouldn't be an everyday occurrence, or I'd have to go on a strict diet in a few weeks.

The three of us settled into Martin's home office to discuss the threats leveled against him. I was trying to hash out the finer points on how my new job was supposed to investigate and remedy the situation, but little progress had yet to be made.

Martin had received half a dozen threatening letters that Mark had taken to the OIO to run for prints and DNA to see if the sender could be identified through forensic means. This turned out to be fruitless. Along with these death threats, Martin also received some menacing phone calls. A kidnapping attempt had occurred a few weeks back when he was on his way home from the office, and soon after, there had been some low-level sabotage at his manufacturing plant.

"Who have you pissed off lately?" I asked, skimming the file Mark had comprised.

"Besides you?" Martin asked innocently, and I gave him a look.

"Yes. Besides me." My tone conveyed annoyance, but he ignored it.

"No one really stands out. People are always pissed about something though. I develop a new eco-friendly product, and my less eco-friendly competitors take issue. If I win a government or private contract over a competitor, I make an enemy. But this is just the nature of business. It shouldn't be a matter of life or death."

"Money rules everything," Mark piped up. "You know this, Marty. You've been on the other side of this before. Hell, look at all those Wall Street types who took a header out the window when the market crashed. Sometimes people can't see the forest for the trees, or sometimes they feel there isn't anything else they can do. Greed, it's all-consuming."

Martin nodded, but his mind was elsewhere.

"Anyone on a personal level you've screwed?" I inquired. "Not just literally, figuratively too, in case you needed some clarification."

"Well, I don't think there were any displeased parties," he scratched his head, "definitely not in the literal sense, anyway."

"Look, if you aren't going to cooperate, it's going to make it difficult to figure out who's got it in for you." I was getting agitated with his less than helpful responses.

Mark tried to break the tension. "I'm going to get a drink, anyone else?"

"Ooh, I've got a bottle of champagne I've been saving for just the right occasion. I think we should toast to Alex's new job." Martin went to retrieve three champagne flutes and the bottle, and I looked at Mark.

"Really, you think that's helpful?" I asked sarcastically. This night had been one irritation after another, and I was tired of it all. I didn't think adding more alcohol to the mix would improve our productivity. It was like pulling teeth to try to get a straight answer out of Martin, let alone the fact we had yet to even discuss exactly what it was he wanted me to do.

Earlier, it was decided it'd be best to first figure out where the threats were focused and then determine the best way to improve his security, instead of defining my job role and then discussing his problem. However, there had been minimal helpful discussions about anything so far.

Mark shrugged. "Look, I've been talking to Marty about this situation since it began five weeks ago. It started with a letter, which isn't at all uncommon, and then it began to escalate. The kidnapping attempt two weeks ago was a high point, and when that failed, there was the sabotage at his plant. It seems business related, but as we both know, not everyone can separate business from personal."

"So, we have to check everything out," I concluded.

"Okay, Jabber's made up a file of all the relevant information I think you'll need," Martin said, pouring champagne into a flute and handing it to me.

I placed the glass on the table and reached for the file instead. While I read, Martin finished pouring and settled onto the couch. Thankfully, he remained quiet as I perused the notes. "Okay." It had been about ten minutes, but I was caught up. Mark and Martin were on their second glass of champagne at this point. "What exactly do you want me to do?"

"Well, you could start by tasting the champagne." Martin eyed my untouched glass.

"Bubbles freak me out." Sarcasm was just as good a response as any. "What is it you want from your security consultant?" I tried again.

"Do you think I need a security consultant?" he asked seriously, and I stared at him as if he had just grown a third arm. "I mean, do I need you to consult, or do I need something more?"

I rubbed my eyes. Could he really be this irksome and unstable? "As a consultant, I can recommend improvements to your current security measures, what works, what doesn't. I thought that was something your Board of Supervisors required."

"Yes and no. They want my personal security updated," he corrected.

"As a security consultant, I can make recommendations to your home security system and personal activities. What else would you need?"

He grinned. If something cheeky came out of his mouth, I would throw my champagne in his face, but he surprised me. "I think an undercover spy or... a mole... or I don't know... something along those lines would be helpful, especially at work." He had watched one too many bad spy movies.

"That might be a good idea," Mark said.

"It won't work," I told them. "At least it won't work if it's me. People at Martin Tech know I interviewed for a security job. Just think about the twenty-something people at the restaurant tonight. With water cooler gossip, it's not a practical idea. You can hire someone else for that purpose, but it has to be kept quiet. No one can know anything about it, and the hiring would need to be under the guise of new office assistant or something similarly innocuous."

"Good point," Mark agreed. "Maybe it's something to consider though. You could always add another person to the mix, Marty."

Martin shook his head. "No. It took long enough to find Alex. We'll stick with her for now." He turned to me. "You can start tomorrow. Come in, get acquainted with people, and see how things work. I'll get you set up as a new consultant, office and everything. I'll leave out the security part and make sure you have access to everything from passwords to the employee lounge, and you can start recommending what needs to be fixed or better ways to make the office safer."

"Okay." We were finally getting somewhere.

Martin held up his hand before I could say anything else. "All the," he paused, searching for the right word, "attacks have been office related. My guess is this is where you'll need to start. After you get comfortable there, we'll expand, and you can start checking out my security here. Maybe see how to improve things. Think you can handle it?"

"Yes, sir. I believe I can." Apparently, my formal OIO training had a bad habit of kicking in at the oddest times.

"Good. Very good." He picked up his champagne flute. "Congratulations on your new job, Miss Parker," he toasted, and I relented and clinked my glass against his.

"Remember, we still need to discuss my salary. Didn't you mention something about a raise?" I quipped, and he got a slightly devilish glint in his eye.

Mark stood up. "I think this is my cue to leave." He gave me a quick hug. "Keep in mind, greed is bad. We discussed it earlier."

"Yeah, and setting up your old friend in a fake crisis situation is worse."

"Marty, it's been fun. Is Marcal still on duty? Figured I could use a lift back to my car."

"No, I let him go home after he dropped us off. Just take the Jag. I'll send someone to pick it up tomorrow." Martin pointed to a set of car keys sitting on the kitchen counter.

Mark thanked him and grabbed the keys. "Always a pleasure," he said to no one in particular and walked out the door.

"You got a second spare car you're going to lend me for the night?" I asked, and he grinned.

"Why? You don't want to stay? I'll cook breakfast in the morning, and I make a killer omelet."

I ignored him. That was one thing I was learning quickly, not to take his teasing, retorts, or double entendres seriously.

He seemed saddened by the lack of verbal sparring, but he continued back on topic. "Okay, I'll pay you this. Half to start and the other half when the job is over." He wrote down a number and slid the paper across the coffee table. "And when you figure out and stop whoever is behind this misery I've been subjected to, I'll give you a five thousand dollar bonus."

"Really? Your life is only worth five grand?"

"Remember, greed is not good, despite what movies might want us to think."

"Says the millionaire in the room." I picked up the paper. Holy shit, those were quite a few zeroes. Hopefully, my eyes didn't reflect my amazement. He assessed me carefully, perhaps suspecting I would faint or rip my clothes off at his generous offer. I somehow managed to resist doing either. "How long do you think this will take?" Was payment supposed to be for a year or a week's worth of work?

"I don't know. Mark thinks you're good at this sort of thing, so I wouldn't imagine too long. At least, I hope not. I'd like to get back to my life without looking over my shoulder. Although, I wouldn't mind having you around for quite some time." He was being somewhat lecherous, but I chose to overlook it.

"To the new job." We clinked our glasses together again.

FIVE

I was dressed and drinking a cup of coffee at my kitchen counter. I looked at the clock on the microwave. The only seven o'clock that should exist ought to be followed by a p.m. It had been a while since I had a job and an even longer while since I had one that required being up in the morning. This would take some getting used to. Good thing someone at some point had decided to run boiling water over processed beans to create a liquid of the gods. I took another sip.

"Let's kick some ass," I said to my empty kitchen, trying to psych myself up for the day. I poured the rest of my coffee into a travel mug, grabbed my belongings, and headed out the door. The drive to the MT building didn't take quite as long as I thought it would, and I ended up arriving a little early.

"Good morning," Jeffrey greeted.

I wanted to downplay the events of last night as much as possible. "Hello," I mumbled, looking around. No one else was nearby. The other security guards were nowhere to be seen. "Do you think we can just not mention yesterday?" I asked, and he agreed.

"Let's get you set up with your permanent security pass." He pointed to a chair behind which was a generic blue screen, reminiscent of the DMV. I sat down. "Smile," he urged, clicking the shutter on the camera, and my picture instantly appeared on a computer monitor. "Look good?"

I glanced at it. "Sure." It didn't matter since it was only for a security pass.

"Okay. I'll be right back." He gestured for another one of the security guards to watch the front door while he went to a small office at the back of the lobby. He entered a number on the keypad and walked into the room. A few minutes later, he returned with my freshly minted ID. "Here you go."

"Thanks." I was about to ask if he had any instructions on where I was supposed to go when a familiar voice sounded from behind.

"Ms. Parker, right this way." The voice belonged to the assistant, Mrs. Griffin, whom I had met yesterday. We went to the elevator banks, and she pressed the button. "Mr. Martin is waiting for you in his office."

We rode up in silence, and she walked me to his door and knocked, which seemed a little ridiculous since his office was a large and spacious room with a glass wall. He had already seen us coming down the hallway.

"Enter," Martin replied. She opened the door and held it for me. "Thank you, Mrs. Griffin. That will be all." She turned and disappeared down the hallway.

"Nice office. But it doesn't really go with the greed isn't good theory, though," I remarked, surveying the room.

He smirked. "No, but you have to admit, it does buy some nice things." He hit a button on his desk, as if to demonstrate, and the clear glass windows turned opaque.

"Recommendation number one, a glass office is asking for a bullet to the brain."

He seemed to take it under consideration for a moment. "Good thing I had them upgrade to bullet-resistant glass." There was a wet bar in the back corner, a nice view of the city from his floor to ceiling windows, a large mahogany desk complete with computer and other work essentials, a few plush leather couches and mahogany end tables scattered about, and a private lavatory. "Do you like the title they put on your badge?" He pointed to the pass clipped to my suit jacket. I hadn't even bothered to look, so I unclipped it and read my name followed by the words private consultant. "I thought it would probably be a better idea. This way, no one has to know what you're consulting on. Maybe you can blend in better. Make it up as you go along. That sort of thing."

"Good idea. You might also want to suggest to anyone you had at the restaurant last night to keep their mouths shut." I thought about Jeffrey.

"Not to worry, it's already done." He glanced at his watch. "I'll show you to your office, so you can settle in and get the hang of things around here. If you need anything, just ask Mrs. Griffin." He hit the button, and the opaque glass returned to clear. He held the door for me, and I followed him down the hall and into the next office over. "Here we go." He opened the door. This office was less than half the size of his with a basic desk, table, and small couch set in the corner.

"Figured you'd keep an eye on me?"

"Maybe I thought you'd like to keep an eye on me." He grinned. "Just part of the job description, right?" Before I could respond, he headed out the door. "I have a meeting, but we'll catch up later. I'd like a full report before end of business today."

"And the fun begins." I closed the door and checked to see if it had a lock. It didn't, but I wanted one installed as soon as possible. I didn't need any random people spying on my work.

In the meantime, I rearranged the room, placing the sofa against the side wall and the table next to it. I scooted the desk farther toward the back wall and angled it so it was facing the door but not head-on. I pulled the rolling office chair behind the desk and looked at the computer sitting on top of it. I turned it on, and the MT logo popped up, asking for a username and password. I would need that information before I could start looking around on the MT network.

I made a mental checklist of things I needed: a door lock, computer passwords, and a non-networked laptop, so I could record my personal observations without worry. I rummaged through the desk, checking the three drawers. All of which were empty. There was a small closet on the back wall. Inside was a mop and bucket, an old vacuum cleaner, and an empty box. Clean out janitor's closet, I added to my list. I sat down in the chair, testing out the seat. A coffeepot and a few mugs would be nice, in addition to general office supplies. When I could no longer come up with anything else I needed, I went in search of Griffin to see what I could mark off my list.

Her office was down the hall in the opposite direction, next to Martin's. I suspected this was so he could call her in at a moment's notice to pour him a drink or rub his feet. I knocked on the door, but instead of asking who it was or telling me to come in, she opened the door.

"May I help you?" she asked, standing in the doorway. She must have been afraid I was going to steal her office supplies.

"Yes." I felt like a child asking for a new toy. "I was wondering if I could get some basic office supplies, pens, paper, paperclips," I paused, "a stapler in case I want to get really crazy and end it all." She didn't seem amused by my joking. She nodded her head, so I continued. "I'm also going to need a username and password to access the computer and a lock put on my door."

"Key or keypad?" She was all business and very serious about her job.

I contemplated the implications of each. "Um...key," I decided since it would be easier to detect if someone broke into my office the old-fashioned way, by tool marks on the lock, instead of trying to figure out if my office had been hacked.

"I'll call the locksmith. The lock will be installed this afternoon. If you come with me, we can get the office supplies now. I will have to schedule an appointment with IT to set up computer access for you."

I followed her to a storage room. Inside were stacks of legal pads, pens, markers, and the like. She handed me an empty copy paper box and asked if I needed any more assistance.

"I'm good." I had the feeling she couldn't wait to get away from me, or perhaps she just needed to hurry back to guard her paperclips.

"Very well." She went back to her office and shut the door.

After loading up on the essentials, I filled my drawers with supplies, left a legal pad and a couple of pens on top of my desk, and began making notes. On the first sheet of paper, I expanded my mental checklist. On the second sheet, I began writing observations about security implementations and improvements to recommend to Martin. The only thing I had come up with so far was the security officers were too friendly.

I needed to get a hold of an employee manifest to begin cross-referencing names to previous criminal records and see if anyone had reason to hold a grudge. An ex-employee list would be even more helpful. I also needed a floor plan of the building, so I could see how things were laid out and where offices and facilities were located. Just as I was getting ready to ask Griffin if she had a map of the building, there was a knock on my door.

"Come in," I called.

Martin poked his head inside. "How's it coming along?" I told him I needed computer access, employee manifests, and a layout of the building, so he logged onto my computer using his own username and password. "There." He clicked open on a few documents. "That should be everything you need for now. We can work on a more detailed list later. I just had a few minutes in between meetings and thought I'd check on you."

"Thanks," I said, not looking up from the screen.

He was halfway out the door when he paused. "My office, four o'clock, okay?"

"I'll be there." I liked all-business Martin a lot better than after-hours Martin.

I spent the next few hours making lists of employees based on seniority and position within the company. I wasn't sure who should be my main focus; therefore, I listed all one hundred and eighty-two full-time, senior level employees and grouped them from mailroom to controlling officer positions.

I studied the building schematic to get a feel for the layout. This would make it easier to check on different employees and also to scrutinize any security weaknesses in the building. There were seventeen floors, and the top was only occupied by Martin, Griffin, and myself. The rest of the floor was empty conference rooms and extra office space. I'm sure meetings were scheduled here, but as for daily activities, the top floor was the least trafficked and theoretically the safest. Every other floor was divided into departments, such as technical support, consumer hotline, accounting, marketing, and so on. I was drawing my own representation of the building when there was another knock at the door.

"Yes?" I asked, not getting up. The door opened, but there was no other sound. I looked up. "May I help you?"

A timid-looking man stood in the doorway. "I'm here to install the lock," he said, chomping on his bubblegum.

"Go ahead. It won't bother me."

The man got to work and in a few minutes was finished. "You're all set, ma'am." He handed me a key.

"Do I have to sign something, escort you back down, or anything?" I was curious if individuals could just wander around the building if they had the proper credentials.

"No, it's all taken care of. The security guys brought me up here to Mrs. Griffin who signed the work order and then sent me down the hall."

"Okay, thanks." He started to leave. "Is this the only key?" I called after him.

"No, the other one is down at security, in case you get locked out."

"Great. I lose things all the time." I tried to sound sincere, but I was unenthused by the fact security likely had keys to every office in the building. It made sense but posed quite a bit of risk for a CEO who was being threatened.

After the locksmith left, I looked at my watch. It was almost four o'clock. Maybe Martin was back in his office. I logged off the computer and took the key to my new lock. I shut the door, made sure it worked properly, and headed across the hallway. Martin's windows were set to clear, and no one was inside. I knocked, although it looked empty, and noticed the door had a keycard mechanism.

"What the hell." I swiped my security badge through the slot to see if I got the all-access, behind-the-scenes pass. Amazingly enough, the door opened. I stood in the doorway, feeling like an intruder. Get over it; you are just checking out his security, remember that. I closed the door and heard the lock click into place. There must be a button at the desk that unlocked the door for any outside visitor who could easily be seen through the glass. Maybe the security protocols were better than I expected. I walked the length of the room and decided to check out the lavatory. It was small and windowless with a sink, washbasin, and toilet. Nothing too fancy. Just as I was getting ready to leave, Martin walked in.

"Making yourself at home?" He went to the wet bar and poured a drink. He reached for a second glass, but I shook my head.

"I'm beginning to think your liver is probably the only thing in danger in this building."

He laughed. "Well, it is five o'clock somewhere. Plus, I'm done for the day. I figured we could discuss what you've learned so far and take it from there."

"Okay, let me grab my notes and belongings. I'll be right back." I was out the door before he could reply.

SIX

I collected my notes and the rest of my things, figuring I could leave after my meeting with Martin, locked my door, and headed back into his office. The door was propped open, and he was sitting on the sofa. His suit jacket was folded over the back of the couch, and his tie was undone and hanging around his neck. The first three buttons of his shirt were open, and he had one leg propped on the seat. For a brief moment, I thought I walked into a life-sized ad for cologne or vodka, but I quickly pushed the thought out of my head.

"Shut the door," he instructed, swirling the ice cubes around his glass. I kicked the doorstop out of the way and placed my belongings on one of the mahogany tables. "Come, sit down." He indicated the other end of the couch, and I sat primly. "You know you can relax. I won't bite," he grinned mischievously, "well, unless you ask nicely."

"Mr. Martin," I began, disregarding his playboy demeanor, "shall we get on with it?"

He cocked an eyebrow up. "Most definitely."

I regretted my wording but continued anyway. I told him what I had noticed about this floor, the security in his office, how I would need to run more extensive background checks on the employees, and that I needed a list of past employees. His green eyes stared intensely as I spoke; it was rather unnerving. When I was finished with my list, he simply nodded.

"Okay, everything seems doable." He smirked at his own

word usage. He glanced out the glass window into the hallway and spotted Griffin leaving her office. He sat up straighter and leaned toward me. "Laugh," he instructed, reaching out and rubbing his thumb across my cheek before tucking my hair gently behind my ear.

I laughed uncomfortably. Now what game was he playing? I noticed out of the corner of my eye Griffin staring at us as she hurried past to the elevator. As soon as she was out of visual range, he leaned back.

"What the hell?" I blurted out, scooting even farther away from him.

"Perpetuating some misinformation. If people think there is something scandalous going on, they won't be too concerned with why you are really here."

"It could backfire, you know."

He waved my warning away. "Trust me. I know how these things work. Gossip mills like juicy stories about private consultants, not new security hires."

"Basically, last night when I told you your idea for an undercover security analyst was a bad idea, you just overlooked that?" Obviously, he was still playing games despite my insistence to be upfront and serious.

"I took it under consideration and then made a unilateral decision. It happens fairly often. You'll get used to it."

I rubbed the bridge of my nose. Any minute the headache would set in. "Fine, we will do it your way." I was tired of arguing. "So, the twenty-something people last night, how much misinformation did you give them?"

"Let's put it this way. You're the only woman who applied for the job, and you got hired. You aren't sitting downstairs in the security office, so maybe it wasn't because of your shooting ability." He cocked an eyebrow up, and I fought the urge to call him a pretentious, chauvinistic pig.

"And of course, you're crazy enough for them to think last night was just you playing an elaborate cops and robbers game for shits and giggles." I was trying very hard not to take things personally or be pissed.

His green eyes brightened. "Exactly."

I wanted to get back to business, so I let it go. His plan did have some merit. Worst case, people would think he hired a security consultant who was also sleeping with the boss, which I wouldn't have minded so much if I weren't the consultant.

We spent the next hour printing out lists of employees, along with blueprints of the building which he kindly marked and labeled based on department and office. I needed to call Mark and see if he could run backgrounds on everyone or give me access to the crime databases so I could do my own checks. I also asked Martin to think of any personal problems or issues with specific employees or departments which might warrant further investigation.

By six o'clock, I was ready to go home. I had more lists and tasks than I cared to think about, and most of these could be done on my own time, away from curious eyes. We rode the elevator down to the lobby together.

"What time does everyone go home?" I asked as the doors dinged open.

"Depends. If we are dealing with foreign business, it might be really late due to time zone differences, but on a normal day, the place is pretty much dead by 4:30. We have a night crew who cleans and provides additional building security. Sometimes we have a stray worker, maybe from marketing or something, working on a presentation or trying to meet a deadline."

"Names would be good."

"I'll have those for you tomorrow," he assured.

"Good evening, sir," a different security guard said as we walked out together.

"Night, Todd," Martin replied, not bothering to glance up. I followed Martin to the parking garage. His car and driver, Marcal, were waiting for him.

"Good night, Miss Parker." He opened the back door. "See you tomorrow."

I headed to my own parked car. I had a lot of work to do. I pulled out my cell phone and called Mark. "Are you still at the office?" I asked when he answered. I didn't feel like exchanging pleasantries. I was tired and still steamed about last night.

"Yeah, why?"

"I'm coming over. See you in a few." I clicked end call and drove to the OIO, figuring we might as well start burning the midnight oil while things were fresh on my mind.

*   *   *

Mark and I sat in his office. He had ordered takeout, and we were surrounded by Chinese food cartons and piles of paperwork.

"You mean to tell me you've already run backgrounds on Martin Tech employees?" I asked around a mouthful of orange chicken.

"Yeah, first thing I did when Marty came to me with the death threats." He put his chopsticks into his carton and rummaged through his notepad, looking for something. "Here." He produced a sheet of paper. "I narrowed the list down to some likely suspects." There were twenty or so names on it.

"Current or past employees?" I skimmed the list, but none of the names stood out. Although after reading almost two hundred employee names earlier in the day, I wasn't sure I would recognize my own name.

"Current. Marty never gave me the list of past employees. I don't think he's much for recordkeeping." Typically, disgruntled past employees posed a threat because current employees didn't want to risk losing their jobs.

"All right, I guess we'll do this the old-fashioned way." I adopted a valley girl accent. "Hi, I'm like totally new here, so I'm going to follow you around and be your friend, and you can tell me like all your deep dark secrets. Have you ever fantasized about the boss or like wanting to kill the boss?"

Mark laughed. "You should work on being a bit more subtle."

"But what fun would that be?" I took a sip of my soda. "How did you determine who made the cut?" I indicated the names on his suspect list.

"Previous criminal records, history of violence, y'know, the usual."

"I thought it was the company line not to profile," I teased, and he rolled his eyes.

"You know, as well as I do, the greatest predictor of committing a future crime is a history of past crimes."

"Wouldn't the company background checks have eliminated ex-cons?" How stringent were Martin Tech's hiring policies and applicant reviews?

"They do a decent job, but some have jackets without convictions. And others might have just slipped through."

"Lovely," I replied sarcastically.

"Honestly, most of this stuff was fairly petty, if I remember right. Minor drug offenses, some domestic disturbances, nothing screamed out conspiracy or murder to me." He flipped through a stack of papers containing a list of offenses by our pool of potential persons of interest.

"Does anyone seem smart enough to pull something like this off?" I asked. "Granted, everything has been unsuccessful so far, so maybe whoever's behind this is stupid or just unlucky."

"I don't know their GPAs or if they are members of MENSA."

"At least it's a start. If anything, it will eliminate some potential suspects." I looked back at the paper. "For my own clarification, are we positive the threats are on the level? Martin is eccentric. Maybe has a few screws loose. Perhaps he missed his meds one day and hallucinated the whole damn thing."

Mark shook his head. "I wish that were the case. It would be a much better alternative. Unfortunately, he's on the level. He might be slightly unorthodox in his methodology, but he's a stand-up guy. Don't let the eccentricity or the playboy act fool you."

"Fine." I tossed my takeout container into the trashcan. "I guess I'll take these," I picked up the list of names and the corresponding files, "and see if I can't narrow this down further."

"Good luck."

"I'm sure I'll need it," I retorted.

SEVEN

The next morning at MT, I moved in some personal effects: a coffeepot, a couple of mugs, a laptop computer, and a side arm and box of ammunition, just the essentials. I was surprised there were no metal detectors to alert security of incoming weaponry, and I made a mental note to discuss this with Martin. Jeffrey greeted me on my way to the elevators, and I slid my ID card through the slot and rode up to the seventeenth floor alone.

I unlocked my office door and placed the box on the table. Shutting the door, I took out the handgun and ammo and stowed them in the top desk drawer, in case I ever needed them. I was just setting up the coffeepot when there was a tap on my door.

"Here's the list you wanted." Martin poked his head in, holding a small phonebook sized sheaf of papers.

I gawked at its magnitude. "You've got to be kidding. This can't be what I asked for."

He entered and closed the door. "That's everyone who has ever been fired, dating back to the beginning. You didn't specify a timeframe, so I figured I'd give you everything." I flipped through the pages. "They're listed chronologically. Hope that helps." He opened the door. "Gotta go, see you later."

"Holy crap." I put the list on my desk with a resounding thud. Mark had obviously been incorrect when it came to assessing Martin's recordkeeping skills. At least it was chronological.

I turned the coffeepot on and sat behind my desk. The ex-employee list dated back a decade. The last two years would be an arbitrarily good starting point, moving from the most recent backward. I knew what Mark and I would be doing tonight. I called and left a voicemail telling him I had the list and would be stopping by after work. As I flipped through the pages from the last two years, I didn't find many names. A few dozen tops. This might be more manageable than I imagined.

Deciding it was best to get better acquainted with the building and the other employees, particularly the ones with criminal records, I double-checked that my consultant badge was clipped on and headed to the elevator. It was time to take a tour.

I spent the entire day snooping around the building. I talked to people from every department. The questions I asked seemed innocent enough, but they served to make me more of an everyday fixture. I wanted the MT employees to be comfortable and accepting of my presence. Infiltrate and gain trust, that was my plan.

Around lunchtime, I located the employee lounge and sat there for four hours. I used a half-eaten candy bar and coffee as cover. It apparently worked since I was greeted by everyone who came in during break. The gossip had already spread about the existence of a new girl working for Mr. Martin, and I was positive Griffin had told everyone about my after-hours exchange with Martin in his office yesterday.

I tried to play the part and questioned my co-workers about their jobs and experiences at the company since I was new and didn't know what to expect. No one had any grudges or serious grievances, or none they were willing to share, but they all seemed particularly interested in me.

"What do you do here?"

"How long have you known Mr. Martin?"

"What department do you work for?"

I kept my answers vague and tried to paint myself as a glorified personal assistant. By the time I left the employee lounge, it was almost four o'clock. It felt like I talked to everyone, or at least the majority of lower-level employees. Unfortunately, none of the board members had shown up in the employee lounge. They must be just as busy as Martin, or they enjoyed staying in their plush offices instead of fraternizing with the help.

Unlocking my office door, I decided to wait for Martin, so we could meet again today. While I was waiting, Mark called back.

"Glad you got the list," he said when I answered.

"Hello to you, too," I teased. "Yeah, it's a fucking phonebook though. I guess we should start with the last two years and see if it leads anywhere."

"Just drop it by, and I'll look into it."

"Okay." Before the conversation could continue, Griffin knocked on my door. "I've got company. I'll see you later." I hung up the phone and smiled at her. "How can I help you?"

I left my door slightly ajar, but when she entered, she shut it behind her. Somehow, I resisted the urge to hide the paperclips.

"I wanted to see how well you're settling in." She looked around nervously.

"Everything's good. People here seem friendly." I tried to make her feel at ease, but it wasn't working.

"I just wanted to tell you to be careful." She paused, unsure if she should continue.

"How so?" I pushed. Maybe she knew something I didn't.

"It's just, you seem like a nice young lady, and I don't want you to get hurt." She briefly contemplated if it was her place to say anything more. "Mr. Martin is a great boss, and he does right by his employees, but I've seen a lot of pretty, young things come and go around here. You don't need to get caught up in that."

"I'm just consulting. There is nothing going on."

"I saw you two yesterday," she insisted. "Do what you like, but," she faltered, "I like my job so don't expect to one day replace me." Before I could respond or ask her to elaborate, she retreated from my office.

Once again, I was alone in an empty room. Maybe

Martin wasn't the only crazy one around here. They really should test for lead paint, radon, or something equally toxic. My musing was cut short when there was yet another knock on my door. At this point, someone should hang a Grand Central Station sign outside my office. Or worse, it could be Griffin coming back with a highlighter to finish me off. Instead, it was Martin.

"Grab your stuff and meet me in my office." He left the door open and walked across the hall to his suite.

I collected my purse and laptop and made sure the top drawer was locked before locking my office too. Martin buzzed me in. He was behind his desk with his jacket off, sleeves rolled up, tie knot hanging loosely, and feet on the tabletop.

"Comfortable?" I asked, putting my belongings down and taking a seat in his client chair.

He considered my question for a moment. "Getting there." He unbuttoned the top button of his shirt. "Yeah, I guess so."

"I just had the strangest conversation with Mrs. Griffin." I filled him in on what transpired.

He placed his fingertips together and tapped his pointer fingers against his chin as he listened. "She's probably afraid you're going to be my new personal assistant. She's been here for years, getting close to retirement age. She probably just thinks you're the newer model."

"Perhaps because you have a reputation for liking newer models."

"It happens, but I'm not as bad as she made it out to be."

Ignoring that comment, I decided it was best to get back to business. I informed him about the lack of metal detectors, the ease of bringing a gun into the building, and also how I was familiarizing myself with the employees. Apparently, I was doing a satisfactory job in his opinion, even though I had no real plan and was running in circles, but at least one of us was pleased with my work. We walked out together as we did the night before.

"Good night, Miss Parker." He climbed into his chauffeured town car.

"Good night, Mr. Martin."

I drove straight to Mark's office and gave him the updated list. There was something going on at the OIO because he accepted it and showed me to the door.

"I will get back to you after I run backgrounds," he promised.

I went home and made dinner and notes about Griffin. I double-checked to make sure she didn't have a criminal record and wasn't connected in any way with anyone on the list who did. Was she actually just looking out for her job and my morality, or could she be part of the threat against Martin? I put the news on and fell asleep halfway through. Getting up early didn't agree with me.

*   *   *

Over the course of the next week, I spent every day trying to get a feel for the employees. I was beginning to be accepted, and I heard gossip about which of the board members were schtupping which secretaries, who was gay and in the closet, and who was hired because she dated someone in human resources. I liked the inclusion, but none of it led anywhere. Griffin was cordial if we bumped into one another in the hallway or the elevator, but she never said another word about the conversation we had.

Martin and I had a ritual of meeting for lunch and grabbing a quick bite from one of the street vendors near the building. We would meet sometime between eleven and noon. We'd grab a bite and talk as we walked to and from the food carts, not about work but just small talk about life in general. He had a little more substance than I originally suspected. These brief rendezvous would last for only ten or fifteen minutes but were enough to further perpetuate the ruse of a budding relationship, especially in front of many curious onlookers. The two of us would meet again at the end of the workday, discuss any important discoveries, and leave together. It probably added to the illusion we were a couple or at least having a clandestine affair. Although, no one ever directly asked about it; maybe decorum wasn't dead.

It was now Thursday, and I had been in Martin's employ for eight days. No more threats had come in, but besides marking some names off the list of potential suspects, no real progress had been made either. Maybe we were looking in the wrong direction, and it wasn't an employee or ex-employee but someone unrelated to his work life. Kidnappings were usually personal, and that could be key to figuring out who was behind this.

Martin knocked on my door. "Ready for lunch?" he asked, glancing at his watch. "I have a meeting at 12:15, so maybe we can just grab whatever's out front."

"Sure." I picked up my purse and locked my office door. I wasn't picky, especially since I spent so much time in the employee lounge. I could get a sandwich or snack out of the vending machines if I wasn't satisfied with our dining option.

"Enjoy your lunch," Jeffrey said as we passed the security office.

We were just exiting the front door when I thought I saw a light glinting off of something from the building across the street. I wasn't sure if I was seeing things or not, but my training kicked in. My brain screamed sniper, and I grabbed Martin's arm and pulled him back through the doorway. I pushed him against the wall and threw myself against him.

"What the—," he exclaimed but didn't get to finish his statement because, at that moment, the hot dog stand parked in front of the building erupted in a sea of flames. I turned my head away as shrapnel from the cart blew everywhere, breaking one of the glass doors to the MT building. Something stung my arm, and I turned to see what had happened.

Outside was pure mayhem. My ears were ringing, but screaming could be heard over the din. I cautiously poked my head around the corner, trying to make out a sniper or more reflective glare, but I didn't see anything. Although, it was hard to see through the smoke and raining debris. I hoped no one was hurt, but I was almost positive the hot dog vendor must be dead, likely incinerated by the explosion. What had caused it? My mind was going in a hundred different directions. *Focus*, I commanded my brain to obey.

"Call 911," Martin yelled to the security guards.

I wanted to go outside to help, but I heard sirens on the way. My first priority was to protect Martin. "We need to get you secured." He seemed to want to argue but saw the look on my face and agreed. "Secure the building," I told Jeffrey, "try not to let anyone in or out. But if you have to let people in, keep them in the lobby. And keep an eye on them. Don't let anyone leave. The cops will want to question everybody."

Martin and I headed for the elevators. Climbing seventeen flights of stairs is never fun, and although protocol and training would dictate to use the stairs in an emergency, I needed to get him away from the danger ASAP. However, I didn't want to risk the elevator stopping on a different floor either. He bypassed the elevator call-stop function, and I pulled out my phone to call Mark. The circuits were temporarily jammed, and I cursed myself for leaving my gun in my desk drawer.

I turned to Martin. "Are you okay? I didn't think to ask. You weren't hit, were you?"

He snorted despite the seriousness of the situation. "No. I'm intact."

"Good." I took a breath. We were getting close to the seventeenth floor. So I pushed him to one side of the elevator, and I stood on the other. When it opened, I cautiously peered out. It was like nothing had happened. "Stay behind me." I went into my office and retrieved my side arm before continuing to his office. Again, I went in first, checking to make sure no one was there. "Privacy windows," I instructed as I searched for armed men in the buildings across the street. "Bullet-resistant glass?"

"Yes."

"Good." I did a quick sweep of the washroom. Then I picked up my phone to call Mark again. This time the call went through.

"I heard. Are you both okay?" Mark responded before I even spoke. The wonders of caller ID. "I'm on my way. Stay put, and don't let anyone in but me or the police."

"We're okay. Waiting for you." I hung up.

"You're bleeding," Martin pointed out as he tenderly touched my arm.

"It's nothing. Although, those bastards owe me a new jacket." I felt trapped, and I didn't like it one bit.

"Come here, and let me see that." He was trying to be helpful. I never pegged him for calm in a crisis situation.

"It's fine."

"It's not fine." He sounded frustrated. "I can't do anything right now, so let me do this." I knew that feeling all too well. I sighed, and he gently took my jacket off. "Apparently, they owe you a shirt, too."

"Lucky me."

He went to the washroom and came back with a wet towel, wiping away the blood from my gash. "You might have a piece of glass in there."

"Leave it. It's not that bad."

He took the towel and tied it around my arm. "There." He felt better having done something, even though it wasn't much of anything.

"Thanks." I scanned the room, still hyper-vigilant. I could have kicked myself for not taking more precautions earlier.

"No, thank you." His voice sounded exceptionally sincere. I looked at him. His bright green eyes stared at me. "If it weren't for you," he hesitated, "you really notice a lot. How did you know?"

"I didn't." It was the truth. "I saw a flash, like from a scope, across the way. I thought a sniper was going to shoot you. I never expected the cart to explode."

I fell silent. Those poor people outside. I shut my eyes for a minute, trying to recall how many were out there. Had there been a line? I couldn't remember.

There was a knock on the door, and I leveled my gun at the sound. "Who is it?" I asked, jerking my head toward the washroom, and Martin took cover inside.

"The big bad wolf," Mark said, followed by the much more serious response of, "police, open up."

I went to Martin's desk and hit the unlock button. My gun remained in my hand. I wasn't positive everyone entering was on our side, and I wanted the opportunity to return fire if need be.

"Ma'am, drop the weapon," were the first words I heard as the door opened.

EIGHT

I laid my gun on the desk and raised my hands in surrender. The group assembled consisted of Jeffrey, Mark, two uniformed officers, and someone else, likely a detective. One of the uniformed cops took my gun off the table and checked to see if it had been fired recently.

Mark just shook his head. "She's one of us."

Martin emerged from the washroom slowly. "Thanks, fellas, for coming down. I hate to put you out." He was being ever cordial. What was his default setting? Businessman?

The cop unloaded my weapon and handed it back to me. I placed it on the desk, seeing no reason to be armed with an unloaded weapon in a room full of policemen.

"What's going on out there?" I asked, unable to wait any longer. I wanted to know what happened.

The uniformed cops kept quiet, letting the detective speak.

"Detective Nick O'Connell." He held out his hand, and we shook. "It's a mess down there. We've got crime scene, arson, bomb squad, fire, paramedics. It's a fucking circus, not sure about the number of casualties yet." Grim news, just what I expected. He shook hands with Martin, too. "Please, make yourselves comfortable. We'll be here a while." More good news. O'Connell noticed my oddly toweled arm. "Would you like a paramedic to take a look?"

"Nah, I'm good. It's just a scratch."

O'Connell looked unsure, as did Mark. I swear men

probably think they need stitches when they get a paper cut.

"You might as well send someone up, just in case," Martin told them, and Jeffrey began to leave the office.

"Jeffrey," my tone was serious, "make sure everyone else is taken care of first before you bring anyone up here. You got that?" I gave him a sharp look, and he nodded.

"So," O'Connell said, trying to rein us in, "I need you to tell me what happened." The two uniforms had their notebooks at the ready, prepared to write down anything we had to say. "May we interview you separately?"

"That's fine." I moved toward the door. "My office is right over there." I exchanged a quick glance with Mark. "Stay with Mr. Martin. He's had a rough afternoon."

Across the hallway, I gave my account of the events from the time we exited the elevator in the lobby until the police came knocking on the door. I left out the previous threats to Martin since I wasn't sure if it was my place to say anything, but the police officer realized there was more to the story.

"Why would you think there was a sniper?" he asked.

I informed him of my background, which I was sure Mark had already done, and told him I was hired to investigate threats and protect Martin. So much for keeping my mouth shut. He took some notes but didn't ask for any details.

"I guess that's pretty much it. Seems like you might have been some kind of hero today."

"I'm just doing my job." I shrugged it off.

When Martin finished answering questions, we went back into his office, and Det. O'Connell questioned the two of us together to cross-check our stories.

"What does the OIO have to do with any of this?" O'Connell asked Mark.

"Officially, nothing. But I've been looking into things for James since he first received the threats."

O'Connell looked at me. "Which explains why you work here, why you noticed the sun reflection, and how you got Mr. Martin out of the way."

"Guess so," I said. "Did you find anything on the other

building? I don't know what I saw, but like I said, I was expecting shots fired, not an explosion."

He hesitated because it wasn't something he should be able to discuss, but I didn't know if he was a bend the rules kind of guy or not. "We'll let you know what we find," he finally decided. He looked at Mark. "We can read your office in, but just remember, this is our show. It's a local crime on local ground. You have no jurisdiction, and I don't want to start a turf war."

"I appreciate the favor," Mark said.

Jeffrey appeared in the doorway with a paramedic. "Is now a good time?"

No one disagreed, so the EMT cleaned my arm, removed a shard of glass, and bandaged the wound. He remained silent since he had already seen way too much today to think of this as anything that needed detailed questions or conversation.

"Well, gentlemen, if that's it, I have a company to run and employees who have been through hell," Martin said.

I was reluctant to let him go anywhere without an armed guard. I was still being hyper-vigilant and felt guilty for not taking the situation more seriously sooner, before things started exploding.

"If you remember anything else or get any more threats, let me know." O'Connell handed Martin his card.

Martin looked at it and put it in his pocket before walking out. I caught Mark's eye and jerked my head in the direction of Martin's fleeing back. Mark got up and followed him out.

I looked at O'Connell. The two uniformed cops had already left. "I know I can't ask anything about this case, but if you had to guess, would you say it's related to his threats?"

"I don't know. What do you think?"

"Coincidences don't happen often. Are you checking into the employees?" I asked.

"You say you understand I can't talk about the case, and yet, you still want to talk about the case. Kinda funny how that works, don't you think?"

"I'm asking about procedure, not the case." I was

splitting hairs, but he let me get away with it.

"We interviewed everyone in the building and everyone outside. We're canvassing the area to see if anyone's seen anything. And don't worry, we will check into what was going on in the other building. If you had to guess, what floor would you say?"

"Maybe seven. I can't be sure."

"It's a start." He handed me his card. "You think of anything else..."

"I'll let you know," I finished for him. He smiled politely and left.

I sat alone in Martin's office. I didn't realize how much time had passed; it might have been a few minutes or a few hours. The floor was dead. *Bad choice of words*, I scolded. Griffin was either hiding somewhere or maybe she left for the day. I wasn't sure. Eventually, Mark and Martin came back to find me in the same spot.

"Are you sure you're all right?" Mark asked, concerned by my lack of movement.

"I'm fine. I was just letting everything seep in." After the initial adrenaline rush had worn off, I had shut down, but they didn't need to know that. "Some coffee would be nice, though."

"I'll go make some," Mark offered. "You have a pot in your office, right?"

I nodded. My door was open since I hadn't bothered to shut it after being questioned.

Martin sat next to me. "Hell of a day. Are you sure you're okay?" He absently brushed his fingers against my bandage.

"I'm fine, just adrenaline crash. Nothing some caffeine can't fix. Are you okay?"

"Thanks to you, but I'm sick of this bullshit."

I was too. Maybe I had signed on to a job I wasn't prepared to handle. All leads had been dead ends, and now we probably had some dead bodies to add to the mix.

Mark returned, balancing three cups of coffee in his two hands. "Here." He handed out the mugs. "I think you need to up your security here and at home. I can have some of my guys keep an eye on things for you. They are always looking for opportunities to moonlight and make a little extra cash."

Martin was going to protest, but before he could say anything, words started pouring out of my mouth without my permission.

"I'll do it," I announced to everyone's surprise, including my own. "If you want, I can stay with you around the clock until we stop the asshole or assholes behind this. You'll probably want to have more security than just me, but…"

Martin cut me off. "Okay." He almost sounded relieved.

Stupid, I screamed at myself. *What in the world are you thinking?*

I looked at him quizzically. "That was too easy? What's your endgame?" I was getting a feel for my boss, and if he was relieved, then he must have planned it all along. I narrowed my eyes at him.

"Well, isn't it just the natural next step for the girlfriend to move in, especially after a life-threatening experience?" he asked innocently.

Mark almost choked on his coffee. I continued to stare at Martin. Was he really this good at manipulation? After Mark recovered from his sputtering coughs, he turned to us.

"Anything you want to tell me, Marty?" he asked.

"You mean besides the fact the whole undercover security idea we agreed was a very bad idea still got enacted?" I asked, recounting how, despite my protestations, Martin still implemented his covert plan with me being the undercover security in spite of my positively overt position at his company, but Martin shushed me.

"It seemed like a good idea at the time," he insisted.

"Too late to back out now," Mark said, "but really, Alex, I thought you had better taste in men."

"What can I say? I must be slumming it with millionaire CEOs." I smiled winningly at Martin. "Darling, if you expect to keep me happy, I could use some diamonds. They are a girl's best friend."

Mark chuckled, and Martin rolled his eyes.

"Guess we should probably be on a first name basis,

sweetheart," Martin replied coolly.

My diamond comment must have struck a nerve, and I acquiesced begrudgingly but only for use in public. The last time I referred to him as James, he staged a fake robbery. "Okay. I guess I'll grab my things and settle in at your place," I said.

We locked up the offices, and the three of us headed downstairs. Police officers were stationed in the lobby, along with MT security personnel. Outside was roped off with crime scene tape, and investigators continued to work the scene. O'Connell stood outside, talking to someone from the bomb squad. I glanced at him as we walked around the crime tape on our way to the parking garage.

"I'll take Marty home," Mark said as we got closer to the garage. "Gather your things and meet us there."

I agreed, and we went our separate ways. *Roommates are always so much fun*, I thought wryly.

NINE

The drive home had been peaceful, but I was beginning to think this was the worst idea I ever had. *Back out now*, the voice in my head kept repeating. I did my best to ignore it and instead grabbed my go-bag, which was already full of a weekend's worth of supplies. Something I learned at the OIO, you could be whisked off at a moment's notice, so always be prepared. I pulled out a suitcase and put more practical items inside: work clothes, a hairdryer, makeup, a side arm, and a box of bullets. Then I unplugged the unnecessary appliances and adjusted the air conditioner, put a timer on the light in the living room, and picked up my gym bag.

With my three bags in hand, I left my apartment for what I hoped would only be a few days. Realistically, I knew it would be a few weeks, at the very least. Our leads in the case were nonexistent. It was time we started overturning different stones or maybe just breaking a few until answers appeared.

I drove to Martin's, enjoying the last few minutes of solitude. Arriving at his compound, I was once again amazed at its magnitude and architectural design. It was a large estate on the outskirts of the city, secluded from passersby and traffic by a hidden private road that led to a long driveway. The building itself was four stories; the bottom consisted of a completely finished garage resembling an expensive car dealership's showroom.

Everything was password and key code access only. I dialed Martin's cell phone.

"I'm outside," I said when he answered. "Can you buzz me in or something?" I needed to further analyze his home security measures, but first, I had to get into the house.

"Sure, south side garage?"

I glanced at the electronic compass on my dash. "I think so." There was a possibility I was directionally challenged.

"Okay, be there in a minute."

The garage door opened, and Marcal directed me into a parking space. Next to the expensive custom cars, my inexpensive subcompact looked painfully pathetic and homely. Marcal came around and opened my door.

"Carry your bags, miss?" he asked in a polite tone.

"That's okay. I can do it." When one is born with a silver spoon in his mouth, like Martin was, it was probably easy to grow accustomed to having help for the simplest tasks, like carrying bags.

Marcal went back to whatever he was doing, probably standing around waiting for someone to need the garage door opened. I felt sorry for the man, but I was sure, despite all of his faults, Martin was very generous in his employees' compensation. He had been with mine.

The door at the top of the staircase opened, and Martin stuck his head into the garage. "Care to join the party, Miss Parker? Alex," he corrected. "That's going to take some getting used to."

"I'm on my way." I headed for the staircase, but to my surprise, he descended the stairs and took the duffel and gym bag from my shoulder and carried them up. I gave him a sideways glance and followed him into the house.

Mark was inside setting up some type of surveillance camera feed on a monitor, and he waved in my general direction, never looking up from the screen.

"Do you have a floor preference?" Martin asked as we passed the kitchen and living room on our way to a back staircase. I had only been in the house once and was quickly realizing how unfamiliar it was. Just another reason why this was a bad idea.

"Floor preference?" I repeated, unsure what he meant.

He grinned. "Here at Chateau Martin," he adopted a French accent, "our guests have a choice of either a second or third floor suite."

"It doesn't really matter." I wondered if he missed his life's calling to be a bellhop or hotel concierge.

"Third floor it is then." He returned to his normal speech pattern. We went up another flight of stairs, and he showed me to the guest suite in the eastern wing. It was a spacious room, larger than my apartment. It had a sitting room, bedroom, private bathroom, and French doors that opened onto a terrace overlooking an Infinity pool. "There are clean towels in the bathroom and under the cabinet. The bedclothes are fresh, but if you need additional pillows or blankets, they're in the closet." He pointed to a doorway.

"You didn't have to go to so much trouble. I could have slept on the couch."

"Nonsense, you're doing me a favor, so you should be comfortable. I'll let you get settled, and you can meet us downstairs whenever you're ready."

I nodded, and he left the room. I opened the closet and then the drawers. I checked out the bathroom and the cabinets. Everything was where he indicated it would be, and the rest was empty space. I took out my gun, debating whether I should be armed at all times, but I decided to see what Mark was setting up before I walked around the house like Rambo and stowed the gun back in the bag. I made sure the French doors were locked and pulled the curtains over the doors and windows. I didn't like having an outside entrance or exit in my room. It didn't seem like a great option when there were people trying to kill you or, in this case, Martin.

"That was quick," Martin said as I descended the stairs.

"Well, I didn't think I needed to dress for dinner," I retorted. "What are we working on?" I leaned over Mark's shoulder to look at the screen.

"I've set up a constant feed on a single screen that way all entrances and exits can be monitored. I've also installed a few cameras in the hallways and around the exterior, and I have the feed alternating on this monitor." He indicated a second screen I hadn't noticed. "I've set it up so Marty can wire it directly into his home security system and use the cameras as motion sensors if need be."

"Is there a direct line to the home security firm or 911 dispatch?" I tapped a key to manually alternate the camera feed.

Mark looked at Martin. "Where does your home security system direct a problem?"

"It's a two-step process. First, the security firm checks to make sure it wasn't accidental, and then the police are notified."

"ETA in the event of an emergency?" I asked. It felt good to be in control again.

"Not sure. They've promised within five minutes, but I've never had to use it," Martin replied, rubbing the stubble on his chin as he thought about it.

"Okay. Hopefully, we won't have to test it out," Mark echoed my thoughts exactly.

"I'll need a tour of the house and grounds," I piped up. "I need to know where you have security and what types of security. How many employees do you have? Maids? Cooks? Personal bodyguards? What kind of access do they have? The whole shebang."

Martin almost laughed. "Do I really seem that pretentious to you?"

"I'm going to assume that's rhetorical." I refused to give him a straight answer, and he feigned being insulted. Mark laughed.

"There's Marcal. He's my go-to guy. You." Martin counted people off on his fingers. "There's a cleaning lady, Rosemarie. She comes in twice a month, and Marcal lets her in. Anyone else I'm missing?"

"You mean there are people trying to kill you, kidnap you, or blow you up, and you don't have any personal security?"

"What do you think I hired you for?"

Okay, so maybe he had a point, but one person was not a security detail. Plus, I wasn't originally hired to be a twenty-four hour bodyguard. "Decoration?" I suggested. "Had I known, I would have recommended hiring full-time bodyguards. Some big, burly men with names like Bruiser,

Brawler, and Killer."

"Brawler and Killer were busy." He smirked. "Plus, you're much smarter and a lot easier on the eyes."

I glared at him.

"Okay, kids, play nice," Mark interrupted. "Let's take a tour of the house, see what blind spots we might have missed, if there are any doors ajar or windows open." He stood between us.

"Oh." Martin grabbed a tablet off the table. "We can bring this along. It's a mobile version of the monitors. We can watch ourselves walk the perimeter." He seemed like a kid wanting to play cops and robbers once again.

Over the next two hours, I got a very detailed view of the entire estate, inside and out. Martin's sleeping quarters and private office were on the fourth floor. He also had French doors with a balcony, but being that high up wouldn't pose too much of a risk, I hoped.

The security system and additional cameras Mark set up did a decent job covering the grounds. Each entrance was keypad and card required. It made sense why Martin never felt the need for more personal security or staff; his house was well-protected. Any unwanted entry would be loudly announced, and the police would be called.

Mark assured me Rosemarie and Marcal were on the level, and both had worked for Martin for at least a decade. Once we were all satisfied the compound was secure and I was familiar enough not to wander into the garden while looking for the bathroom, we returned to the second floor.

"Everything's set. I'll try to get some of my guys to patrol around or at least drive by periodically to make sure everything is okay," Mark reassured us. "Plus, Alex is here. She's like a pit bull, only scarier."

"Gee, thanks."

"It's been a long day. Things are as secure as they can be, at least for now. I would stay to keep an eye out, but I have to get back to work. We were in the middle of planning an op when I got the message about the explosion. I will check in with you in the morning," Mark promised.

"No problem. I'm sorry I kept you this long, Jabber."

Martin extended his hand.

"Not a problem. Catch you tomorrow."

After Mark left, Martin turned to me. "Alex, can I interest you in some dinner?" He seemed to deflate as he slumped into a chair. The events of today weighed on him, and he had been going nonstop since it all began.

"Sit down, relax." I got up and went into the kitchen. "I can probably scrounge something up for both of us."

"You don't have to do that."

"Don't get used to it. Just because I'm pretending to be your girlfriend doesn't mean I'm going to start cooking or cleaning for you, not on a regular basis, anyway. But today things blew up, literally, so I got this."

"Okay."

We had a lot to discuss, but tonight, neither of us was up for it.

TEN

I awoke with a start. There was someone in the room. I heard a noise. My thinking was garbled, and I grabbed my gun from the table and pointed it directly at the cause of the sound as I tried to blink the sleep from my eyes.

"Don't shoot. It's just me," Martin said in a soothing voice, his hands slightly raised. He was wearing swimming trunks and nothing else.

"What are you doing? What time is it?" My brain wasn't functioning. Where was I? How did I get here? I thought back. Last night, after dinner, I stayed downstairs on the couch, checking out the surveillance feed and trying to work out new leads. I had gotten my handgun, just in case. "I must have fallen asleep."

"I'm sorry. I didn't mean to wake you," he apologized. "I didn't know you were down here. You know you really didn't have to sleep on the couch. I gave you the guestroom for a reason." He remained frozen in place. "Can you put the gun down?"

"Sorry." I felt hungover even though I didn't drink the night before. My brain and body were both sluggish. I clicked the safety on and put the gun down. "What are you doing?"

"Just going for an early morning swim before work," he replied as if this was simply what he did every morning. Maybe it was.

I rubbed my eyes. "You're going to work? I assumed after yesterday you were giving everyone the rest of the week off. Today is Friday, after all. It could have been a nice three day weekend." We should have discussed some things last night.

"I told everyone to use their best judgment when deciding to come to work today. If they took the day off, they would still be paid, given the traumatic events of yesterday. But it doesn't mean I'm not going to show up. I'm in charge, and I have to put on a brave face."

"But you're the face they were trying to blow up."

"Can't let the bad guys win," he replied matter-of-factly, heading for the sliding door. I got up and followed him outside. The sun was barely over the horizon. It was definitely too early to be awake, let alone arguing. I sat down on one of the chaise lounges as he got into the pool. "Care to join me?"

"No. I'm attempting to be your bodyguard. I want to make sure no one is intent on drowning you."

He glanced around the enclosed pool area. "Looks all clear to me."

"Good." That was enough conversation for this early in the morning. I fought the urge to sleep, but eventually, I gave in and dozed on the chair until the splashing stopped. I opened one eye and watched him exit the pool and grab a towel. I had to admit it wasn't necessarily a bad sight to wake up to.

*　　*　　*

Martin and I were riding to the MT building together in the back of his town car. He was reading the newspaper and ignoring me.

"What's so important that you need to go to work today?" I asked.

He slowly folded the paper and placed it neatly on his lap, giving me his full attention. "I have an acquisition meeting this morning, and the Board and I are set to meet this afternoon to discuss yesterday's events."

"Fine, but I'm following you around all day. Maybe yesterday was just a warning or perhaps another failed attempt. Either way, I'm sure they will try again. The

longer this goes on, the more desperate they will become."
He needed to realize I was speaking from experience and
not being dramatic.

He considered my point for a few moments. "How's
your note-taking?"

"I suppose it should be sufficient." I knew exactly what
he was thinking, and I didn't like it.

"Wonderful." He smiled slightly, picked up his paper,
and resumed reading. I gave the paper a dirty look and
continued to sit quietly for the rest of the ride.

Marcal dropped us off in front of the building instead of
in the garage. The crime scene tape still surrounded much
of the sidewalk, and a few police officers loitered nearby.
The damaged glass was replaced with cardboard, and
security was beefed up inside. Instead of being greeted by
the laid-back Jeffrey Myers, we encountered metal
detectors and an employee ID scanner. Two armed guards
were standing by, and a few local LEOs were posted in the
lobby.

"You set all this in motion yesterday?" I whispered.

"I'm more than just a pretty face." Martin swiped his
card through the scanner and headed through the metal
detector.

"Um, Mr. Martin," I stammered. I was carrying today,
and the metal detector would loudly take note of this fact.

"Right this way, Miss Parker."

I swiped my card and approached the metal detector.
"I'm not sure these things agree with me."

But he just stood there, grinning like a Cheshire cat. I
walked through the metal detector, and nothing happened.
Great, it's broken. What was the point of having a metal
detector if it didn't even work properly? We continued to
the elevator, and once the doors closed, allowing a moment
of privacy, I spoke up.

"Your metal detector is broken."

He laughed. "No, it's working just fine. I had the
computer programmed to disable metal detection
temporarily after certain IDs are swiped."

I thought about this for a moment. It seemed practical,
but it left gaps in the security system. "Not a good idea. It

leaves loopholes. You need to get that changed."

He shrugged noncommittally. Martin and his damn unilateral decisions, I wanted to hit him.

When the doors opened on the seventeenth floor, Detective O'Connell was waiting in the hallway. "Mr. Martin. Ms. Parker," he greeted us, and I gave him a wary look.

"What can I do for you?" Martin asked as he swiped his card and opened his office door. "Please." He held the door for the detective, and I followed the men inside.

"We've identified the cause of the explosion," O'Connell said. "It was a small incendiary device, similar to a pipe bomb, with a remote detonator. The device was fairly simplistic, and the radio detonator needed to be within a two hundred foot radius. The bomb squad believes it must have had a few seconds delay from the time the detonator switch was flipped until the bomb actually exploded."

"You think the sun glare I saw was from the bomber?" I half-asked, half-stated.

"We do. Our crime scene guys recovered a lens on the sixth floor balcony, most likely from a binocular or monocular. The bomber was probably lying in wait. Do you normally follow the same routine?" O'Connell asked Martin.

"More or less, at least during business hours."

"I see." O'Connell frowned.

"How much of a lag between the switch and the explosion? Do you think the delay was due to the distance and radio frequency transmitter or intentional to make getting away easier?" I asked.

"No way to know for sure," O'Connell said. "Either seems to be a reasonable explanation." I bit my lip, thinking. "I'd like to advise you to lie low for a while, Mr. Martin. Stay out of the public eye. Maybe take a vacation. It's reasonable to assume the hot dog stand exploding was meant for you. We are still investigating other avenues just to make sure, but...," he trailed off.

"Thank you for the concern, Detective, but I will be just fine," Martin said curtly, and the detective headed for the door.

"O'Connell," I called, and he turned on his heel, "any suspects?"

"Sorry, I'm not at liberty to discuss an ongoing investigation. Have a good day."

I sighed. I hated the company line, especially since he had already thoroughly discussed certain aspects of the investigation.

"Did Mark call this morning?" I asked as Martin settled in behind his desk, looking for the materials he needed for his morning meeting.

"Huh?" He looked confused. I was amazed at how quickly he could lose himself in business.

"Mark. Did he call?"

"Not that I know of." He returned to tapping away at his keyboard.

I hit the top of his desk lightly with my palm to get his attention. "I'm going to my office for a minute to check on some things and give Mark a call. Do not go to your meeting without me. Understand?" I felt like I was talking to a child.

"Okay."

I went to my office and opened the door. Then I unlocked my drawer and made sure my side arm and bullets were still secure. Maybe I was a tad bit obsessive. I fished my cell phone out of my purse and called Mark's office. When the call went straight to voicemail, I tried his cell phone. After five rings, he answered.

"What?" he mumbled into the receiver. It sounded like he had been asleep.

"Any news?"

"Parker, do you realize what time it is?"

"It's morning. You said you'd talk to us in the morning."

"Cute," he replied, sounding disgusted. "How 'bout I come by in a couple of hours? We'll talk then."

"Thanks, sweetie." If he thought I was being cute, I might as well go with it.

He mumbled something about a sarcastic bitch and hung up.

I was on my way to Martin's office when he met me in the doorway, legal pad and pen in hand. "Let's go acquire some acquisitions." He beamed brightly, seeming somewhat manic.

Despite the fact I had traversed the building numerous times over the last week, I had never seen the Marketing/Research floor this empty. Apparently, most employees decided it was better to stay home with their loved ones than go to work where bombs might ruin their lunch hour. Martin led us into a large conference room equipped with a flat screen television mounted to the wall.

"Blake Denton, meet my...," he paused uncertainly.

"Alexis Parker." I introduced myself.

"Mr. Denton is our vice president. He's in charge of foreign acquisitions," Martin said.

"Pleasure to meet you, Miss Parker." Denton gave my hand a slight squeeze. "I heard you two were very close to the accident yesterday. I'm glad you're okay. It's disconcerting. No wonder so few workers came in today." He seemed to be talking to neither of us, and I suspected he might be shell-shocked.

"I gave everyone the option of having the day off. I didn't want to further traumatize anybody in the wake of such unfortunate events," Martin said sympathetically. "I'm glad to see you didn't abandon me today, too." He winked at Denton. "You know how cunning our colleagues in Dubai are."

"We're in negotiations to open some manufacturing and processing plants in the Middle East." Denton tried to catch me up to speed. "It will be highly lucrative for both MT and our foreign partners, if we get approval for the acquisition."

"Alex is here to take notes for us," Martin interjected. "I figured we might be short a few assistants."

Denton grinned. "Have a seat then. We're just waiting for them to call."

I spent the next hour and a half attempting to take notes on things I didn't understand. Hopefully, Martin and Denton were paying attention. After the call was over, Martin and I returned to his office.

"Has Mr. Denton received any threats?" I asked.

"Not that I'm aware of."

"I just figured since he's a board member and VP, if this was company related, maybe he had gotten some threats, too." I was pulling at straws, but it was another angle to consider.

"I think I'm the only lucky son of a bitch here," he said bitterly.

ELEVEN

As promised, Mark showed up a little before lunchtime. "Place seems like a ghost town," he said, taking a seat in Martin's office. "It's still a good thing you have the enhanced security, just in case."

"Any news?" I was impatient.

"O'Connell called this morning, a little while after you did. He passed along a casualty list and some bomb specifications, but nothing in terms of persons of interest," he said matter-of-factly.

"How many?" I asked, even though I really didn't want to know.

"Two. The hot dog vendor and a woman. She seems random. Doesn't work at MT, no connection to Marty that I'm aware of. Probably just wrong place, wrong time."

I felt awful. I hated to think people had died, especially since I should have stopped this from happening. I felt sick to my stomach.

"What was her name?" Martin asked, concern evident in his voice.

Mark pulled out his notepad and flipped through a few pages. "Jillian Monroe," he read as I watched Martin's expression carefully for signs of recognition.

"Never heard of her," Martin confirmed. "Poor woman. The hot dog vendor, too." He was solemn and looked exactly how I felt. It was obvious we both felt responsible for these deaths.

"The two of you need to remember you didn't do this." Mark focused on me. "You will track down this motherfucker. You got it?"

"Damn straight."

"Okay, good." Mark was acting as cheerleader today. He probably thought we could use it since it felt like we were on the losing team. Unfortunately, from my score sheet, we were the losing team. "I'm going back to work, but I'll come by tonight to bring some things I think you can both use." He looked at Martin. "And you, sir, need to consider taking a break until we get some things straightened out, or at the very least, start wearing your bullet-resistant suits. You had those custom-made for a reason."

Martin hedged. "I'll think about it. I had some important meetings today, and I didn't want to come in looking sub-par." I gaped at him. Could he be this shallow? "See you tonight, Jabber." Martin walked him to the door, and I waved to Mark as he left.

But as soon as the door shut, I dove in head first. "You and your unilateral decisions can kiss my ass." I turned on Martin like a rabid dog. "You will start taking precautions, and you will take some time off. You can tell the Board today when you meet with them. Your security consultant insists."

"You work for me," he snarled.

"Yes, but let me make one thing perfectly clear. If you don't listen, I can walk away. No one is trying to kill me, and quite frankly, I don't want to get shot because I'm standing too close to you." I wasn't being completely fair. I was taking the two deaths out on him, but I didn't care. He was still playing games, and he needed to realize just how serious this matter was.

"So go," he growled. We were standing inches apart.

"Un-fucking-believable." I prepared to leave but stopped myself and turned back. "Your business means more to you than your life?"

"It's all I have."

"Get over yourself. You are a living, breathing human being, at least for the moment, and if all of this came crashing down tomorrow, you would still be the same person."

He didn't respond, and I expected death rays to shoot from his eyes. "No. I wouldn't. I would be nothing," he said in a low bitter tone as he went back to his desk, trying to busy himself with work.

I stormed out of the office, slamming the door. "Narcissistic prick." I wasn't going to leave, but staying and fighting wasn't helping either of us. I had a job to do, and despite my better judgment, I planned to see it through until the end. I stomped back to my office where I sat smoldering for a couple of minutes. Finally, I opened my door and stared across the hallway at him. He was behind his desk working as if nothing had just transpired. I half-expected him to call security and have me removed from the building. However, that would have been bad for business, and business was obviously the only thing he was capable of thinking about.

After twenty minutes, he grabbed his portfolio and opened his office door. "Let's go. The Board is waiting." He wasn't asking. He was ordering, and I didn't say a word.

I grabbed a pad and pen and followed him to the elevator. We rode in silence, neither of us acknowledging the other. I followed him down the hall to yet another conference room. There were ten people assembled around the rectangular table. I recognized Blake Denton, but he was the only one.

I was going to take a seat in the back of the room, where the other assistants were gathered, but Martin put his hand on my arm. I looked up, confused. He was no longer acting as if I was a total stranger, but I could see the anger still resonating in his eyes.

"Ladies and gentlemen of the Board, I need to make an announcement," he began. "As you are aware, recently I have received numerous threats. Yesterday's explosion, while still under investigation, may have been intended for me." He took a breath and stared into my eyes, looking for reassurance. "Therefore, I think it is in the best interest of our employees that I take a vacation or sabbatical, if you will, until this situation is resolved."

Some of the board members had questions, but he

continued speaking, ignoring them. "I discussed the issue with my security consulting firm, and they agreed it would be wise for the situation to be resolved before anyone else is endangered. I trust you are capable of running the company for the next few weeks in my absence."

"What about the Dubai acquisition?" a woman asked.

"Blake and I had the meeting this morning. I think they are ready to sign, but I will still be close by if issues should arise. In the meantime, I will appoint Mr. Denton as acting Chair until further notice." Martin waited for additional questions.

"Why are you leaving now? Things have been going on for weeks, and we don't even know yet if the food cart explosion had anything to do with you? It might have been an accident," Denton argued, trying to get him to stay. That was one hell of a friend, or perhaps he was afraid of screwing up if he was left with the keys to the castle.

Martin's expression was forlorn. "My girlfriend, Alexis," he wrapped his arm around my waist, and I resisted the urge to beat him to death with it, "has been filling in as my personal assistant, and yesterday, if it hadn't been for her, we both might have been hurt or worse. It's time I take these matters more seriously for everyone's sake. I don't want anyone else getting hurt or killed on my account."

"Mr. Martin," an older, balding man addressed him now, "what about the banquet?"

He pondered this for a moment. "I will contact legal and have the papers drawn up for Mr. Denton to temporarily replace me, but I am still planning to attend the banquet. Our charity work is very important, and nothing should detract from it. Afterward, I will hold a press conference announcing my sabbatical in hopes of helping to insulate the company from any further threats."

Another woman spoke up. "We shall take a vote. Those in favor of temporarily placing Mr. Denton as acting Chair until Mr. Martin's return say aye."

Everyone agreed, Denton slightly begrudgingly. I couldn't tell if it was for show or if he honestly had reservations.

"Good. I'm glad everything is settled. Now, if you'll

excuse us, it's been a rough day." Martin led me out of the room and to the elevators. "Later," he whispered, and I remained silent for fear someone would overhear what I had to say.

As we waited for the elevator to arrive, Denton came down the corridor. "James, hang on," he called, rushing to get to us. "Are you sure about this? I've never been in charge of quite so much before."

"You'll be fine, Blake." Martin patted him on the shoulder. "You've got the entire Board to back you. Come by my office in an hour, and you can sign the paperwork."

"See you then, sir," he said respectfully. "It was lovely meeting you, Alexis. I'm glad James found someone who makes him realize there is more to life than work."

I tried to look coy, but I wasn't sure how well I conveyed false emotions. It wasn't easy to feign romance when murder was on my mind. Luckily, the elevator provided an escape from the awkwardness.

"An hour, don't be late. It wouldn't look good for the acting Chair," Martin teased as the doors closed, and we began our ascent back to the seventeenth floor.

"Are you out of your fucking mind?" I hit the stop button, and we were halted between floors.

"I must be to do exactly what you told me to do."

I resisted the urge to slap him across the face. "If you agreed, you could have said so ahead of time instead of blindsiding me, especially with the announcement about your girlfriend." I used air quotes. I was pissed because this asshole just slapped a target on my back, but I didn't want to say it. I knew it was a possibility when I signed on to the job.

"Sorry, sweetheart," he spat, "but you got what you wanted. So be happy about it." He hit the resume button, and we continued to the seventeenth floor. "I could lose everything doing this. So get off your high horse and do your goddamn job." He stomped to his office while I remained in the elevator, stunned.

Was I being completely unreasonable? Oh, that manipulative son of a bitch. The doors started to close, and I shoved them aside and went straight to my office to call

Mark.

"I need everything you have on those ex-employees. I also need you to cross-reference anyone suspicious with any type of gang or criminal organizations. Check out drug and arms dealers working near Dubai. If there is any connection to anything or anyone, I need to know. It's a long shot, but I want to get this job over with before I shoot the bastard myself."

TWELVE

I sat in my office, rubbing my temples. The fighting needed to stop, especially before I killed Martin. The main reason I was angry at him was because I was angry at myself. Two innocent people died because I was sitting around playing secretary and babysitter instead of tracking down leads. Sure, Martin was eccentric, he didn't listen, and he could go from serious to teasing at a moment's notice. I knew this when I took the job, but I still took it. That was my mistake.

Perhaps I was also afraid the little voice in the back of my head telling me I had no idea what I was doing was right. I didn't have any idea what I was doing; if I did, things would be different now. Although thoughts like this led the other little voice inside my head to point out if I wasn't here or if I didn't know what I was doing, Martin would be a chalk outline of some goo on the pavement. I sighed audibly and put my head on my desk. If only all the voices in my head could just get along. I laughed at the absurdity. I must be clinically insane.

I sat up in my chair and turned on the computer, clicking open on the company e-mail and selecting Martin as my contact. *I'm waving the white flag. Can I come over?* I typed the message and hit send. It was incredibly childish, but I couldn't blame him any longer. And I was too proud to apologize in person.

He responded immediately. *Cease-fire accepted.*

I took a deep breath. Be calm, try to understand, and resist the urge to argue. I repeated these things a few times before opening my office door and going across the hall.

He buzzed me in, and I sat on the couch closest to his desk and watched as he worked. Checking the time, I knew Denton would be here in a few minutes.

He glanced up at my still form. "Nice to see you back to work."

"I'm sorry. This is the only way I know to keep you safe." That was as close to an apology as he was going to get.

We locked eyes. He opened his mouth as if to speak and then decided against it and went back to reading the forms for temporarily signing over his company.

"I guess you can be the witness." He stared at the paper. "Someone from legal is coming up to notarize it, but it's good form to have a third party witness the event."

"Okay."

"Maybe you could also play the part of doting girlfriend when Denton's up here. It might help sell the fact you aren't my added security."

"Sure."

"Look." He dropped the paper on the desk and was about to say something, but there was a knock on the door. We both turned at the intrusion. "Never mind," he mumbled as he changed the glass from opaque to clear and buzzed in Denton and someone else, presumably from legal.

The papers were signed, and the formalities were completed rather quickly. "Let's toast to your temporary job." Martin went to the wet bar and poured scotch into two glasses for himself and Denton.

Denton picked up a glass. "No," he raised it in the air, "to returning to your rightful position as quickly as possible." They clinked glasses together, and Martin turned to look at me. I was leaning against his desk, playing with the hem on my jacket.

"I'm sorry, Alex." This was his way of apologizing. "What would you like?"

"Nothing, dear." I beamed at him. The sweetness factor would give me cavities; I was sure of it.

"C'mon, Alexis," Denton poured liquor into a glass, "drink with us, at least to the good fortune of having

Jimmy around more. I know it must be tough being in a relationship with such a workaholic."

"It is tough." I walked over to the men, eyeing Martin, and Denton handed me the glass.

"To us," Martin toasted.

"I'll leave the two of you alone, but if you need anything, man, let me know." Denton was almost to the door when Martin spoke up.

"Just so you know, the office doesn't come with the job." He grinned, trying to convey it was in good fun.

"No problem. I already have a nice office," Denton said as he left.

"So, Jimmy," I couldn't resist, "are we okay with this arrangement?"

"As long as you never call me Jimmy again."

"Deal."

He didn't want to fight anymore either, and what was done was done. It was time to move on and wrap this thing up so we could both get back to our lives.

We spent the rest of the afternoon packing up anything he deemed essential or private. I went to my office and retrieved my laptop, notes, and handgun since the cleaning staff didn't need to think I was part of the threat.

It was before four when we walked out of the MT building. The police were still in the lobby and patrolling the area out front. It would probably be a few more days before they were gone, and then it would be as if nothing happened at all. Marcal brought the car around, and we got in and rode back to Martin's compound in silence.

* * *

A few hours later, Mark arrived with a truckload of equipment. He had some surveillance cameras, flak jackets, a shotgun, box of shells, and motion sensors.

"What did you do? Raid the supply van?" I asked as he unceremoniously dumped the equipment across the dining room table.

"It's nothing we needed. We've updated our equipment since you were there, and I thought you could use some hand-me-downs on loan, of course."

"Of course," I mimicked, breaking down the shotgun to make sure it wasn't loaded.

"I figured we could set up some more cameras or sensors in those blind spots we found the other day, just to make things more secure."

"Great." Martin seemed less than excited. "I love living in a fishbowl."

Mark ignored him and hauled a camera and mounting equipment to the western exit. Martin and I exchanged a look.

"You want to help or should I?" I asked.

"I'll go. I need to make sure he doesn't set up surveillance in my bedroom or bathroom. I don't need any sex tapes hitting the internet." He seemed so sincere I just stared at him, trying to determine if he was kidding.

"I wouldn't advise having any guests over, at least until this is straightened out." I chose serious, which was obviously the wrong choice.

He looked at me like I was insane. "Have you ever heard a joke before?"

I didn't comment, and he went to find Mark. I took the shotgun and box of shells and placed them in the kitchen. The box of shells went under the kitchen sink and the gun on top of the cabinets. I wanted them within reach but not any place overly obvious or in the way. I would have to remember to tell Martin to inform Rosemarie before she came to clean. If not, she might have an unpleasant surprise. The flak jackets I hung in the coat closet on the second floor near the stairs.

I went out to check on the guys. Mark was on a ladder, and Martin was handing him various tools. "You got a handle on this?" I hoped they wouldn't want help.

"Yeah, we have it covered," Mark responded. Before he could ask for anything else, I continued.

"I'm going to check into some things. Can you keep an eye out?"

"Yeah, we'll manage while you're gone," Mark replied.

"Okay, I'll be back later."

"Take the remote access key," Martin said as I reached

the door. "It's in the crystal bowl on the counter. It'll get you in and out of the garage."

I retrieved the remote and took my car back to my apartment.

*   *   *

"Feels good to be home." I took my notes out and began to re-evaluate the employees. I was looking for anyone with criminal connections who would have the know-how to make a bomb. As far as motivation went, I was still stumped. Maybe they, whoever they were, didn't like Martin for personal reasons, or perhaps the Dubai acquisition was motivation enough to threaten him. Anything could be motive, especially when dealing with irrational people, and irrational people were the ones most likely to make bombs or shoot up a place.

The employee files I had were limited. MT employed people of all races and ethnic backgrounds, none of which struck me as particularly radical or having obvious gang or terrorist ties. I looked for anyone with potential organized crime connections. Still no luck. Finally, I considered who might have dealings with weapons or drug trafficking. This, of course, was a much more difficult avenue to pursue. Did I have any ATF or DEA friends who owed me a favor? My brain was sluggish. I could feel a thought gnawing at the corners of my mind, but it just wouldn't surface. It felt like I was trying to think my way through quicksand.

"This is ridiculous," I said to my empty room. "Think, Parker." I ran through the list of things I knew: threatening letter, kidnapping attempt, manufacturing sabotage, a bomb. All of it happened near work or at work. The letters weren't sent to Martin's residence. The kidnapping and the explosion both happened outside MT. Was it someone with a beef with the company or a beef with Martin?

They don't know where he lives. The thought flashed across my mind like lightning. Obviously, I didn't know this for a fact, but it would make more sense to attack someone at a private residence than in broad daylight in front of potentially hundreds of witnesses. I grabbed the dry erase note board I kept on my fridge and scribbled out the thought. Another thought struck me. Unless the attacks are supposed to be in public to scare Martin into stepping down from his job. Maybe isolate him at home and finish him off. Too much speculation on my part. I went back to the original thought; they didn't know where he lived.

I started back over. Everything's been at work. I sprawled out on my bed and lay against the pillows. Okay, everything happened at work. Can the motive be work related? The only work related thing I was aware of was the Dubai acquisition. Evidently, there must be more going on than just one acquisition. I needed to ask what other big projects were in the works at MT. I added that to my note board before closing my eyes to try to clear my head.

Opening my eyes, I glanced at the digital clock on my nightstand. "Dammit," I swore and got out of bed. I had fallen asleep. These late nights and early mornings were counterproductive. I picked up my note board and everything I brought with me, locked my apartment, and drove back to Martin's compound. It was a little after one a.m., and I hoped Mark was still filling in as bodyguard and wasn't too pissed about the inconvenience.

I arrived at Martin's quickly, given the almost nonexistent traffic, and I used the remote to pull into the garage. I shut the door and took the steps up to the main level two at a time. I didn't see Mark's car and suspected he must have left for the night. The house was dark, and I was paranoid about tripping some new unforeseen security measure. But no alarms blared as I entered the living room. The table lamp was on, and Martin was sitting on the couch. His arm was outstretched over the back of the sofa, a half empty glass in his hand and an almost empty bottle of single malt on the coffee table.

"Sorry, I was checking on some things and lost track of time. Did Mark leave?"

"S'okay," he slurred. He tilted his drink-holding hand, as if to examine his watch, and spilled the contents onto the couch cushion. "What time is it?" In his intoxicated state, he was unable to focus or notice the spilled drink.

"It's time for you to get some sleep."

"No." He looked up with those green eyes, reminding me of a wounded animal. "I'm going to finish my drink first." He put the glass on the table and poured the rest of the bottle into it. I sat down on the non-soppy cushion and decided to wait him out.

"Y'know what?" he slurred, his tone semi-hostile. "They already fucking won."

I didn't like drunk people, but when running low on sodium pentothal, drunk could be helpful in finding out some truths. Although, I would have preferred a quiet night of Martin sleeping and me staring at the surveillance feed, especially after our fight earlier.

"Who?" I tentatively asked.

"Whoever." He took a sip. "The faceless, letter writing, hot dog bombing bastards, and I liked those hot dogs, too."

I swallowed, trying to avoid focusing on the casualties. We sat sullenly for a moment.

"We're going to stop them." I didn't want to go into details and start asking questions when he was in this state; it was enough trouble getting him to focus and stay on topic when he was sober.

"Yeah, Mark said that, too." He slurred the s badly. "Mark's a good guy. Did he ever tell you about Panama?"

"No." I was getting curious now. "What happened in Panama?"

"It's been almost ten years now. I was just starting out." He stared off into nothingness, but it seemed he was watching something which occurred in a different time and place. "I had just inherited the company from my father and decided I was going to change the world. I was in South America, trying to bring clean water and food to the smaller communities there." He took another sip. "I was working my way back up through Central America. I had some transport issues and ended up buying my own boating company." He paused, smiling devilishly. "Do you like boats?"

"Sure."

"We should go out on my boat. It's a yacht. It's got cruise control." I rolled my eyes. He was making no sense. "And some really nice suites. King-sized beds." He waggled an eyebrow suggestively.

"A boating company in Panama." I was trying to get him back on track.

"Yeah, so as I was saying," the 's's were getting worse, "Jabber was tracking some stolen art, and the dude was apparently not only an art collector but some cartel bigwig. Needless to say, the Federalis were in on it, and no one would help get him or hissteam out."

Hissteam? I was deciphering in my head. Oh, his team. I nodded for him to go on.

"They were trapped, but I had the boats." He raised his finger in the air to emphasize his point, looking incredibly self-satisfied.

"You rescued them from the cartel," I concluded for him. "You brought them back to the States. You did save Mark's ass." Despite everything, I couldn't help having a slight fondness for Martin.

"Guns going off, people screaming, so many bullets." He was lost in his memory. "So many bullets."

"Come on." I got up and took him by the arm. "Let's get you to bed. You need to sleep this off."

He focused on me and stood up, somewhat wobbly. "I shot him. I didn't have a choice."

"Shot who?" I draped his arm around my shoulders, and we headed for the stairs.

"The guy who was going to kill Jabber." I was completely shocked and turned to him. "I don't want anyone else to get hurt because of me. I'm sorry I put you in the middle of my problems." His story seemed to have temporarily sobered him.

"I know what I signed on for."

"It doesn't make it right. You were doing Jabber a favor, and he was doing me a favor." He touched my bandaged arm. "You should go before anything else happens."

I swallowed, uncomfortable with the entire exchange. He leaned against me, rubbed his thumb across my cheek, and gently tucked my hair behind my ear, like he had the first day in his office.

"I'm not going anywhere," I tried to reassure him. He leaned in and kissed me gently. I could taste the liquor on his lips. I shut my eyes. *Don't do this, Parker,* the voice in my head warned, and I slowly pulled away. "You need to get some sleep."

"That I do." He half-crawled, half-stumbled up the two flights of stairs. I was glad when we finally made it to his room, and he flopped onto the bed. "Join me," he mumbled, seconds away from unconsciousness.

"In your dreams," I retorted, making a mental note to check on him in a while just to make sure he didn't aspirate in his sleep.

THIRTEEN

I checked on Martin twice during the course of the night. On my first trip, I brought him a glass of water and left it on his nightstand, along with a bottle of aspirin. I was relieved to find him still alive and breathing. The second time was during a routine walkthrough of the house. I was antsy and had started walking the interior of his compound as I pondered the best way to find the answers I was so desperately seeking. Having spent a good portion of the evening napping in my own apartment, I took advantage of the quiet and continued to work on those few fleeting thoughts from earlier.

I settled into Martin's office on the second floor and used his concept board to start listing suspects, motives, and opportunity – the holy trinity of crime. However, there were obvious gaps in the information, and I had no suspects at all. The only thing I could do was use broad categories to describe potential suspects. Ex-employees, co-workers, board members, personal relations, and random individuals seemed the most likely.

I knew whoever was behind this had to have a reason, so I went once more for the typical motives: money, revenge, passion. Whoever was behind it either figured the best way to destroy Martin was to destroy his business or they only had access to him through MT. This made limiting the suspects and motives much more difficult.

Under opportunity, I realized I needed a list of

employees who were out of the office during the time of the explosion and those who had the ability or the means to compensate someone to create a bomb. I would need a breakdown of the chemical composition and the difficulty of ascertaining such materials. O'Connell might already have access to this information, so either Mark or I could potentially weasel it out of him. I batted my eyelashes as practice for that prospect.

The brilliant thoughts from earlier were starting to unravel back into a mesh of uncertainties. The problem was there were still too many possibilities. *Work backward*, I told myself, but I couldn't think clearly. A fog was settling in over the lightning storm of perceived progress. I glanced at the clock; it was almost six a.m. No wonder things were quickly coming undone.

I could afford a couple hours of sleep, so I double-checked to make sure the security system was live and headed up to my room. I didn't even bother to change out of my clothes as I got into bed. As I began to drift off, my mind wandered back to Martin's story of Panama and the kiss. I never would have pictured this perfectly manicured, business professional to be the type ballsy enough to open fire in the defense of another. I also wouldn't have expected to be so turned on by just one simple kiss. I forced the thought out of my mind. You've got a job to do, Parker.

I drifted in and out of consciousness for a couple of hours, but by 8:30, I gave up since sleep was being too elusive. I got out of bed and took a shower, trying to refresh my mind. It was Saturday, so I put on jeans and a t-shirt. No more business attire needed. I went downstairs and made some very strong coffee and some eggs and bacon, figuring Martin needed something to soak up the remaining hangover.

I retrieved the employee files and brought them into the kitchen and began crossing off those individuals who could not have been responsible. Unfortunately, there weren't many names I could mark off. I was almost positive I wasn't the mastermind behind the threats, but my name wasn't on the list. Jeffrey had been working the desk, so he couldn't have been in two places at once to set off the explosion.

My mind seemed to have gotten the jump-start it needed. I realized I didn't have the surveillance feed from the lobby. If I could get a hold of it, then I would know who left the building and possibly had time to set the bomb and get across the street. I wondered if O'Connell had gotten the MT surveillance feed or any video footage from the numerous cameras outside on nearby buildings. I made a note at the top of the page to call him and see what he had found. There might just be a break on the horizon.

I grabbed another sheet of paper. The manufacturing sabotage and corporate espionage had to be an inside job. I hadn't focused on either of those because they weren't direct physical threats to Martin, but now I was positive whoever was doing this had to be an MT employee or ex-employee. How long did they keep surveillance tapes of the manufacturing plant? I was getting very excited and tapped my fingers against the table. How could I have missed all of this? I should have started with the manufacturing issues and went from there. I picked up my phone to call Mark and see if he had pursued this avenue, but I stopped myself. It was Saturday morning, not even ten a.m. yet; Mark would either be asleep or working. I put the phone down, trying to determine if the giddy jitteriness I was experiencing was because I was on to something or because I drank too much coffee this morning.

"We will figure this out," I said to what I thought was the empty room.

"Well, it is why you're here." A response came from the next room. Martin walked in with his hair sticking up in a hundred different directions, looking like hell. "Do you think you can speak a little softer?" He stumbled into the kitchen and went straight to the coffeepot, pouring himself a cup. "I feel like I was hit by a train."

"Yeah, it was the Macallan express. I made some eggs and bacon, thought the grease might help with the hangover." I wasn't sure if he would be able to eat without getting sick. "There's toast, too." I went back to sipping my coffee. He sat down across from me, drinking his own coffee and looking absolutely miserable.

"Strong coffee."

"Helps with hangovers and sleep deprivation." I glanced up at him, unsure what he remembered about last night. It'd probably be best to act as if nothing happened.

Yesterday had been an emotional rollercoaster with our fight in his office and then his confession later that evening. I was just going to pretend I didn't know his deep dark secrets and we hadn't kissed. That would be the best course of action, remain professional. He got up, after finishing his cup of coffee, and made a plate with eggs, bacon, and toast. He picked at it while I reread my notes.

"I used your office last night. It's a bit of a mess right now. Sorry." I didn't sound very sorry, and he simply grunted. Nodding was probably too painful.

"You brought me water and aspirin last night?" He watched me flip pages.

"Yeah, I checked on you to make sure you were still alive and figured might as well, since I was already on my way. Not a big deal." I put my plate and mug into the dishwasher. Being a bit cold might be the most professional course of action to follow.

"Thanks. I hope I didn't make too much of an ass of myself last night." His eyes were bloodshot, and he reeked of alcohol. But I could tell he was trying to determine what he did or didn't do. Maybe he thought I was angry.

"Not any more than you do on a regular basis." I smirked.

"I'm going to take a shower." He got up and headed for the stairs.

I straightened up the kitchen and organized his office, but I left my notes on the concept board. I was trying to keep busy until he came back down. I wanted him to be functioning, so we could get to work. Dragging him to the MT building today didn't seem like a good idea, but I wanted the surveillance footage now.

An hour later, he re-emerged, looking slightly more human. His hair was brushed and styled. He had shaved, doused himself with cologne, and probably used half a bottle of eye drops to erase the red inkiness from around his green irises.

"Feeling better?" I asked, and he made a so-so gesture with his hand.

"Getting there, slowly." He retrieved a bottle of water and a couple of aspirin and swallowed. "What's going on?" He took a seat across from me at the kitchen table, eyeing my notes.

"They have to be MT employees or ex-employees," I blurted out. "I don't know why I didn't see it before. The manufacturing sabotage, it's where we need to start." The words spilled out of my mouth, and he put up a hand to halt my verbal onslaught.

"Hang on. I'm only slightly functional right now." I sat quietly, staring at him. He realized this was a losing battle since the dots weren't connecting for him the way they had for me. "Why?" he finally asked.

"Who has access to your manufacturing plant and knows what to do to sabotage it?" I wasn't really asking; I was just pointing out the obvious.

"Anyone could have walked in off the street." He still seemed confused. "We don't have much security in manufacturing. It's a separate building across town from the MT building, and people come and go all the time. Deliveries, exports, imports, repair guys." This was why I hadn't started there, because it was the most accessible place to attack.

"True, but they," I was using the term they because we didn't know the gender of the assailant or the number of those potentially involved, "also knew where to find your corporate design secrets. They had to have access to that data or know how to get access, and they also had to know your daily schedule. Whoever is behind this has to work for you." I realized during my explanation it must be a current employee or else they wouldn't be aware of our daily lunch dates. Before I began working for Martin and playing the role of doting girlfriend, he rarely went to lunch, like most of the other higher-ups.

He rubbed his temples and closed his eyes. His head was pounding, but I needed him to focus. The longer we waited, the greater the chance whoever was behind this would either get away with whatever they were after or succeed in eliminating him. Although, in all actuality, the reason I was so anxious was because I just realized I was five steps behind and wanted to play catch up to make up for my blunders. I had been working for almost two weeks, and now it dawned on me what was really going on and who could be behind it.

"I need the surveillance footage from the manufacturing plant from the day the sabotage occurred. I also need a report of exactly what happened and who in the company possesses the knowledge to know what to sabotage and how to do it, and I need the surveillance from before we tried to leave the office on Thursday. A list of who called in sick would be great too. I don't know how well you monitor your employee attendance, but you must keep records to determine paychecks, right?" I rambled. Way too much caffeine, Parker.

Martin looked a little pale, as if he might pass out or throw-up. Luckily, he didn't do either. "Okay." He swallowed unsurely. "Go down to MT. Tell whoever is working security to give you a copy of the surveillance from Thursday. There should be a few extra copies on disk in the security office because the cops and the other alphabet soup agencies wanted our video footage as part of their investigations. Take my ID with you, just in case you encounter any problems. I'll give them a call and let them know you're on your way to pick it up."

"What about you?"

"I'll be fine. I'll make the call and then probably throw-up a few times."

I didn't want to leave him alone, but if I was right, whoever was threatening him didn't know where he lived. So it should be safe to leave. "Okay." I was about to ask about the manufacturing footage, but he read my mind.

"We'll have to go to the plant to get the other tapes. Separate systems. Today things are shut down, so that'll have to wait until Monday."

"All right." I got my keys and picked up our ID cards. "Make the call. I'll be back soon. If there is any problem, call 911 first, then me or Mark." I pointed at my handgun sitting on the kitchen counter. I had started keeping it with me at all times. "Worst case, point and shoot. Don't hesitate."

*   *   *

It took about an hour to get to the MT building. Saturday traffic was never fun to negotiate. I arrived and scanned my ID as I entered the building.

"May I help you, ma'am?" the security guard asked.

"I hope so." I gave him my winning smile, even though he called me ma'am. "I'm here to pick up some things for Mr. Martin, surveillance footage and a list of the employees in attendance from Thursday. I believe he called earlier about this."

The security guy looked pleased. "Sure did. I have it all right here. Can I see your identification?" I showed him both cards, and he looked from my picture to me. Granted, I did look somewhat different in casual dress, but he seemed to be doing his job very thoroughly. "Oh," recognition dawned on him, "you're Mr. Martin's new girl. I remember seeing you leave with him in the afternoons. Tell him Todd said hi, and we can't wait for him to be back at work."

"Thanks, Todd. I will." It was better to make friends with the security personnel and continue the ruse than to be enemies or arouse suspicion.

I left the building and headed back to my car. The police tape was still out front, but only a couple of officers remained. By Monday, things would appear to be completely back to normal. I went to my car feeling paranoid and decided to take a circuitous route to Martin's. It never hurt to be cautious.

An hour and a half later, I pulled up to the compound and entered through the garage. As I went up the stairs, I resisted the urge to call out *honey, I'm home.* "I'm back," I announced loudly to make my presence known in case Martin decided to be a bit trigger-happy and shoot any and all intruders. There was no response, so I put my belongings on the coffee table and headed up the stairs. Maybe he didn't hear me.

"Martin?" I tried again. Still no response. I was beginning to worry and stopped in my room and glanced around. Nothing looked like it had been touched. I took out my backup handgun and continued to the fourth floor, knocking on his bedroom door.

"Martin?" I heard a muffled response, so I opened the door slowly with my left hand, my gun held in my right. He was lying in bed on top of the covers, apparently trying to sleep off the rest of the hangover. At the sound of the door, he opened his eyes. The nine millimeter I left him was on the bedside table. "Still alive in here?" I hid my weapon against my thigh, glad he had taken my suggestion seriously; at least he listened some of the time.

"For the moment." An icepack was pressed against his forehead. "Did you get what you needed?"

"For now." I shut the door.

FOURTEEN

I set up shop in the living room. I was seated on the couch, avoiding the scotch-stained sofa cushion and watching the surveillance feed on Martin's big screen television. The employee manifest was opened, and I kept hitting pause every time someone exited the lobby. It was slow going, matching names with faces, and I desperately missed the facial-recognition software the OIO used. I was making a list of employees who had exited the building from 10:30 until the time of the explosion.

So far, there were fifteen people who left the building from 10:30 to 11:00 a.m. However, the same fifteen people returned to the building within a fifteen to thirty minute time span. I got up and retrieved Det. O'Connell's business card and dialed his number, hoping to discover what time the hot dog vendor parked in front of the MT building.

"O'Connell," he responded after the third ring.

"Hi, this is Alexis Parker. I work for James Martin."

"Yes, Ms. Parker. Did you remember any additional details you wanted to share?" He sounded suspicious on the phone, probably realizing I was only calling to get information from him.

"Just wondering how the investigation is going, Detective."

"Okay." There was an awkward silence. "What do you need?"

"Any idea what time the hot dog vendor set up shop

outside the MT building?"

"Hang on," I heard some papers being shuffled around, "10:45, why?"

"Just needed a good starting place," I replied, somewhat unhelpfully.

"Yeah, well, you come up with some persons of interest, you pass it along."

"Absolutely, Detective." I debated if I should ask about the bomb materials but decided to wait and see if Mark had gotten any news yet. After all, he would have the resources to track down the bomb maker. "Maybe you could do the same."

"Have a good day, Ms. Parker."

At least my arbitrary starting point wasn't quite so arbitrary after all. I continued through the rest of the footage until the explosion occurred. I had a list of sixty-one employees in total who left the building between 10:30 and noon. Of those sixty-one employees, forty-three returned within fifteen to thirty minutes. I circled the remaining eighteen names on the list.

I just pulled out the employee attendance sheet to see who was scheduled to leave early or work half a day when I heard footsteps behind me.

"Feeling better?" I asked, not bothering to turn around.

"Yeah." Martin sat down on the couch. "What are you watching?" He stared at the paused, grainy, black and white surveillance footage.

I turned to see if he was attempting to make a joke or if he really was clueless. "Surveillance from the lobby."

He looked at the list I made. "You sure do like to make lists, don't you?"

"It helps." I didn't know why I did it. It was just part of my process since I didn't necessarily trust myself to remember things that might seem innocuous but turn out to be important.

"What do the circles mean?" He seemed interested, so I explained what I was doing. "Are these the timestamps?" He pointed to the times written next to the names.

"Yeah."

"I think you can cross these off." He took my pen and

marked off six more names. "Lunch is thirty minutes. They left too close to the explosion to have set a bomb." I tended to agree with his rationale. Maybe he was more than just a snazzy suit.

"So, out of the twelve suspects on the list, recognize anyone as potentially dangerous? Holding a grudge for something? Smart enough to create a bomb?" I hoped he could point us in the right direction.

He reread the names. "I don't know everyone, but really, Suzanne Griffin?" He gave me a look. "Come on, don't you think you can mark her off as a suspect?"

I had been so consumed with identifying people that I hadn't consciously realized her name was on the list, but I was getting a bad feeling. "Have you seen her since the explosion?"

Martin rubbed his hand down his face, thinking. "No. I don't think so."

"I didn't either." I remembered sitting in his office and wondering where she was. Reaching for my phone, I dialed O'Connell.

"O'Connell," he answered again.

"It's Parker." I was done with the pleasantries. "There's a Suzanne Griffin who works at Martin Tech. We haven't seen her since the explosion Thursday."

"Afraid something happened to her? Or thinking she's involved?"

I thought back to the strange conversation Griffin and I had on my second day at work. "I don't know. See what you can dig up, and let us know." I hung up.

"C'mon," Martin said dismissively, "she's worked at the company for years. She's getting close to collecting her pension. Why would she have done this?" He narrowed his eyes. "You're still upset about the conversation she had with you."

"You are being ridiculous and letting your personal feelings get in the way," I retorted. "Seriously though, we need to know where she is. I'm not saying she did this, but she never came back either. Didn't call or anything." I flipped through the absentees. "Does that seem like the reliable woman you know?"

"No. Do you think she's hurt?"

I didn't have an answer for him. I opened the employee manifest and found her phone number and address. Picking up my phone, I dialed the number, but there was no answer.

"I'll call Mark, and we'll check her place. You are going to stay here. If O'Connell calls, find out what he knows." I grabbed my keys while I dialed Mark's number. I put on my shoulder holster, snapped my handgun into the slot, and put a jacket on over it. "Stay put."

Martin stood up, seemingly ready to go with me. "But...," he began to protest.

"It's probably nothing." I wanted to downplay my bad feeling. "I'll be back soon, and I'm taking Mark with me. Remember, you're the body I was hired to guard. Don't make my job more difficult." I tried to joke, and he resigned himself to house arrest and sat back down on the couch. I went down the stairs to retrieve my car as my phone finally connected with Mark's. "Where are you?" I asked.

"I just got home. What's going on?"

I shut the car door before replying, afraid Martin might overhear. "I'm not really sure, but I might need some backup. Griffin, the secretary, just got bumped to number one on my suspect list. No one's seen her since the explosion. I'll pick you up on the way."

"Okay. Did you call the police?" he asked as I drove away from Martin's compound and onto the main road.

"I called O'Connell, but who knows how long it'll take him to check things out. I have a bad feeling about this."

"Woman's intuition?"

"Years of training." I could hear Mark checking to make sure his service pistol was loaded.

"That's what I was afraid of."

We ended the call, and within fifteen minutes, I was honking my horn outside his house. He got into my car, and off we went.

The GPS got us to Griffin's address in twenty minutes, and I parked on the street. The neighborhood seemed quiet. Mark and I approached the front door. It appeared no one was home. He rang the doorbell, and we waited. I tried to peer into the front window, but the blinds were closed.

"Try it again," I insisted, stepping away from the porch and going toward the driveway. There were no cars parked there, but that didn't mean Griffin hadn't parked in the garage.

"Nothing," Mark said. He knocked a couple of times. "Mrs. Griffin?" he called. He turned to me and shook his head.

"I'll check around back." I walked around the house, but everything seemed normal. I reached the back door and tried to turn the knob, but it was locked. The back windows were closed, and there were no signs of anything amiss. I returned to the front of the house.

"Anything?" he asked, and I shook my head.

"Want to do some canvassing since we came all the way here?"

Mark seemed annoyed but played along, anyway. I took the house to the right; he took the left. We knocked on a few doors, asking if anyone had seen Mrs. Griffin since she didn't show up to work. The neighbors were less than helpful. No one remembered when they had seen her last. Mark and I were getting ready to leave when I saw flashing red and blue lights.

"Did you call in the cavalry?" I asked. We turned and waited while O'Connell and another detective pulled up behind me and shut the lights.

"Ms. Parker, funny running into you here," O'Connell said. "You too, Agent Jablonsky."

"Just in the neighborhood," I replied. "What brings you down here?"

O'Connell gave me a no-nonsense look. "Checking out a lead, not to mention dispatch got a call about some suspicious looking people snooping around their neighbor's house."

"Hmm. I don't remember seeing anyone suspicious. Did you, Mark?" I asked, and Mark glared at me.

"Need I remind you this is our investigation?" O'Connell threatened.

"Just checking on an employee," I responded. "Y'know, part of my job description at Martin Tech."

O'Connell shook his head slowly. "Find anything?" he asked. I guess he decided if you can't beat them, join them.

"No one's home, and no one's seen anything. Well, except for some suspicious people walking around for the last twenty minutes, apparently." I couldn't help but be sarcastic. "I showed you mine. Want to show me yours?"

"We've got a plane ticket under the name Suzanne Griffin. She was supposed to fly out today, one-way to Nova Scotia, but she never checked in at the airport."

The detective with O'Connell knocked on Griffin's door. "This is the police, ma'am. Please open up." After a few moments, he turned to the three of us. "No response."

"Maybe we heard some screaming for help coming from inside," Mark suggested. "It might be part of your job to enter, just to check things out."

O'Connell considered it for a moment. "No. We're doing things right. I'm not screwing up an investigation that will end up being dismissed in court for improper procedure." Well, at least now, I had my answer about what kind of guy O'Connell was. "You got anything else which might make getting a warrant easier?"

"All I know is she is always at work, and she left before the explosion and hasn't been back since. Not on Thursday and not on Friday. Martin's worried. He says it's not like her."

"Can you get me access to her work office?" O'Connell asked. I agreed and called Martin.

"Call the office. Tell them Detective O'Connell needs to get in to check out Griffin's office," I instructed Martin as Mark and I followed the police car back to the MT building. "I'm so glad I don't have to go to the office anymore," I said ironically as we parked and got out of the car, and Mark gave me an odd look. "I've already been here once today." My ID and Martin's were at home, but luckily, Todd picked up an extra shift and was still working security.

"Ms. Parker," he greeted.

"Hey, Todd, you know why we're here."

He came around the desk. "I'll take you to her office."

He kindly unlocked the door. "I'll be downstairs if you need anything else."

I thanked him, and the two cops entered Griffin's office.

"Stay outside. We don't need you potentially contaminating anything." O'Connell spoke as if I were incompetent. I sighed but stood in the hallway, trying to peer inside.

"Did you leave your door open?" Mark asked, getting my attention.

"No, why?" I turned to see my office door cracked open. Mark pushed it open a bit more with his foot. It was obvious someone had been inside. Everything was slightly askew. The papers on the desk were scattered everywhere, and the trashcan was dumped on the floor. I was about to step inside when Mark grabbed my arm.

"O'Connell," he called. The detective poked his head out of Griffin's office. "We might have a problem."

O'Connell approached us, not understanding what was going on until he saw the mess inside. "Thompson," he called to his partner, "lock that up for now. We have another issue."

They entered my office and carefully checked to make sure no one was still inside. O'Connell approached the storage closet while Thompson covered him. I was outside in the hallway where I was instructed to remain with Mark. We were prepared to rush in if need be when I heard a loud thump as the closet door opened.

Please don't be a dead body, I thought as I reached for my weapon and stepped into the office.

FIFTEEN

"You should talk to Martin about hiring better janitorial staff," O'Connell teased as the four of us stood over the ancient vacuum cleaner that had been stuffed in the closet.

"Clearly." I looked around, positive someone had gone through everything looking for information. Information on what, I didn't know. Perhaps someone was checking to see if I was investigating Martin's threats or maybe looking for information on Martin or me. Good thing I cleaned everything out yesterday before we left.

"It just looks like the janitors got called away before they finished cleaning up," Thompson said.

I wondered how long he had been on the job, or if he had any clue how serious this could be. I wanted to strangle him.

O'Connell eyed me curiously. "Are you sure you shut the door? It doesn't look like anything was really disturbed or damaged." He didn't seem concerned.

"Maybe you're right." I wondered what the surveillance tapes would show. Whoever was up here had less than twenty-four hours to get into my office, look around, and leave. Maybe the security cameras caught the culprit in the act. Maybe he was watching us at this very moment. Parker, you're being paranoid.

Unfortunately, things weren't adding up. Griffin was missing, and my office had been searched. I was sure of it. I learned long ago, just because you're paranoid, it doesn't mean people aren't after you. Mark looked at me skeptically. He didn't buy this was a cleaning oversight any more than I did.

"I guess I'm losing it. I must have left the door open, and maybe the janitors got distracted and didn't get a chance to take out the trash properly. My mistake," I lied through my teeth, and Mark knew it.

"Maybe we should check to see if the cameras have anything on them, you know, with Mrs. Griffin being gone and all," Mark suggested, and I had a feeling he wanted to know who had been inside my office just as badly as I did.

"That would be most helpful." O'Connell smiled sweetly. "If you could get us a copy, it would greatly help our investigation." He was relieved I had something else to do with my time besides make him go on scavenger hunts.

I went back to the lobby and found Todd in the security office. "Hey, I have another favor to ask. The police want a copy of the video for the seventeenth floor from Thursday through today."

"No problem." Todd typed commands into the computer.

"Mr. Martin would also like a copy. He wants to keep up with everything going on around here, especially in his absence."

"Of course." Todd saved the files to a disk and copied the same information to another. "Here you go." He handed me both disks.

"If you see anyone from cleaning, can you tell them they never finished in my office? It looks like they got distracted before they were done." I wanted to appear naïve and ignorant. It never hurt to play dumb.

"Sure thing." He seemed uneasy but didn't say anything more.

I went back upstairs and found O'Connell, Thompson, and Mark inside Griffin's office. I slowly edged my way into the room. "Here." I handed the disk to O'Connell, expecting him to berate me for entering the office, but he didn't.

"Thanks." He took the disk and put it inside his jacket pocket. "We didn't find anything. The only information here is work related, schedules of meetings and appointments for the board members, errands to run, mostly run-of-the-mill stuff."

"It was worth a shot," Mark responded.

"She's still missing," I said. The detectives were losing sight of the problem. "She's not at work. She's not at home, and she didn't show up at the airport for some trip no one was aware she was taking. There is something seriously wrong."

"We'll look into it," O'Connell said firmly. "If she doesn't show up to work Monday, maybe Martin or someone from the company can file a missing person's. But you told me Friday was an optional workday, and it's the weekend now. She's not missing, not yet anyway."

I sighed. His hands were tied, and so were mine. I turned and walked out of the office. I was sick of the bureaucratic red-tape. Mark told the cops to do as they liked and to keep him informed before catching up with me at the elevator.

"Someone isn't playing well with others," he chided, but I didn't say a word. We left the building and went back to my car in silence.

Once we were on our way to Mark's place, I finally spoke. "There was someone in my office looking for god knows what, and despite what the cops say, I'm positive something is very wrong when it comes to Griffin."

"I agree, but there is nothing you can do right now. Check out the feed, see if you can spot who was in your office, and Monday, if Griffin hasn't shown up, then the cops can start searching. It's all you can do."

"Just for the record, playing by the rules sucks. For all they know, she's the bomber, or she's dead. What good is any of this waiting around doing?" This was exactly the reason why I didn't work at the OIO anymore. I pulled up to Mark's house and stopped the car.

"It's a start. You will figure this thing out. Come on, you've already made better connections and have more leads than I ever did." He patted my shoulder.

"It took long enough to get to this point."

"You got this." He opened the car door. "Just tell Marty

to keep his head down until it's resolved."

I drove around randomly for a while, thinking about things. Griffin was missing, and my office had been broken into. I was one hundred percent certain whoever was threatening Martin was a current employee at MT. Could it be Mrs. Griffin? Initially, that's what my gut said, but now with her missing and the unclaimed plane ticket to Nova Scotia, I was beginning to think something horrible had happened to her. I mean honestly, who the hell plans a trip and doesn't go? *You're just going to have to let the cops do their job, Parker*, I reminded myself.

When I arrived at Martin's compound, I heard him talking on the phone. "Thanks, I appreciate it. If you need anything else, let me know." I shut the door, announced my presence, and looked at him. He held up a finger, indicating I should wait a minute. I put my belongings down and took off my shoulder holster, waiting for him to hang up. "That was Detective O'Connell," Martin answered my questioning look. "He found a bus ticket confirmation under Suzanne's maiden name. Someone is checking into it. He'll let us know."

I sighed and sat down. "I'm glad he called." I closed my eyes and leaned my head against the back of the couch. The seat next to me sunk in slightly as he sat down. I turned to look at him. He looked like a lost puppy. "We don't know she's behind this. We don't even know if she's involved. Maybe she just got scared and took off." It felt like I was coddling him, but I didn't need him melting down again, or worse yet, having a replay of last night.

"While you were gone, I watched the surveillance a few times and checked into the employee records of our possible suspect list." He held up the notepad to show me the list he made.

"I thought you didn't like lists."

"I guess I learned from the best." He handed me the notepad. "Anyway, I've done some digging into the employee files." He had crossed off about a third of the names. "It doesn't seem likely these individuals would have access to manufacturing, let alone the knowledge to sabotage anything at the plant. Monday, we'll get the surveillance, and hopefully, it will narrow this down further." He hedged, and I suspected he might be hiding something.

"What?"

"I gave the list to O'Connell, figured he might as well do some checking."

"It's okay. We scratch his back, and maybe he'll scratch ours." It wouldn't hurt to have some professionals looking into things, especially given the bang-up job I had been doing. "Why didn't you go to the cops in the first place, when you received the first threat?"

"I didn't want the publicity. Bad press is never a good thing for a company. Plus, things like this happen all the time. Despite what you might think about me crying wolf, I'm not one of those people."

"Fair enough." It didn't explain why he didn't call the cops after things escalated, but I didn't push the issue. I informed him about the trip to Griffin's and to the office. Finally, I told him about the break-in.

"If you want to back out of this, you can. No hard feelings."

"Like I said, I'm not going anywhere. This is what I do, and things like this come with the territory. I'm not one to run and hide whenever there are a few bumps in the road." We were heading toward dangerous ground, flitting around last night's conversation, so I tried to steer us clear. I pulled out the new surveillance disk. "But we might be able to figure out who it was."

He smirked and got up from the couch. "I'll let you get started on that, and I will start on dinner." A man who cooks, I could get used to this.

I popped the disk into the DVD player and flipped my notepad to a new sheet of paper while Martin rummaged around in the kitchen, pulling out pots and pans.

"Hey, what do you know about Todd?" I asked.

"Todd?"

"Yeah, security guard, Todd. I don't know his last name." Why didn't I look at his name tag? Did it not say? I thought about it for a moment and realized I didn't remember seeing a name tag on him.

Martin came back into the living room with an apron tied around his waist, and I tried not to laugh. "Jackson, I think." He considered it for a second. "That's it. He's normally there when I leave in the afternoons. He's just the night shift guy. Seems friendly. Why?"

"No reason. He was just really helpful today."

Martin nodded in an 'I see' fashion and went back into the kitchen. He continued to cook while I stared at a mostly boring screen.

There was a single camera positioned at the end of the hallway on the seventeenth floor, and the only people on the footage were Martin and me as we walked from my office to his or vice versa. I hit fast forward and watched as we exited our offices in a Laurel and Hardy fashion and got into the elevator. The tape continued without any movement until 2:17 AM, according to the timestamp.

At this point, the elevator doors opened, and a person wearing overalls and a baseball cap pushed a cleaning cart into the hallway. He kept his head down as he pushed the cart toward my office. The man stood in front of my door for a while before getting it open. It probably took him a few minutes to pick the lock, but then I remembered no one had noticed scratches or telltale tool marks on the doorknob. He must have gotten the key from security.

"Do the janitors have keys to all the offices?" I called into the kitchen.

"I think so, or they just borrow the master set from security. I'm not really sure. I've never worried about it."

I ignored Martin's unhelpful response and continued watching the footage. Maybe what had taken so long was the guy trying to find the right key to get the door opened. Once he got into the office, I couldn't see anything else since the camera only covered the hallway. It was 2:33 when he exited. He left my door open and headed down the corridor, his face still obscured from view, and into Griffin's office. He opened her door faster than mine, and within ten minutes, he left her office, carrying something. I paused the playback and stood directly in front of the television, but I couldn't make out what the item was.

"What is that?" Martin asked, and I almost jumped out

of my skin.

"Don't scare me like that. Do you want me to shoot you?"

"Jumpy," he sounded amused. "Who else would be behind you?"

"I didn't hear you." I stared intently at the screen. It looked like a shoebox. "You need better cameras. Some color HD ones would be a vast improvement."

"I'll add it to my list," he mocked.

I hit play, and the man on the camera headed back to my open office door. He was almost inside when the elevator opened again. He turned and dropped the item into the garbage bag on the cleaning cart and ducked his head.

"Who's on the elevator?"

Martin squinted at the television. "I'm not sure." He got a little closer. "Looks like another janitor. See?" He pointed to the uniform. "And isn't that a cleaning cart in the elevator with him?" He pointed to another indecipherable object.

"I'm guessing shoebox-janitor guy wasn't supposed to be working the seventeenth floor."

"Probably not," he agreed.

"So who the hell is he? And what the hell is in the box?"

SIXTEEN

I sat across from Martin at the dinner table. We were eating the pasta primavera he made and bouncing ideas off of each other. Mark and I had done this numerous times at the OIO, and I figured it wouldn't hurt.

"Did the bomb squad check out the building?" I asked around a mouthful of angel hair.

"Yeah, Thursday evening." He took a sip of water. I was relieved he wasn't drinking with dinner. "I gave them permission to do a full sweep."

"So the box more than likely wasn't a bomb."

He shrugged and helped himself to another serving. We ate in silence for a few minutes. "Run through it again," he said after we finished eating.

I rolled my head from side to side to work the tension out of my neck. I was getting sick of going over the same things and not getting different results. Wasn't that the definition of neurotic?

"Okay, Mrs. Griffin is missing, last seen on the surveillance tape from Thursday, pre-explosion. No word from her except for a plane ticket and a bus ticket, different locations. LEOs are working on that." I stopped to make sure I hadn't forgotten anything.

"Friday late night, shoebox-janitor guy." Martin wanted me to continue the run-through.

"Right, he enters my office, looking for god knows what, then goes back into Griffin's office, retrieves a box, and plans to take it back to my office." I looked at him curiously. "Why?"

"Why what?"

"Why put something in my office. I mean if it were a bomb, okay. I open it, ka-boom. Or maybe it was addressed to you. I give it to you, ka-boom."

"Stop saying ka-boom. We know it wasn't a bomb. Suzanne hasn't been at work since Thursday afternoon, and the box he retrieved from her office was on Friday. No one had been in there in the meantime, except the bomb squad."

"What would she have possibly needed to have surreptitiously placed in my office?"

He leaned back in his chair and looked up at the ceiling. "Blackmail?"

"What in the world have I done to warrant blackmail? Plus, why the need to hide whatever it was from the actual janitor? Couldn't fake janitor have just said he was delivering a misplaced package or something?"

"Maybe the blackmail was against me," he said quietly.

"Explain."

He shrugged and got up to clear the table, trying to avoid the conversation.

I followed him to the sink, cornering him. "I'm waiting."

"It's nothing, just speculation on my part." He was backpedaling quickly, and I gave him a serious look. "It's just, I have a bit of a past. Wealth and power make a great aphrodisiac. Assuming anyone believes you are my permanent romantic liaison, maybe they are trying to encourage you to abandon me." He was serious, but I couldn't help giving him my 'yeah, right' look.

"Oh, please," I rolled my eyes, "unless you have a dead hooker in the closet or some stripper who overdosed on blow, I don't think your sexual escapades are that important."

"Perhaps because you're not really dating me," he practically spat.

"Speaking from past experience?"

Obviously, he must be since he ignored me and began scrubbing the pots and pans.

I waited him out, and once the water shut off, I tried again. "Are there any serious skeletons in your closet? Dead employees? Back-stabbing deals? Under-handed business practices? Illegal drug use? Prostitution?"

"No."

I looked into his eyes, but I didn't think he was lying. "Are you sure? Maybe something from college or a vacation? Anything? Family secrets?"

"There's nothing. Anything even remotely scandalous has all been aboveboard."

"We are back to square one. What's in the box?" I really couldn't stand his mood swings, but I tried to get us back on track. I picked up a towel and dried the dishes. As I was doing this, I thought about the blackmail suggestion and the conversation Griffin had with me my second day on the job. There was more to the story. I could feel it. I nudged him with my elbow. "Maybe you're right. Griffin didn't want me around since I was just the most recent in your line of newest models. So let's say she had a box of pictures of you with Bambi, Bimbo, and Bunny. Why didn't she drop it off? Why tell anyone else about it and then have them break into my office to deliver it, especially after you and I weren't going to be working out of the office any longer?"

"Maybe whoever it was figured you'd go back to work, even if I wasn't," he suggested, and the familiar gnawing returned to the corner of my mind.

"If you are right about this, and clearly there is no way to tell," I provided my disclaimer, "then Griffin is involved, and maybe whatever is in the box is motive."

"Motive?"

"Yeah, to frame me for killing you." As the words left my mouth, a chill traveled down my spine.

"We don't know any of this," he began, but it was my turn to interrupt.

"True. Until we have more concrete evidence, we'll stick with Occam's Razor." I waited, making sure he understood my point.

"Least amount of new assumptions, got it. Or if you prefer, pluralitas non est ponenda sine necessitate," he quoted the Latin and graced me with a self-satisfied smirk.

"Wiseass. But this brings us back to the current problem. We still don't know where Griffin is, what the hell is in the box, or most importantly, who is behind everything."

I left him to finish cleaning up while I went into the living room to re-watch the surveillance tape again. I still wasn't getting anything more out of it. Switching to the Thursday morning tape, I let it run through. The wheels in my head were spinning, but I was stuck in the mud. I turned off the DVD player and the television and stared at the blank screen.

"Dammit." Picking up the remote, I threw it across the room. I wasn't getting anywhere, and I didn't know where else to go.

"Very lady-like," he said, entering the room.

Rubbing my neck, I looked at him. "Sorry," I muttered.

He stood behind the couch where I was sitting. "Let me." Before I could ask what he was talking about, he began massaging the kink out of my neck. I closed my eyes. God, that felt good.

"You don't have to." I opened my eyes and tried to lean away from his insistent hands, but he continued. "I just feel like we're on the edge of something, and I'm not seeing it. I've watched this damn tape a hundred times, and I'm not seeing anything new. It has to be there, or I must have missed something."

"Take the day off. Actually, take the rest of the weekend off. No more surveillance footage. No more checking on leads. Nothing. Just hang around here. Go for a swim, have a drink, do whatever it is you do for fun, and Monday, when we get the plant footage, you can start this whole process over again. Just don't throw the remote next time. It's hard to find replacements."

"I can't do that." I finally pulled away from his massaging grasp.

"Too bad." He came around the couch, taking the notepads and moving them onto the coffee table before sitting down beside me. "I have a banquet to attend tomorrow evening. It's more of a ball really, black tie, very formal. Since you insist on working all weekend, I guess you'll have to escort me." He winked as I tried to determine if he was serious.

"I thought you were lying low. And if you wanted me to take the weekend off, I don't see how having to work bodyguard duty can be considered time off."

"True, but you rejected my offer of time off. Plus, it's a party. Parties are fun." He raised an eyebrow. "Do you need me to define the word fun for you?"

"Depends, you seem to have a pretty fucked up concept of what fun is." I was already dreading the thought of being any place in public with him, given the explosion, the mystery shoebox-janitor, and the unknown whereabouts of Mrs. Griffin. "I thought you were going to keep your head down and avoid the crosshairs. If this is a planned event," I remembered him briefly talking to one of the board members about it on Friday, "then there could be a bull's-eye on your back."

"Good thing I've got my bodyguard then."

"But you said I could have the rest of the weekend off," I whined, trying to get his previous offer back on the table. I was attempting to make an unreasonable man see reason; clearly, this was a hopeless endeavor.

"You already said you're incapable of taking a day off, so instead, it's a workday based on my work." He seemed pleased with himself. Damn manipulative bastard and his unilateral decision-making. I could feel the kink returning to my neck, and I sighed loudly to express my displeasure. He grinned. "You'll have fun. I promise."

"What's the security going to be like?"

Pleased I had given up, he said, "That's the spirit." He spent the next thirty minutes explaining where the event was being held, what it was for, and how incredibly stringent security would be. I spent the same half hour trying not to go into a coma from the boredom. "Are you even listening?"

"Huh?" I had been semi-listening; apparently, the gala was going to be in a ballroom at a five-star hotel with valet parking, cater-waiters, and things like that. Those in attendance were supporting bringing food, water, or medicine, some type of necessity, to third world countries. The guest list included the Martin Tech board members, their investors, their honored guests, some B and C-list celebrities, and other similar types. All very social and civil with the Muffys and Buffys of the crowd. He sighed and got up from the couch. "I'm sorry, what did you ask? I got the gist of it."

"I asked if you had anything to wear." He seemed annoyed, which annoyed me; it was a vicious cycle. He was the one manipulating the situation in the first place, and now he was annoyed because I wasn't paying enough attention to his monotonous discourse.

"Um." I made a mental assessment of my clothing. I could do business professional or business casual, but when it came to cocktail dresses worthy of an event of this magnitude, shopping seemed to be required. "Not exactly. Unless I can go as a former OIO agent or maybe a cater-waiter, but I'd probably need to borrow a tux for that. So I guess we can nix the cater-waiter idea." I looked innocently at him, hoping we could nix the entire event.

"That's what I thought." He seemed consumed by his own thoughts.

"So, no party?"

"No, we're definitely going." He waggled an eyebrow. "But maybe I can be persuaded to cut out early." He was back to being a lothario, and we had been making such progress too.

It was decided, somewhat unilaterally, that I needed to get a good night's sleep. Apparently, Martin didn't want to attend such an important function with a zombie. He set the motion sensors on the alarm system for the first two floors of the house. This was meant to encourage me to stay in my room and actually sleep, instead of patrolling the house late at night. However, I ended up lying in bed, listening to every creak and groan of the house settling as if it were an attacker in the shadows preparing an assault. The light began to filter in from outside before I actually fell asleep.

I dreamt I was on the seventeenth floor of the MT building, chasing after Mrs. Griffin. But the hallway was never-ending. I could see her running away, but I couldn't catch up. The chase continued as we ran past some cops, then janitors, and finally a slew of strippers.

"Knock, knock," Martin called from the hallway. I jumped up in bed and squinted at the clock. It was almost noon. Despite having slept five or six hours, all the dream-running made me feel even more exhausted. He slowly opened the door a crack. "Are you awake?" he asked, which I found to be a ridiculous question since I was sitting up in bed.

"Yeah." I stretched. "I didn't mean to sleep so late. Perhaps, I was just imagining I had the day off. Crazy notion, right?" Not that I was annoyed or bitter or anything.

He ignored the jibe. "I brought you a present." He held out a garment bag and shopping bag. "Don't worry, I didn't go anywhere. Marcal ran some errands this morning."

I eyed the designer logos as he hung the garment bag from the doorframe and put the shopping bag on the floor next to it. "Party's tonight at eight. We'll leave around 7:30. I like to be punctual, but you might want to make sure I got the right size." He scrutinized my face. "Did you even sleep?"

I glared at him. My hair was probably all over the place. I had no makeup on, and he was commenting on my looks. "Get out," I growled.

He smirked and closed the door. "Hurry up. I'm making brunch, and I don't want it to get cold."

SEVENTEEN

I took a quick shower, threw on an oversized t-shirt and a pair of shorts, ran a brush through my still wet hair, and went down to the kitchen to meet Martin. His continued insistence to do and act how he pleased without any regard for his own safety or mine fueled my irritation toward him. I hoped he realized I wasn't part of the Secret Service and he wasn't the President because I damn sure wasn't going to jump in front of a bullet to save his life and sacrifice my own, especially when he couldn't take my advice on keeping a low profile.

I walked into the kitchen. The table was set nicely. Coffee was already poured, and there were flowers in a vase. I looked at him skeptically; perhaps this was a peace offering, a bribe, or someone had died.

"Sleep well?" he asked, flipping through the newspaper.

"Sure," I replied sarcastically. I sat down and picked up a bagel and put some scrambled eggs on my plate. "Y'know, I'm getting the sneaking suspicion you like to cook."

"That's just the kind of thing that makes you such a great investigator." He folded the paper and put it on the table.

I resisted the urge to stick my tongue out like a three-year-old. We ate in silence for a few minutes.

"This is actually really good." I scooped up the last forkful.

"Thanks." There was an awkward pause, and it occurred

to me if we weren't talking about his threats or his job, we really didn't have much to say to one another. "So, what did you think?" he asked. I was confused. Didn't I just compliment him on the meal? He sensed my confusion and clarified. "The dress?"

"Oh." I hadn't bothered to unzip the bag. "I haven't looked yet." He sighed, trying hard not to lose his patience. "I'll go check it out, now." I was getting tired of conceding. Was I just stubborn? Probably.

I trudged up the stairs, leaving him with the dishes. Unzipping the bag, I found a deep purple dress, so dark it was almost black, with a plunging neckline. At first glance, I thought the back was facing forward.

"You've got to be kidding me." I took the dress off the hanger, figuring I might as well try it on before I murdered him. Oddly enough, he had gotten my size just right. Then again, he probably only spent time with models, so being a size two didn't require too much guesswork on his part. The dress had a fairly modest back, considering, and a halter top front with a neckline I would have never chosen in a million years. It fell to my ankles, and the slit on the right side came to mid-thigh. "Sexist pig," I muttered to my reflection. Okay, so maybe I looked good in a designer dress that would have been a month's salary at my last job, if I liked the slutty look.

The curiosity got the best of me, and I looked in the shopping bag. Inside was a fabulous pair of Jimmy Choo's with small diamond studs glistening off the straps. These I could work with as long as I didn't have to run. Thoughts of my dream re-entered my mind, and I cringed at the possibility of having to run in stilettos. Hopefully, tonight would be nothing more than a fun night out, like he kept insisting. I tried the shoes on and walked around the room. Not as uncomfortable as I would have imagined. Finally, I noticed a smaller bag inside the shopping bag.

I took the dress off, hung it up, and put my clothes back on. I placed the shoes safely in their box, grabbed the third bag, and went downstairs in a huff. *Sarcasm or anger*, I debated, descending the flight of stairs.

Martin was in the living room, waiting expectantly. He

seemed disappointed I wasn't prancing down the stairs to model for him. Instead, I threw the small La Perla bag at him.

"Either you left your undergarments in the shopping bag by mistake, or this is sexual harassment." What do you know, sarcasm and anger can coexist.

He didn't even miss a beat. "If you rather I wear these, that can be arranged." The arrogant son of a bitch smiled.

"Fine, we'll go with sexual harassment then."

"I just thought you might want to dress to the nines completely."

"Thanks, but no thanks." Our natural state of existence was bickering.

"How was the rest? Did it fit? Did you like the shoes? Diamonds are a girl's best friend." He really was unperturbed and quoting me no less.

"It's fine for Bambi the Whore. The shoes, well, I can work with those." A small smile crept onto my face as I spoke. He was pleased. "Really, though," I said seriously, "tonight is not a good idea on any account. I strongly discourage attending."

But he waved off my warning. "It will be fine. It's a charity event. We rub elbows with the other affluent members of the community, put on a good face for the company, and do something philanthropic. It's a win-win-win situation."

It's all fun and games until someone gets murdered; I didn't share that thought aloud.

"Security is on high alert, right?" I double-checked, and he reassured me of this fact. "Okay, whatever you say, boss." I wasn't happy about the situation.

The rest of the afternoon was spent re-watching the security footage. I called Mark and Det. O'Connell but neither answered. I didn't have anything new to tell them, but I hoped they had some news. Mark was likely at work. Maybe it was O'Connell's day off, or he was afraid I might send him on another wild goose chase and just didn't want to answer his phone.

Martin made himself scarce for most of the day, remaining on the fourth floor to primp for the evening or work on something. I was glad for the break. He was a difficult person to get along with, but at the same time, he was a difficult person to completely dislike. He was just frustrating, and after being forced to play his girlfriend all night, we would probably be sick of one another soon enough. It was a good thing he was giving me some space now. The less time we spent together, the better off we'd be; I tried to convince myself.

Unfortunately, I was getting restless. It was a little after four when I knocked on his bedroom door. There was no answer, so I walked down the hallway to his private office and knocked again.

"It's open," he called from his desk as he went over expense reports.

"Sorry if I disturbed you."

"What's up?" He put down the sheet of paper.

"I wanted to make sure you were okay here since I was thinking of going for a quick run." It felt like I was asking permission, and I guess, in a way, I was.

He rubbed his eyes and leaned back in the chair. "Give me five minutes." Apparently, he thought I was inviting him to go for a run.

"Okay."

I went to the guestroom and put on some sneakers and tied my hair up. I grabbed my waist pack and put my side arm and cell phone in it. Never could be too careful. I was downstairs stretching on the floor when Martin came down. He had changed into a t-shirt, running shorts, and sneakers. My initial impression of him had definitely been accurate. He did have a runner's body; although I had been reassured of this the morning he had gone swimming. I pushed those thoughts out of my mind.

"You don't have to go if you're busy," I told him.

"Nonsense, I was staring at expense reports completely unable to figure out where the money went." He stretched too. "Sorry, I didn't mean to bore you with work on your day off, Alex," he teased.

We exited the back door, and he set the alarm system on the way out. We started out with a slow, comfortable jog, pacing nicely with one another.

"What do you mean you can't find the money?" His work was one of the safer topics to discuss.

"Remember the Dubai acquisition?" We circled the house and headed for the driveway. "There is a specific account set aside for company acquisitions, but the money for Dubai isn't in the account."

"But if you already acquired Dubai, wouldn't the money have been spent?" I didn't have an accounting background, so my thinking was likely too simplistic.

"Not yet. We agreed upon the price, but we are still in the midst of finalizing the sale. Final payment has not been made. It's kind of like buying a house. It's a slow process with a lot of steps in between."

"Do you think it's just a bank error? Or maybe Mr. Denton expedited the sale?"

"I don't see how that could be." We picked up the pace slightly as we jogged from the end of the driveway and onto the private road. It was much cooler here with the trees providing ample shade.

"Do you think someone stole the money?" I didn't know what else to ask.

Martin chuckled. "No. It was probably just misappropriated to another fund, but I have to go through all the accounts in order to figure out where it went."

Conversation was getting more difficult as we continued to increase our speed. We made it down the private road, almost to the connection to the main thoroughfare, when I announced through my huffing and puffing we should turn around. Thankfully, he was in complete agreement.

"Race you back?" he asked, and even though I was slightly winded, I was too competitive for my own good.

"Okay." We both ran full-out back to the house. He got there before I did and was unlocking the door when I came up behind him. "You have longer legs," I protested as we went inside. "And you're a guy. It's an unfair advantage." My complaining amused him.

He went to the fridge and retrieved two bottles of water, handing one to me. "Thanks for getting me out of here and away from the paperwork. I know I give you a hard time about just relaxing. I need to follow my own advice and do the same." Post-workout Martin was much more amiable than everyday Martin. I would keep that in mind. He glanced at the clock; it was close to five. "I'm going to shower and give you some time to get ready."

He went up the stairs to his room while I drank some water and stared out the window. Was Martin always so isolated from people, hiding in work, or was he doing this because of the threats? Granted, I shouldn't be the one to talk since I tended to hole up in my apartment far too often. Deciding I needed to get ready, I made my way to the stairs, glancing at the La Perla bag still sitting untouched on the armchair. Just in case, I retrieved the bag and headed up to my room.

EIGHTEEN

I checked my reflection in the full-length mirror. The dress fit nicely, and the shoes complimented it perfectly. I curled my hair and clipped half of it up. I put on more makeup than normal and tried to decide if there was any place to strategically hide a weapon. I'd just have to hope security was on their toes tonight. Worst case, I could brain an attacker with the heel of my shoe.

Trying to make sure I didn't trip on either the dress or the shoes, I descended the stairs slowly. Martin was already downstairs, his back to me. He was on the phone, speaking with someone. I tried to eavesdrop to see if it might be Mark or one of the detectives calling, but I quickly realized it was someone from the accounting department at MT.

"If you can fax over the statements, that would be most helpful." Martin paused, and I could hear muffled sounds coming from whoever was on the other end of the conversation. "Yes, I know it's Sunday night." Another pause. "No, I will not be in the office tomorrow. I'm on vacation." He was agitated, so I busied myself with checking my phone for any missed messages. "Okay, thanks. Have a good night." He hung up.

I turned partially away from him, listening to my voicemail inform me there were no new messages. When I turned back around, he smiled.

"You look absolutely breathtaking."

Right back at you, I thought. He wore a charcoal gray suit with a slight silver sheen and a light lavender shirt accented by a coordinating striped silk tie and matching pocket square.

I blushed slightly and hoped he didn't notice. "Thanks. I guess you have good taste in women's fashion." I couldn't help but joke; that's what nerves did to me. "You don't look too bad yourself."

My compliment delighted him. He glanced briefly at the empty armchair and then back at me, but he remained silent. "Shall I call Marcal and have him bring the car around?"

I shrugged. "Whenever you're ready."

He smirked, and I could see the devious thoughts swimming around in his mind. "I'm always ready," he looked at his watch, "but we have some time. I need to check on a fax. Want to make yourself a drink in the meantime?"

"I'm working." I thought he was going to argue, but he decided better of it and continued out of the room and into his office to check the fax machine.

"Want to make me one, sweetheart?" he called, attempting to be charming, but I resisted.

"Actually, if you could do me a huge favor and not get shit-faced tonight, that would be great." I sounded passive-aggressive. "Don't get me wrong, I'm not a teetotaler, nor do I really care what you do on your own time. It's just, if things go haywire, I want to know you're functioning well enough to get out of the way of anything." I wasn't entirely sure what the anything could be, but given his recent history, anything seemed to be the appropriate word.

He came back into the living room, carrying a few sheets of paper. I wasn't sure he heard a word I said. He frowned at the papers and put them down on the kitchen table. "I'll deal with this later." He looked up, perhaps seeing if I had poured a drink for him. "Agreed," he conceded.

* * *

The ride to the hotel was uneventful. Marcal and Martin

made small talk, and Marcal asked how I was enjoying staying at the manor, his term for Martin's compound. This was the first real conversation I had with Martin's chauffeur, and I discovered he had a wife and two daughters. He and his family went shopping for my dress which his wife picked out.

I glanced at Martin. "I thought you were up on women's fashion, secretly staying up late to watch fashion shows and subscribing to all the magazines." Martin chuckled, and I turned to Marcal. "Tell your wife she has exquisite taste, and I appreciate you taking the time out of your day to do this."

Marcal waved off the gratitude. "It's not a problem. Mr. Martin's always been good to us. We don't mind helping him out." Maybe I was the only person who wanted to slap Martin on an hourly basis.

The car pulled to a stop at the hotel entrance. Cameras were going off everywhere as I watched warily out the tinted window for anyone suspicious. This entire thing was surreal. The valet came toward the door, and I looked nervously at Martin.

"Just try to play the part." He seemed worried I wouldn't blend in, but I was more concerned with someone shooting him.

I gritted my teeth. "Fine. Let's just get inside as quickly as possible."

He shrugged, and I had a feeling as quickly as possible, in Martin speak, meant posing for a few photos. The valet opened the door, and Martin stepped out and waved briefly to the crowd of onlookers, mostly press, before turning and offering me his hand.

"Inside quickly," I hissed, taking his hand as he helped me out of the car.

"Smile," he whispered, beaming brightly at the press. He put his hand on the small of my back to guide me inside.

A few people, likely reporters, shouted questions to him. Things like are you really going on a vacation, is the leave from work because of the recent bomb scare, how long have you been dating this mystery woman, and are you traveling to Dubai for the recent acquisition. But he shrugged them off, and once we reached the entrance, he addressed the crowd.

"A public statement will be issued in the coming days, but tonight, let's focus on the good we are doing for those less fortunate."

He led me inside the hotel. As we passed through security checkpoints, I noticed hotel security and a few LEOs in the lobby.

"You're one hell of a public speaker." I admired his cool, collected demeanor.

"Just part of the CEO persona." He dismissed my compliment and offered his arm as we walked toward the ballroom where the banquet was being held.

The room was decorated exquisitely with numerous large, round tables skirting the edges. There was a bar at the back, a podium and stage set up at the front for speeches and toasts, and a dance floor in the center of the room. This felt like a very elaborate wedding reception or Bar Mitzvah. Martin led us through the room to one of the head tables.

Almost everyone greeted him as we passed with nice to see you and glad you could make it. He would stop momentarily to introduce me, only to see someone else and politely maneuver away, as we continued to make the rounds. We eventually made it to our table. He was in his element, but I couldn't stop scanning the room for possible danger.

A familiar voice came up behind us. "It's lovely to see you, James, and you brought Alexis, how wonderful." The voice belonged to acting-CEO Blake Denton.

"Mr. Denton." I turned, trying to appear pleased to be here.

Martin stood and shook his hand. "How is everything?" Martin was asking mainly about the office. Just business as usual for him, and he said I couldn't relax.

"Things are great," Denton reassured him. "The office is fine. No major crises to report." He smiled. "You realize I've only been in charge since Friday afternoon. It's Sunday, and the office is closed on the weekend."

Martin looked a little sheepish but said nothing. I wondered if he was going to discuss the accounting discrepancy, but surprisingly, he kept his mouth shut. A server walked past with a tray of champagne flutes, and Martin motioned him over and took two, handing me one.

Denton took the hint. "We'll catch up later. Lovely to see you again, Alexis." He disappeared into the throng of guests.

I looked at Martin, slightly confused. He scooted his chair closer to mine, despite the fact no one else was seated at our table or anywhere near us. "Are you having fun?" he asked. Once again, I wondered if he had multiple personalities.

"It's fine. Things seem secure." What exactly was I supposed to say? It's not like we were on a date. "Why do you seem wound so tightly?"

"I'm not. Things are great."

I didn't believe him for a second. Things were fine until Denton appeared. "So why do I feel like Denton makes your skin crawl?"

"He doesn't. Everything's fine."

I dropped it but filed it away to ask about later. We sat in an uneasy silence for a few moments.

"Shouldn't you be networking or whatever it is people like you do at events like this?"

"And shouldn't you be acting like you're into me instead of casing the room?" he retorted, so I laughed and touched his arm.

"You're so funny, honey." The sarcasm dripped from every word, and he shook his head. Luckily, our awkwardness was cut short by the announcement to take our seats.

Speeches were made, and information was given about how much money was raised and the good it would do. Martin got up somewhere in the middle and gave a brief speech about the efforts of his company and thanked his employees for their continued support. Luckily, no shots were fired. He concluded by mentioning he was going on a sabbatical of an unknown duration, but during his absence, he was positive Mr. Denton would continue to ensure

Martin Tech made the same charitable contributions. Once he finished, Denton took the stage to deliver a speech of his own.

"I thought you were having a press conference or issuing a statement?" I whispered when he came back to the table.

"No need. The press is covering this. They'll pick it up and run with it. The PR department can deal with the fallout and issue the official statement tomorrow morning." He was determined to be okay with the situation, but I couldn't help but think of the drunken man from Friday night pitying himself or the angry man in the office proclaiming he was nothing without this job. I reached over and put my hand on his arm. He looked down at it and then at me.

"Just playing along."

He put his hand over mine, and we sat through the rest of the speeches, toasts, and self-congratulations. When the formal portion of the evening was over, the house band began to play. People moved around, chatting in small groups, or dancing. Martin got up and led me to the bar.

"Scotch and soda, lots of ice," he ordered for himself and waited for my order.

"Lemon drop martini?" I asked the bartender. One drink couldn't hurt.

He prepared our drinks, and Martin put a fifty in the tip jar. A group congregated behind us.

"Alex," Martin turned to me, "these are a few of the board members. You might remember meeting them on Friday. Yuri Oskilov, Samantha Miller, Marcy Ryan, and Charles Roman."

"Nice to officially meet all of you."

"James, how long are you going to be gone?" Samantha asked curiously.

"And where are you going?" Marcy chimed in.

"I don't know yet." Martin wrapped his free hand around my waist and held me close. I played along and clung to his side, placing my arm around his back and my martini-holding hand against his chest, carefully so as not to spill, like the doting girlfriend would. "We'll figure something out though." He spoke as if we had a romantic vacation planned.

"Of course, we will." I tried not to act as confused as I felt. The Board knew of his threats and required his additional security, so why the secrecy? Maybe Martin had the same inkling I did; the person or persons responsible could be his trusted board members.

"After all that threat business and the explosion outside, it's good you're getting away while you can," Yuri said knowingly. "Are you still working with the same security firm?"

I tensed slightly. Obviously, the Board was oblivious, but Martin played along. "Yeah, they've updated my personal security and are working on a few leads. It's all very hush-hush, though."

"Well, a trip will be good. Get away, and maybe they'll nail the bastards before you get back," Charles interjected.

"We can only hope," Martin said. "If you'll excuse us, I owe someone a dance."

"So lovely to meet all of you," I said as he dragged me away. We put our half-empty glasses on a tray as a server walked past. "You realize now we actually have to dance," I muttered, less than enthused.

He grinned and pulled me onto the dance floor, drawing me close. One hand rested on my waist, and the other held my hand. "It won't be so bad. I'm an excellent dancer."

"Modest, too."

"Don't be snarky."

He attempted to lead, and I failed to follow. This was our constant problem. Whether we were dancing or not, we both wanted to be in charge. Eventually, he gave up and dropped my hand. I wrapped my arms around his neck, and he put both hands on my waist. I leaned in close; my lips inches from his ear.

"What was that about?" I asked. "Do you really have a boardroom of complete idiots who can't put two and two together and get four?"

"They believe what they like." His lips brushed against my ear, sending chills down my spine. "But they bought that you're my personal assistant. Just some girl I hired, and it has nothing to do with the threats I was getting.

Mission accomplished. I mean, really, they wanted updated personal security, not office security. Why would my bodyguard go into a building where we already have hired guards?"

I wasn't sure if I should be offended. "That's why you needed to hire Bruiser and Killer," I reminded him.

"It's a party. Let's just have fun."

He was tired of arguing. I laid my head against his shoulder as we swayed back and forth. I was tired of this too.

"Mind if I cut in?" Denton's voice cut through our peaceful moment. I turned and looked at him and then back at Martin, who was already stepping away.

"Be my guest," Martin told him. I gave him a questioning look. "Come find me when you're finished dancing." He winked and headed back to the bar.

"I have to warn you I'm not much of a dancer, Mr. Denton."

"Please, it's Blake." He put his hand on my waist and took my hand, giving it a slight kiss. I could smell alcohol on his breath, and I wondered if drinking was part of the CEO's job description. "Maybe you just don't have a strong enough partner." I remained silent. "How long have you and James been together?"

He's just making polite conversation, Parker. I tended to be suspicious even when things were completely innocent. "Honestly, I've lost track." Denton considered my words but didn't say anything. "Are you here with your wife? Girlfriend? I don't want anyone to get jealous." I hoped to find an excuse to go find Martin. I didn't like leaving him unguarded, despite the secure setting.

"No, I'm the consummate bachelor, as of recently. The last girl I dated, Jill, didn't work out so well."

"I'm sorry to hear that." I couldn't have cared less. Denton's hand traveled lower than my waist, and I resisted the urge to break his fingers. "I need to get some air. It's a bit stuffy in here." *Do not cause a scene, especially with the acting-CEO of the company*, I instructed myself as I tried to escape without incident.

"What a good idea. I'll join you." Denton followed me to

the balcony, which was the absolute last thing I wanted.

A couple was making out in the corner, but we paid them no heed. Leaning over the railing, I checked for guys in combat gear who might be hiding in the bushes. Denton was uncomfortably close and getting closer by the second.

"So," he leaned in further, "what exactly did you have to do to get the job at MT?"

"Excuse me?"

"You know what I mean." He ogled my cleavage. "Come on, you gave it to the boss real good, and you got a nice cushy job, I bet."

"Not quite." I struggled to remember I was the girlfriend and not an ex-federal agent who could put this guy on his ass at a moment's notice. "It just happened M...James knew I needed a job, and there was an opening."

"Oh, I bet there was."

"If you'll excuse me, Mr. Denton, I need to find James."

But he blocked my path. "You know, if you still want a job, you could come back and work for me since it doesn't look like you'll be working anytime soon with Jimmy," his voice dripped bitterness, "being on sabbatical for an extended amount of time. If he gets tired of you, you'll be back to nothing. Whatever your existing arrangement is, I'll double it. If you give me a raise, I'll give you one."

That was it. I backhanded him across the face. It took almost all my willpower not to punch his lights out or throw him over the balcony.

"Go to hell, you sick fuck."

Dazed, he leaned against the balcony railing for support. Had it not been there, he'd be on the ground. I turned toward the door. Martin was making his way quickly across the room. He must have seen the whole thing, along with the large group of gawking guests.

"Are you okay?" Martin asked anxiously from the doorway. I clung to him, trying to resume the role I was supposed to be playing.

"Can we get out of here?" I hoped to avoid any further incidents. He held me in his arms, glancing at Denton.

"It was just a misunderstanding." Denton apparently recovered somewhat. "I misspoke. Probably shouldn't have drunk so much."

Martin moved to push me aside, seeming to want to go out there. I didn't know if he would help that horrible, vile creature or knock the guy's teeth out, so I remained blocking his path.

"We should go," I whispered insistently.

"Get yourself cleaned up, and stay the hell away from Alex," Martin growled, his voice dripping venom. He took a breath and addressed the crowd. "Nothing to see here. Blake's just had a few too many. Someone make sure he doesn't drive himself home."

Martin put his arm around my shoulders and escorted me through the crowd toward the front door. Hotel security came inside to check on the commotion. *Too little, too late, guys*, I thought as they ambled past. The group of board members from earlier gathered near the exit.

"Never a dull moment around here," Marcy said to us.

"Everything okay, sweetie?" Samantha asked, but before I could answer, Martin replied.

"It's fine. I'm taking Alex home. Blake can be licentious when he's drunk."

"Did you see how she slapped the shit out of him?" Charles seemed impressed, and I resisted the urge to grin.

"Just keep an eye on him at work, and make sure he doesn't get handsy with the business or the employees," Martin warned them.

We bid the group good night and exited the hotel lobby. Marcal was waiting for us out front. When we emerged, he started the car and brought it around. The photographers were still outside, and I was temporarily blinded by the flashes going off. Hopefully, the incident wouldn't be in the paper. The valet opened the door, and I slid into the car. Martin tipped the man and joined me inside.

"You know, if you wanted to leave early, we could have, without all the dramatics." He tried levity. I shrugged and fidgeted with the seatbelt. "What happened?" he asked, the concern evident in his voice.

NINETEEN

I gave Martin the play-by-play of what happened from the time Blake cut-in until I slapped the hell out of him. Martin listened, never interrupting, until I finished the story.

"Son of a bitch." His green eyes were on fire. "I'm sorry. I never should have left you with him. I didn't know."

"It's okay. You didn't know," I parroted his words back to him. "Plus, what's not to love about getting to assault someone?" I paused. "Do you think he'll press charges?" I was making a joke, but he ignored it. I felt degraded by the horrible things that despicable man said, but I wasn't Martin's girlfriend or secretary. It was part of the role I was playing. "I never realized I was such a damn good actress, did you?" Humor and sarcasm were my go-to responses in difficult situations. "Maybe I should be nominated for an Oscar, or at least the Golden Globes. Hell, he stared at them long enough."

"He has no right to talk to you or anyone else like that." Martin was livid, and his anger helped keep mine in check. "I should fire him or request his resignation. I wish I had gone out there and kicked his sorry ass."

That answered my question about what he had intended to do on the balcony. I leaned my cheek against the cool glass of the window. I wanted to apologize for putting him in this position, but it was not my fault. Parker, you did not do this; you didn't do a damn thing. To avoid any more theatrics, I took a deep breath.

"Who would have thought you'd be saving me tonight?" I asked, and he cracked a smile.

"Does this mean I get to wear the tights and cape for once?"

I punched his arm playfully. "Don't start. I already took down one guy tonight. That number could easily double."

"I'm sorry."

"I know." I crossed my arms across my chest, and he took his jacket off and wrapped it around me, scooting closer. I rested my head against his shoulder, and he put his arm around me. It was nice not feeling like a piece of meat. "What are you going to do?" Causing more waves or forcing him to go back to work wasn't the best plan.

"I don't know. The Board can keep an eye out, short-term. We'll just see what happens."

"Any previous complaints against him?"

"Not that I know of."

"No history of sexual harassment or history of substance abuse?" I needed to figure out where the off switch was to my questioning.

"I don't think so."

I nodded, even though he couldn't see it from the angle we were sitting. "Maybe it's just the job."

"If I've ever come off that way, I'm sorry."

"You could be worse." I poked him in the ribs. "If you were that bad, I wouldn't be here, and you would have been slapped a long, long time ago." We rode the rest of the way in silence.

Marcal pulled the car into the garage and wished us a good night. I took my shoes off and carried them up the stairs. No need to walk in them any longer than necessary. I had already dealt with enough tonight.

I headed straight for my room and changed into baggy sweats, unpinned my hair, and washed my face. It was my way of counteracting the sleaziness of the evening. I hung the dress on the hanger, put the shoes in their box, and put them in the closet before returning downstairs. Martin had taken off his tie and unbuttoned his shirt, but he was already staring at the faxes he received earlier.

"Workaholic," I muttered, making my way to the

kitchen.

I rummaged through the cabinets and pantry, looking for something to eat. When stressed out, eat, yet another one of my philosophies. Not to mention, with the exception of a few hors d'oeuvres, I hadn't had anything since breakfast. I found a box of crackers and some hard cheese in the fridge. This would suffice.

I was slicing the cheese when Martin entered the kitchen. "Hungry?" I asked, not looking up.

"Yes," he said in an odd tone.

I turned to find a puzzled expression on his face. "What?"

"Why are you eating that?"

"Because I'm hungry. Didn't we just establish this?"

"Yes," more bewilderment, "so why aren't you eating a real meal?"

"Seriously?" I couldn't get a break tonight. I pointed to the clock. "It's after eleven. I'm not in the mood to cook, and you have no microwavable dinners. Cheese." I held up the cheese. "Crackers." I held up the box. "Works for me."

He chuckled. "Sit down." He took the knife from my hand and put it on the cutting board. "Sit." He gently pushed me toward the table.

"Fine, but if I break a tooth chewing on the tabletop, I'm holding you responsible."

He begrudgingly handed me the plate with the cheese and the box of crackers. I smiled sweetly and opened the box.

He got out a skillet, chopped an onion, and tossed it into the pan. He grabbed a bag of pre-cooked shrimp and set it in the sink with the water on to thaw. He cut and chopped more ingredients, and within twenty minutes, he presented me with a meal.

"Showoff." I went to get the dishes, but he stopped me.

"Relax." He turned around and got the plates. He wanted to make up for what happened earlier.

"I'm fine."

"I know." I could hear the smile in his voice, even though his back was to me. We sat down to eat. It always felt so formal, sitting at a kitchen table and eating meals together. "Tomorrow, we'll get the manufacturing plant footage and maybe make some headway."

"Hopefully. I know it's been about a month or so since it happened. Are you sure you still have the footage saved?"

"We should. Everything is backed up and stored in case of anything." He sounded slightly unsure. I guess we'd find out tomorrow.

"Well, on the bright side, it can't make things worse." Something else was bothering him. Given the list of things that had been going wrong in his life, I didn't think I was a good enough investigator to determine exactly what the cause of his current distress was without asking a few key questions. "What's wrong?" My deductive skills knew no bounds.

"Nothing. I'm just stumped by the missing funds. They don't appear to be anywhere."

"As in they never existed?"

"They existed," he insisted. "They were earmarked for this acquisition, but I can't trace them. I thought they might have been in a different account, but I don't see a surplus in any of those."

"Could there have been a loss from a different account that was nullified by reallocating the acquisition funds, so maybe you wouldn't notice they were moved?" I grasped at straws. Accounting was not my thing.

He thought about it for a moment. "No, it would be very unlikely the same amount would be involved."

"True, coincidences like that aren't very probable." I bit my bottom lip, trying to come up with some out-of-the-box explanation. The problem was, when money went missing, it was almost always because someone took it. "Who had access?"

"Denton, the accounting department, the other board members, and me."

"Pretty much narrows it down. I'm going to rule you out, just for argument's sake."

"Thanks."

"Given my current feelings toward Denton, I say let's add embezzlement to his list of attributes and call it a night, but just in case I'm letting my personal opinion get in the way, I have a forensic accountant friend at the Bureau. She can follow the money. I'll give her a call in the morning and see if we can get this figured out."

"Maybe tomorrow we can kill two birds with one stone."

"Here's to hoping."

We cleaned the kitchen in a comfortable silence. The night had worn me out. Once again, the ball was rolling, and things were about to be set in motion. Maybe life would return to normal sooner rather than later.

I settled on the couch, flipping through channels until I found a movie to watch. Martin was down the hall in his office, still going over the accounts. I glanced at the monitor to make sure the security system was operating. Everything looked quiet. I stretched out and closed my eyes, listening to the dialogue and thinking about the night's events.

A few minutes later, Martin poured himself a drink from the bar. "Make that two," I said, sitting up.

"I thought you fell asleep." He filled a second glass.

"No, I was just thinking."

"About?" He handed me the drink.

"Life. Nothing important."

He chuckled.

"Don't let me disturb you," I jerked my head toward his office, "get back to work."

"I'm done for the night. What are you watching?"

"*Sherlock Holmes.*"

"Looking for pointers?" he teased.

"Couldn't hurt." I played along.

I wondered how the hell we became so buddy-buddy in such a short amount of time. Wasn't this the same man I was screaming at two days ago? Maybe tonight had changed him for the better, or maybe it made me more tolerant since he wasn't the worst person to deal with. Either way, it was an improvement on the way things had been, if it lasted. We watched the movie for a while. When it was over, he looked at me.

"I'm going to get some sleep." He got up from the couch. "You know, you are allowed to do the same."

"I know." I wasn't a great sleeper in a strange

environment, and I had the tendency to feel the need to patrol the premises since I was both security consultant and personal bodyguard simultaneously. I turned the television off and stood up.

He seemed surprised, erroneously believing I was giving in so easily. "Good night." He headed for the stairs, but I grabbed his arm.

"Thanks." Despite the incident with Denton, tonight had more good moments than bad. I gave him a hug, and he wrapped his arms around me. "Good night," I whispered in his ear and gave him a friendly kiss on the cheek before pulling out of the embrace and heading down the hall toward his office to stare at surveillance footage for a little while longer.

TWENTY

It's Monday, finally. This was the first thought that popped into my head when I woke up. I squinted to make out the time. It was just before eight. I rolled on to my back and stared at the ceiling, trying to collect my thoughts. Martin and I would get the manufacturing plant footage then check in with Mark and O'Connell to see if there were any new developments or if Mrs. Griffin had been located. If not, I would make sure a missing person's report was filed. I also had to call Kate Hartley to check into Martin's missing funds. It was going to be a long day.

I got out of bed and headed for the bathroom. Splashing came from outside, and I opened the drapes and stepped onto the terrace. It was the first time I used the French doors since arriving at Martin's. He was already up and swimming laps. I watched him for a couple of minutes before heading back inside.

By the time I got downstairs, Martin was coming in from his morning swim. "Good morning," he greeted too cheerfully for this early hour.

"Morning," I mumbled in response.

"I have some good news." He seemed excited, but he noticed my half-asleep demeanor and decided it best to turn down the cheeriness. "I'll be back in twenty, and I'll tell you all about it." He practically skipped up the stairs.

Whatever he was on, I wanted some. Although, I was

sure he just happened to be one of those morning people. How they existed was baffling. Thankfully, the coffee was already made, and I poured a cup and brought it into the living room. I noticed a missed call on my phone, but it was from a blocked number. Maybe it was just a wrong number.

Martin came back down the stairs in dress pants, a white shirt, and a tie. I stared at him expectantly, waiting for this supposed good news. "Jeffrey Myers called this morning. Guess who showed up to work today."

"Griffin?"

"Yep, just like normal."

"Wait. Did you call O'Connell?"

"He's on his way. I have Myers keeping an eye out to make sure she doesn't leave the building."

I wanted to kiss him and also hit him for not telling me twenty minutes ago. "What are we waiting for?" I thought better of my comment. "Correction, you should stay here. I should go."

"No, you shouldn't. As far as Suzanne knows, you are not my security consultant. You are my girlfriend, and a girlfriend does not go traipsing down to the office to confront a suspect."

"Person of interest," I automatically corrected.

"Same difference."

Okay, so the good news was we had a lead, a living, breathing opportunity to get answers. The bad news was I wasn't supposed to go near her.

I narrowed my eyes. "O'Connell told you to keep me away, didn't he?" I didn't think Mr. Big Shot would waste an opportunity to get answers and his old life back sooner rather than later.

"Perhaps, but it makes sense." He waited for an argument, but I didn't give him one. I already decided I'd wait a couple of hours and then go to the precinct and see what I could find out. Maybe I'd bring Mark along. "In the meantime, we can get the plant footage and take it from there."

"Fine, but we might need to make a stop on the way back."

*   *   *

Marcal drove us to the manufacturing plant. It only took a few minutes to get the video footage. The problem was there was absolutely nothing helpful on it. The cameras in the factory were posted on the ceiling, and everyone on the floor wore the same jumpsuits and hardhats. Unless the saboteur looked directly up at the cameras, we wouldn't be able to identify him.

"This was fun." My sarcasm reared its ugly head again, but Martin wasn't quite as quick to give up.

He turned to the worker helping us. "I need the sign-in sheets." The man searched for the proper file folder and flipped through a few dozen pages before finding the one with the proper date. "Where can I get the payroll list for that date?" Martin asked once the sheet was provided. The man went back and found the corresponding payroll list and handed it to Martin. Martin copied the documents and handed back the originals. "Thanks."

"Good thinking."

Between the footage, the sign-in sheet, and the list of those who were paid for working the day, it would be easier to narrow down how many unaccounted individuals were loitering in the factory. Martin seemed pleased with himself.

We were heading back to the car when my phone rang. "Who is it?" he asked as I looked at the caller ID. Still blocked.

"I don't know." I hit answer and held the phone to my ear. "Hello?" No one responded. I tried again. "Hello?" I heard a click. Frowning, I put the phone back in my purse. "Apparently, it was no one." I didn't like getting unknown calls, and this one caused a funny feeling.

"It was probably just a wrong number or one of those automated things," he suggested.

"Yeah, probably." I wasn't convinced. As I got into the car, I called Mark. Luckily, he answered. "Hey, Griffin's back," I told him.

"I know. O'Connell gave me the news," he said. Great, I

was the only one not included. "I'm heading down to the precinct now. Care to join me?"

"I'll be there." I hung up and leaned forward in the car. "Marcal, can you drop me off at the police station before taking Mr. Martin home?"

"Sure thing," he replied, and Martin glared at me. Obviously, he wanted to be the one in charge of our destination.

"You are going back to the house and staying put until I get back. Mark can give me a ride," I said.

"I wasn't going to argue. I need to go over the expense reports again and maybe conference call with the accounting department to get things straightened out."

"Okay. If not, I'll call Kate and see if she can look it over for you," I promised.

Marcal dropped me off at the precinct, and I met Mark in the lobby. "Are they here yet?" I asked, hoping Mark knew more than I did.

"Yeah, O'Connell has her in the back." He drummed his fingers impatiently against the counter. "I'm waiting for him to escort me up."

While we waited, Mark filled me in on the digging he had done. My Friday afternoon call requesting backgrounds on the ex-employees and any and all possible gang or drug ties had turned out to be completely fruitless since it was now very obvious our suspect list was down to current MT employees only, and no ties to gangs had turned up. I felt ridiculous for having made the call in the first place, seeing as Martin and I had been in the middle of a knock-down, drag-out fight which was what led to my hysterical plea for assistance. I admitted this to Mark, and he laughed. Evidently, he understood how irritating Martin could be.

I checked my watch and impatiently tapped my foot against the tile floor. The precinct was quiet, probably because it was a Monday morning. Finally, I spotted Thompson and O'Connell. They appeared to be joking about something. O'Connell saw us waiting and came over to the front desk.

"Ms. Parker," he didn't seem surprised, "Agent

Jablonsky. I'm guessing this is a package deal."

I shrugged. "If you want me to stay out here and wait, that's up to you."

O'Connell turned to Mark. "Let me guess, whatever you see or hear, you're just going to tell her, right?"

"Most likely."

"Fine, you both go up, stay on the other side of the glass, and have no contact with Griffin. Do you hear me?"

"Loud and clear, Detective," I replied.

He led us upstairs to the observation room on the other side of the interrogation room. A police tech recorded the video and audio of the interview. Mark and I stood in the back, watching as Detective O'Connell asked Griffin a few questions.

"Ma'am," O'Connell was seated across from her, his back to us, "there was some concern over where you disappeared to since you didn't show up to work, and there had been no word from you after the explosion on Thursday afternoon."

Griffin seemed startled. "Am I in trouble? I didn't do anything wrong." I was beginning to have doubts she was the criminal mastermind behind this.

"Can you tell us what happened Thursday afternoon?" O'Connell asked gently, and she cleared her throat.

"I went to lunch and walked a couple of blocks to get a sandwich when I heard a really loud noise. With all the dust and people screaming, I hightailed it out of there. I went straight home. I thought it was some kind of attack."

Mark and I exchanged glances.

"Why would you think that?" O'Connell asked, standing up and slowly pacing the length of the room.

"Mr. Martin has a target on his back."

I leaned closer to the glass, watching her expressions.

"You seem to know a lot about that." O'Connell feigned intrigue.

"I am the senior personal assistant at Martin Technologies. I know what goes on with all the board members." She puffed herself up with false importance.

"She can't be serious," Mark whispered.

"She thinks she's some hot shit," I replied.

O'Connell tried a redirect tactic. "Was anything missing from your office today when you returned to work?"

Griffin seemed slightly flustered. "I'm...I'm not sure. I wasn't in my office very long."

I didn't believe a word she said.

"Really?" O'Connell baited his hook. "There were reports of a break-in on the seventeenth floor from Friday night. Your office and Ms. Parker's were both hit, according to the surveillance tape we watched." How far was O'Connell going to take his fictitious scenario?

"What was taken from her office?" Griffin tried to play innocent, but we weren't falling for her act. What was her motivation for asking that particular question?

O'Connell opened the file folder, flipping through the pages and pretending to read the report. "Nothing of any significant value. A company laptop and coffeepot were missing, but I shouldn't be discussing this with you."

"Really, he thinks she's going to believe someone stole my coffeepot?" I spoke out loud to myself, but Mark chuckled. Perhaps O'Connell didn't want to tell her what really transpired in case she got caught in a lie of her own creation.

"What a shame." She tried to appear sympathetic. "My computer was untouched, Officer."

"Detective," he corrected.

"She just lost some brownie points," Mark commented, and I tried not to laugh.

"What about everything else? Was anything missing?" he asked again.

She considered the question, internally debating if she should say anything. "I don't think so," she concluded.

"I see. That's good to hear." O'Connell sat across from her. "So, where have you been these last few days?"

"I went on a trip," she answered a little too quickly.

"Where did you go?" O'Connell leaned against the table in front of Griffin.

"I was going to visit a friend, but I decided at the last minute to go on a road trip. I stayed at a lovely B&B not far from here."

"Where does your friend live?" O'Connell asked,

seeming curious and friendly and not at all interrogative. Maybe he practiced his good cop/bad cop routine in the mirror.

"Nova Scotia, Canada, but I thought it'd be too cold to go up there this time of year." Griffin had all the answers, didn't she?

"That's understandable." O'Connell continued to play the friendly role. "What B&B did you visit? My wife is always pestering me to take her somewhere nice."

"It's called the Cat's Cradle, just off Route 9."

He would check to see if she had been there. "Thanks. I'll have to make a reservation. We're almost through here. I just need to see if my partner finished his paperwork. Can I get you a glass of water or some coffee?"

"Coffee would be nice with cream."

"Sure thing," O'Connell said and headed out of the room. He opened the door to our room and told the tech to get a coffee with cream and bring it back.

"Perks of being a detective," I commented.

"Damn straight," he replied. "So what do we think?"

"She's involved." I didn't hesitate. "I just don't think she's behind it."

"Griffin was uncomfortable when I told her about the break-in," O'Connell pointed out, "and her plans for leaving town don't make sense. Why would someone waste a plane ticket and bus ticket just to drive to a B&B forty miles from here?"

"It's almost as if whatever was supposed to have happened on Friday failed, and she had to come back," I pointed out. "Did you ever find out if anyone used the bus ticket?"

"It was never cashed in or redeemed. Anything else you think I should ask?"

Something still didn't sit right between her and Martin. "Bring up the acting-CEO, Blake Denton. See if anything shakes loose."

O'Connell took the coffee the tech brought back and headed into the interrogation room. "Almost done, ma'am." He handed her the cup. "I just have one last question before you go. How do you like working for the new CEO?"

"Oh, Mr. Denton is lovely." She was practically giddy about the prospect.

"Good to hear," O'Connell said, throwing a quick glance at us.

"Yes, he's always been the most considerate when it comes to the assistants, Christmas gifts and bonuses. He even gave me his airline miles to use."

Bingo.

TWENTY-ONE

"Really?" O'Connell asked.

"Oh yes, I believe it was two...no, three years ago," Griffin responded.

"Dammit." I hoped the dots would connect. The tech guy turned to me; unmistakably, my outburst startled him. "Sorry," I apologized.

"Well, thanks for your time. If we have any further questions, we'll let you know." O'Connell stopped at the door. "Just between you and me, Mr. Martin seems like a blowhard. Is Denton any better?"

Griffin pondered the question for a few moments. "Mr. Martin is a sweet man, but he's too easily distracted from the important things. Don't get me wrong, he's been a great employer, but Mr. Denton is better for the company."

I turned to Mark. "Does Martin strike you as easily distracted from work?" I asked, considering the Martin I knew was a workaholic.

"Maybe he has an evil twin brother we don't know about," Mark suggested.

Griffin left the interrogation room and tossed the paper cup into the trash receptacle on her way out. O'Connell motioned to the glass before following her from the room and leading her presumably out of the building. The tech put on a pair of gloves and grabbed a plastic bag to retrieve the cup. At least we'd have some fingerprints or DNA in case we ever needed to make a comparison, even though this was definitely not the break I had been waiting for.

O'Connell returned to the observation room a few minutes later. He wasn't pleased by the way things had gone, either. "Why'd you think it was so important to look for her on Saturday?"

"It doesn't add up. She has to be connected. Did you see the surveillance tape with the mystery box, her unexplained disappearance, the fact that she enjoys working for Blake Denton?"

"I'm with you on the first two points. But why does it matter what she thinks of Denton?" O'Connell asked.

I quickly explained what occurred the night before.

"We can check into Denton just to see if there have been any complaints, but it sounds like he had too much to drink." O'Connell dismissed my story easily. "But I agree. There is more than what she's saying."

"We need to find the box," Mark said.

Yeah, but that's not likely to happen, I thought miserably.

"Look, I have a stack of reports to read on the explosion from Thursday, but without knowing the intended target, no obvious motive, and no one coming forward to take credit for it, there's not much more I can do. I have a ton of open cases on my desk that need attention, so unless you have something more concrete, I'm just working this in the background, at least at this stage," O'Connell said. I knew exactly what that meant; there would have to be more threats or worse before he could step back in to investigate.

"Okay," Mark shook his hand, "thanks for doing what you can. If you hear anything else, let me know. If my guys uncover anything, you'll be our first call."

I didn't know what to say. I understood O'Connell's predicament. "All right, but if something important turns up, I'd appreciate a call next time."

Today was turning into a huge disappointment. We headed back to Martin's house, and I leaned back in the passenger seat and closed my eyes. Mrs. Griffin had to know something. I just didn't know how to get her to break.

"Where's her husband?" I asked.

"Whose husband?"

"Griffin, Mrs. Suzanne Griffin." I emphasized the Mrs. "Is she married? Divorced? Widowed?"

Mark shrugged. We had read her employee file and found nothing on her in any of the criminal databases, but as far as marriage was concerned, we were severely lacking in information.

"You'll have to ask Marty. Maybe he knows." We rode in silence for a while before Mark spoke again. "So, last night, you kicked that prick's ass, right?"

I tried to hide my grin. "Something like that."

"Good girl."

We arrived back at Martin's compound, and Marcal buzzed us in. I was just about to ask Mark if he was going to hang around when my cell phone rang. I looked at the phone, annoyed. The caller was still blocked. I hit answer.

"Who is this?" When I didn't get a response, I clicked end call.

"What's going on?"

"I don't know. I've been getting blocked calls all morning."

Mark took my phone and checked the call log. This was the third time today. "Hang on." He picked up his phone and called the office. "Hey, Anita, this is Jablonsky, I need you to do me a favor. Can you find out who the last caller was to this number?" He gave her my phone number. "Okay, call me back whenever you have it. I owe you." He hung up and turned to me. "It'll just take a few minutes, hopefully."

"Come inside. You can stare at some horrible surveillance footage while we wait," I offered.

Martin was in his second floor office on the phone. I could tell from his half of the conversation he wasn't getting very far with the accounting department.

"What's going on?" Mark asked. I filled him in on the missing funds, and he shook his head. "When it rains, it pours."

"Don't I know it?" I found the disk and the corresponding paperwork sitting on the coffee table. I turned the video footage on for Mark to watch as I listed everyone who signed in to work that day and then crossed off all the names which corresponded to the list of people who were paid for working that day. Only three names didn't match up.

"What am I looking for?" he asked. I had already seen the video once when we were at the plant, and there wasn't much to be gained from it.

"Well, ideally, the saboteur. So which of these things or people don't belong?"

We both stared at the screen. Everyone moved with purpose. No one loitered or seemed lost.

"What about this guy?" He paused the screen.

"Looks like everyone else," I responded dismissively.

"No, see how everyone else just mills about." He rewound and hit play. "But," he pointed out the guy, "this one makes sure he keeps his head down. He turns away from the others as he walks past." He rewound and played it again. I had no idea how he noticed that. The guy was so inconspicuous I never would have seen it.

"That's our guy." I checked the timestamp on the tape and double-checked the sign-in sheet. No one signed in immediately before this guy appeared on camera. "I just don't know how to identify him."

"Can I take this?" he asked, indicating the disk. "Maybe I can call in some favors and have our techs run it through, clean it up, see if we can get it cross-referenced with the employee IDs in our facial recognition software."

"There are a million dirty things I'd love to do to you right now," I joked, expressing how incredibly pleased I was to have help identifying a suspect.

"How come you never say anything like that to me?" Martin asked, appearing in the doorway.

"Maybe if you had better surveillance cameras installed, I would."

"Glad to see you're still in one piece." Mark nodded at Martin.

"Yeah, my security's been racking up a lot of overtime hours to make sure I stay that way. What happened with Suzanne?"

Mark gave a brief rundown of the interview, leaving out the part where Griffin expressed her favoritism for Denton.

I didn't know if this was to spare Martin's feelings or not.

"Is she married?" My memory was like a steel trap.

"Used to be," Martin said. "She got divorced years ago."

"I'll head out and see if I can get a rush put on this." Mark held up the security tape. "I'll check in with Anita. She probably got bogged down with other things, but if she gets a number for you, I'll let you know." We said our good-byes, and Mark left.

I turned to Martin. "How are things?" I asked.

"Not so good. Accounting doesn't know where the money went. Oh, and it gets better. They've also misplaced funds from three other accounts."

"When did they go missing?" I had a sneaking suspicion the threats and the money were connected. Maybe this was why I was making the big bucks.

"They didn't even notice they were gone until I had them run through everything."

"Okay, I'll give Kate a call. Do you have the relevant account numbers handy?"

"I'll go get them." He headed back to his office while I dialed the number.

"Hartley," Kate answered instantly.

"Hey, Kate. It's Alex Parker. I know it's been too long, but I have a favor to ask. I'm working private security right now for CEO James Martin. Some funds have gone missing in the last seventy-two hours or so. Do you think you can track them down? See where they went and who authorized the move?"

"Sure, just give me the account information," Kate said. Martin returned and handed me a sheet of paper. I read the numbers off. "I'm a bit backed up, but I'll get to this as quickly as I can."

"Thanks. When this is all cleared up, we'll go out for a girl's night and catch up. Drinks are on me."

"Can't wait." She hung up.

"She'll get to it as soon as she can," I relayed the message to Martin. This seemed to be the story of our lives right now.

Sighing, he sat down next to me. "You realize it's only a little past two o'clock, and there is nothing left to do today.

Everyone else has jobs, and they go to work. But we're waiting on Mark to give us a suspect, and Kate to find the money, and..."

"Stop it," I cut him off. "I know, okay. I know."

"I wasn't criticizing you." He must have realized that's what it seemed like. "But I don't know how to just do nothing."

The wheels in my head were turning around something that had been bothering me for quite some time. "Did you sleep with her?" I turned to face him.

"Who?"

"Mrs. Griffin. Suzanne." It was out of the blue, but it was driving me crazy ever since the conversation in my office. "Did you sleep with her?" I repeated.

"Yes." He got up from the couch and went into the kitchen.

Well, that's just fucking fantastic. "When?" I called into the kitchen. I almost felt jealous. *Quit being idiotic,* I berated myself.

"About five years ago. It only happened once." He stood half in the kitchen and half in the living room, unsure of what to do. I was pretty sure he was trying to find an escape route from this conversation.

"Was she still married then?" I didn't want to ask these questions any more than he wanted to answer them. Get a hold of yourself, Parker. I stared into his eyes, judging the veracity of his statements.

"No," he swallowed, "newly single."

"You remember the part where I said I needed to know about the skeletons in your closet? This would count as a skeleton."

"Sorry, it's something I'm not proud of and would rather forget." He paced in the kitchen, out of my line of sight.

"Was she upset you didn't continue the affair?"

"There was no affair. It was a onetime thing." He came back into the living room. "Everyone makes mistakes. I shouldn't be interrogated because of it."

"I'm not interrogating you." I tried a softer approach. "She's angry at you." He looked confused. "I know. It makes no sense. I get that, but I could tell. O'Connell asked if she preferred Denton to you. She made Denton out to be a saint."

Martin rearranged the liquor bottles at the bar and snorted. "Some saint."

"That's beside the point. Not to mention, the conversation she had with me in the office, the one you so easily dismissed." My accusatory tone crept back into my voice, and I tried to rein it in. "And then your comments on blackmail being in the box, blackmail against you." I touched his shoulder and gently nudged him to turn around and face me. "She has dirt on you, doesn't she?"

"It was a crazy night. I was three sheets to the wind. It was an office party. Things got out of hand. I don't know what she does or doesn't have. It's been years." He emphasized the years.

"Did she ever try to extort you? Why did you keep her at the company?"

"It was never anything that sordid, and I couldn't just fire her. She was a reliable worker, not to mention the potential sexual harassment lawsuit. Hell, she could have sued me if she wanted, but we let it go, I thought. Let bygones be bygones. She got transferred to executive personal assistant to the Board. Her office is still on the top floor, but she works for all the board members and is in charge of the other assistants."

"That's it?" I was unsure if there was anything else to the story or anything else he had failed to disclose.

"That's it. I treat her just like any other assistant. I don't ask for anything special. Most of the time, I get one of the temps to fill in if I need an assistant for something. When I hired you, she just happened to be the only one in the office to make the call."

I resisted the urge to bust his balls over how easy it is to make a phone call. "Ever hear any rumors about her with Denton or any of the other board members?" Before he could answer, my phone rang again. We both turned toward the intrusion. "Hello?" I asked, not checking the name.

TWENTY-TWO

"Hello, Alexis. Please don't hang up," the last voice I expected to hear responded.

I turned and headed for the stairs, looking for some privacy. "I'm listening," I replied, trying to keep my tone neutral.

"I just wanted to apologize for my egregious behavior last night," Denton sounded remorseful. "I don't know what came over me, but I was completely out of line. I hope you can forgive me."

I made it to my room and shut the door. "Okay." I didn't know why he was calling, and I was apt to let him do most of the talking.

"Let me try to make it up to you. Perhaps you and James would like to meet for dinner, my treat. Or drinks? Coffee? Anything? I'm so ashamed." Denton was laying it on thick. He was scared he'd be removed from his position as acting-CEO.

"James has a busy schedule." My mind raced. I wanted answers about Denton's connection to Griffin and if he knew anything about the missing money. "But I'd be willing to meet for a quick cup of coffee." The thought of seeing that slime made my skin crawl; I must have caught that affliction from Martin.

"Really? That would be great. Just name the time and place."

"Coffee shop on Third in," I glanced at my watch, "thirty

minutes?"

"See you there."

I grabbed my purse, slipped my smaller caliber backup handgun into it, along with my MT ID card, and grabbed my keys. I went back downstairs to find Martin still standing where I left him.

"I have to go." I pointed to the nine millimeter, resting on the end table. "In case of anything, remember point and shoot, just like a camera. Call the police first, then me."

"Where are you going?" he asked, confused and somewhat suspicious.

"I have a semi-personal matter to take care of. I should be back soon. Just stay put in the meantime." I tried to leave, but he grabbed my arm.

Spinning around, I confronted him, unsure of what my face reflected. It might have been anger, defiance, or hurt, but he let me go without another word. I went down the stairs, retrieved my car, and headed toward Third Street.

During the drive, I tried to figure out what I should say or do. I wanted to confront Denton, but I didn't want to risk tipping him off either. Finally, I decided to play it by ear as I pulled into a parking spot and tossed a few coins in the meter. Inside, Denton was already seated at a table.

"Alexis, I'm glad you agreed to meet me." He wore sunglasses, and I wondered if he had a black eye or maybe just a bruise across his cheekbone.

A waitress walked past and asked if we were ready to order. I requested a regular coffee, as did Denton. He sat back against the chair and removed his sunglasses.

"You might want to put some ice on that," I suggested, hiding my internal cheering masterfully.

He tried to smile but winced. "I definitely deserved this." He indicated his bruised cheek. "I can't excuse my behavior, but I've hit a rough patch lately. Yesterday might have been my rock bottom. I told you about my girlfriend leaving. And while James has given me an amazing opportunity, I can't shake the fear that I might screw it up." He considered his words for a moment. "I drank too much and jumped to the wrong conclusions, and for that, I am deeply sorry."

"Well, you know the old adage about assuming things." I wasn't sure where I wanted to go with this, so I started with the simplest question I could come up with. "What was your girlfriend's name?" Getting him talking would hopefully lead to more information.

"Jill," Denton said. I thought back, positive he had said the same thing last night. At least he was consistent. "I thought we would get engaged, but...well, things happen."

"Yeah." I tried to figure out how to get onto the subject of work and how personal he might be with the assistants.

"Have you and James made any travel plans or anything? You should enjoy your time off as much as possible. Once he's back to the daily grind, I'm guessing it'll just be business as usual."

"Not yet. You know James, he has to make sure everything works perfectly before he can relax. You're the lucky one." I tried to appear friendly, even though I was fighting the overwhelming urge to throw my hot coffee in his face. *Don't be vengeful, Parker*, my internal voice insisted.

"How so?"

"You have the help of Mrs. Griffin and the other assistants. You have an entire staff of people working under you while I'm stuck at home, simultaneously trying to be travel agent, assistant, and significant other," I over-embellished, but hopefully, he'd latch on to the bait.

"I didn't think of that." He leaned forward and gave my hand a friendly pat. I noticed his watch encrusted with diamonds. That must have cost a pretty penny. "If you want, I can have someone work on your travel plans for you."

"It's okay." I resisted the urge to jerk my hand away and instead forced a smile onto my face.

"If there is anything you and James need, please don't hesitate to ask. I owe him for this opportunity, and I need to make amends with you. Tell me how I can make it right."

"Thanks for the offer." I tried to change topics and find another way to get back on the subject of Griffin. "Is everything back to normal at work today? You know, after the explosion on Thursday."

"Yeah, MT is a tight ship." He assumed, albeit incorrectly, Martin asked that I inquire about this. "You can tell James it's under control."

"And everyone is back to work then? Well, with two obvious exceptions, of course."

"I think everyone is back, at least as far as I know. HR didn't report an abnormal number of call-ins or absentees." He glanced at his watch. He was probably ready to get back to work, or maybe he was hypnotized by the shimmer from the diamonds.

"Have you seen Mrs. Griffin? She must be lonely on the seventeenth floor all alone. I haven't seen her since Thursday morning and never got a chance to tell her we weren't going to be in for," my voice trailed off, "a while."

"I talked to her today. She's doing fine, moved down to some extra offices on the fifteenth in order to help me out."

Before I could continue, my phone rang. This time it was Mark. "Sorry, I have to take this."

Denton nodded.

"Hi, honey," I greeted, trying to imply it was Martin.

"Alex?" he asked as if I had lost my damn mind, which maybe I had. "It's Mark."

"Of course. Did you find what you were looking for?"

Mark still seemed confused by my part of the conversation but understood enough to realize something was up. "If you're in danger, name a type of fruit." I waited. "Fine, you aren't in danger, but you can't talk, I take it."

"Very good, dear." I wanted him to get on with it. "So did you find it or not?"

"Anita got the trace. The blocked calls came from the MT offices. Extension 325. Any idea who it belongs to?"

"I'll have to check, but I'll be home soon. Go ahead and start dinner without me." I waited, positive he was still puzzled by my odd conversation. "Love you, too. Bye." I clicked end call as Denton watched me intently. "I swear I don't see how he managed to survive without me," I said in an exasperated tone. I thought about trying to broach the subject of Mrs. Griffin again, but I didn't want to raise suspicion. Also, I needed to get a running start on extension 325. It would be best to make a clean escape. I left Martin and needed to go back and patch things up. "I should head out. Thanks for apologizing in person. You'll do just fine as acting-CEO."

Denton stood as I slid out of the booth. "You take care of yourself." He gave me a friendly hug, but something about his tone made me cringe.

I pulled away as quickly as possible, exiting the coffee shop. I had just gotten inside my car when my phone rang again.

"Where the hell are you?" Martin asked. I wasn't sure if he was angry or concerned.

"I had something to do." Mark probably phoned him to make sure everything was all right.

"Are you okay? Mark called. He was worried." At least I knew my gut instincts still worked.

"I'm fine. Do you know who uses extension 325 at work?"

"No one. It's a phone in one of the empty offices." Great, anyone could have made the call. "Alex," he sounded anxious. I heard him clicking buttons on his phone as if reading a text message. "Where are you?"

I put the key in the ignition and drove away from the coffee shop. Conceivably, now would be a good time for full disclosure. "I went to gather some information from Denton, and we stopped to get coffee." I waited for a response. When none came, I continued. "I didn't mean to leave you like that, but I just wanted to get some answers." There was an awkward pause over the line. "Do you want me to pick anything up for dinner?" I tried to show my remorse with a peace offering.

"No." There was silence on the phone. "Why didn't you tell me?"

"Because you would have wanted to come, or you wouldn't have wanted me to go." This was starting to sound a lot like a conversation an actual couple would have. "I wanted to see if I could get anything out of him about some persons of interest and thought it'd be easier solo."

"Did you?"

"Nothing earth-shattering. But Denton wants you to know he has it under control."

"His drinking or his harassing my security?" he asked bitterly.

"I think he meant your company, but at least, at the present, the drinking and the sexual harassment are both under control."

"Good to know." His voice still sounded off. "Are you on your way back now?"

"Yes, ten minutes or so."

There was another uncomfortable break in the conversation.

"I need to know I can trust you," he said quietly.

"You don't think you can?" My voice remained calm, but I was getting defensive. There was another painful pause.

"I think maybe you need to get back here." Martin hung up.

Accelerating, I headed straight for his compound. Something wasn't right. I didn't believe for a moment he didn't trust me, not after everything that had already happened, so there was just one possibility left. Something was wrong. I thought about calling Mark back or maybe O'Connell, but it would have been premature. I didn't know the situation. I turned on to the private road and slowed the engine, creeping up to the compound while keeping a constant eye out for any vehicles or signs of movement through the trees, but no one was there. I used the remote access to open the garage door and pulled my car inside. Everything appeared normal. After parking my car, I took out my gun, went up the stairs, and opened the door.

"Martin?" I called, half-expecting to find an assault team in the living room.

"I'm in the office."

My nine millimeter remained in the holster on the table, having never been touched. Walking slowly down the hallway, I pinned myself against the walls as I went, just in case I encountered any problems.

"Are you alone?" Granted if he wasn't, he'd probably be forced to say he was.

"Of course." He emerged from the room,

unaccompanied. Automatically, I raised my gun, and he looked at me like I was crazy. "There's no one here. Just me."

I pushed past him and checked inside the office before lowering my weapon and putting the safety back on. "So what was–" I stopped. Did my leaving actually cause him to question my loyalty? Did he really not trust me? "What happened? What's wrong?"

"I just received these." He opened his e-mail. Inside were pictures from less than twenty minutes ago. In one of them, I was smiling at Denton. In another, he had his hand on mine across the table, and in the last one, we were hugging.

"Shit." Someone followed me. Did they tail me back to Martin's house?

"That's it? You aren't even going to explain why it looks like it does?"

"Someone must have been watching me or Denton. What if I led them to you?" It was best to vocalize these things, so hopefully, Martin could follow along with my thoughts as I did my best to avoid panic-mode.

"Alexis, stop." He grabbed my shoulders. "What is going on? Why were you with Denton," he pointed at the pictures on the screen, "like that?"

"Make sure the security system is active. I want to monitor the outside surveillance just to be on the safe side." Why didn't he comprehend I could have been followed, and he might be in danger now?

"But," he tried to interject.

"Just do it. I'll explain everything, but you have to do this first." I practically pleaded with him.

How could I be so stupid? I tried to think if I had noticed a tail, which I hadn't. But the pictures meant something. What, I wasn't yet sure. Martin double-checked the security system while I went into the living room and turned the television to the input setting, so I could see the security camera feed on the big screen. Everything looked completely calm. Nothing out of place.

"Okay, it's active." He sat down in the armchair across from the couch.

I alternated my gaze between him and the security feed. "The reason I left was because Denton called. He wanted to apologize for the other night and invited us out. I said you were busy, but I agreed to meet him alone. We went to the coffee shop on Third. I wanted to get information on Griffin." Did we not just have this exact conversation over the phone?

"You could have told me that's who was on the phone. Has he been calling you all day?"

"No." I thought about it a moment. "Actually, I don't know. Those other calls came from extension 325. Mark told me that right before he called you."

"What does this even mean?" Martin indicated the pictures he was e-mailed.

"Who sent the e-mail?" That was the more important question.

He shrugged and shook his head.

"Did it say anything?"

Another headshake.

"When did you receive it?"

"While I was on the phone with you," he said. I reached for his phone and checked the call log. "I just asked if you were okay, and then I got the e-mail on my phone. I hit open, and the pictures popped up."

I swallowed. The sender had to have been right there. I must have walked right past him. A shiver traveled down my spine.

"Call Mark. Let's see if he can track down the sender." I watched the monitor, but Martin didn't move from his spot. I shifted my gaze and focused on him. "Honestly, do you think I'm meeting with Denton behind your back, or that I'm trying to sabotage you and your company?"

"No," he didn't miss a beat, which was a great relief, "but I don't know why you didn't tell me you were meeting him."

"I already told you I wanted to ask him questions about Griffin, and after our earlier conversation, I didn't think you would find that reason very valid." There was nothing else to say that would be helpful. It was best to avoid another fight, especially when I had screwed up by failing to disclose my intentions.

"Don't crucify me for one past indiscretion," Martin insisted.

"I'm not. I just need to know these things ahead of time, and you need to come to terms with the possibility Suzanne is involved." I dialed Mark's number and tossed my phone to him. "Give Mark the details. I'm going to check the computer."

TWENTY-THREE

After examining the photos in detail, I was sure the pictures were taken from outside the coffee shop. They were probably from a camera phone due to the size and quality and since I didn't notice anyone hauling around a camera. The problem was I didn't know if our unidentified photographer had been following me or Denton. I also debated the purpose of the photos. Were they designed to make Martin suspicious and cause a rift in our relationship? Maybe get my ass kicked out of his house, leaving him unprotected? Or was it an implied threat with two equally important targets, the acting-CEO of his company and his make-believe girlfriend?

Martin entered the room and sat down next to me. "Jabber has some people running with it. I asked if we should call O'Connell, but he said there wasn't anything worth telling."

"I agree. There's no explicit threat." I leaned back in the chair.

"But there's an implied threat?" he asked. I had to give him credit; he was an expert at reading between the lines.

"Maybe you should call Denton and tell him about the photos. No details, just that you received some photos of the two of us and you were afraid it could be construed as a threat, so you want him to be extra cautious."

He considered this for a moment. "What if he's behind it?"

"If he is, then he'll know the attempt to cause a rift between us didn't work, and if he isn't, it might be good to tell him to watch his back. Someone was following one of us."

"I'll make the call." He picked up the phone.

"Put it on speaker. I want to hear his response." Martin pushed a button. "And, just so you know, I'm not really here," I clarified.

"Got it." He dialed Denton's cell phone and told him about the photos.

"Jesus," Denton sounded worried but not very surprised. "Thanks for warning me. I'll keep an eye out."

"Be careful. If you need increased security, talk to the boys downstairs. I'm sure they'll take some extra shifts," Martin suggested.

"I will." Denton blew out a breath as if smoking a cigarette. "Is Alexis okay?"

I gave the phone a suspicious look.

"She's fine." Martin looked at me, and I held up my hands in a 'now what' gesture. "Call if you need anything." Martin hung up without waiting for a response.

"Not awkward at all." I laughed nervously. From the living room, my phone rang. "We should have been born in the era of the Pony Express. It would make these things a lot easier." I got up to get the phone. "Hey, Mark," I greeted.

"The photos were sent from a burner phone registered to a John Doe. It's already been turned off. We can't track it."

"Thanks for trying."

"Honestly, Parker, what the hell is going on today? You get some blocked calls, and Marty's getting photos sent to him. You guys can't do anything without me, can you?"

"Don't forget you're working on the surveillance tapes from the plant too," I reminded him sweetly.

"Yeah, yeah." I pictured Mark rolling his eyes. "Can you explain why you quit the OIO? Weren't things much easier here?"

"Not really, but I imagine they were for you since I was the one doing all the legwork."

"I miss those days," he sounded nostalgic and hung up.

"That was Mark," I announced. "It's a no go on tracking our mystery photographer."

"And the hits just keep on coming," Martin replied from the office. Something crashed, and I figured he might have just thrown a coffee cup against the wall.

"Everything all right in there?" I didn't want to feel obligated to help clean up the mess.

"Peachy."

He was frustrated, and I briefly considered the possibility his anger might have had something to do with my abrupt disappearance earlier or my chumminess with Denton. But maybe this was just a very self-centered view of things. After all, I was not the center of the universe, especially not the universe Martin lived in. It was best to keep busy and stay out of his way. There wasn't anything else to do at the moment.

I went upstairs and unpacked the few remaining items still stuffed in my bags. I was running low on clothing and other essentials and needed to go back to my apartment sometime soon and replenish my stock. In the meantime, I might as well do some laundry.

The laundry room was on the third floor, down the hall from my suite. As far as I could tell, Martin never used the room. Probably Rosemarie, the cleaning lady, did his laundry whenever she came to clean. *It must be nice to have that many pairs of underwear*, I thought, keeping my mind entertained with my own pointless musings.

I found the laundry detergent and fabric softener and tossed my dirty clothes into the machine, setting it to delicate and not bothering to separate the colors from whites. I didn't have anything nice enough to worry about ruining. The few work items I had were dry clean only and hanging safely in the closet.

I headed back to my room. I had been staying at Martin's since Thursday. It wasn't even a full week yet, but it felt like several months. I tidied up the guest suite and my private bathroom but decided against changing the sheets and towels since it had only been five days. I needed to keep busy to avoid dwelling on the phone calls, the photos, and Martin. I needed a break and a clear head.

Originally, I planned to return to the compound, ask questions about the extension, and see whose offices were nearby. Instead, my plans were derailed by Martin and his tantrum over trust and the pictures. God, the pictures. The crosshairs were no longer solely focused on him. *Perks of the job*, I thought wryly. Some people got medical and dental. I got a target painted on my back.

I entered the security code, opened the French doors, and went onto the terrace. A wicker table and chair were in the corner, and I sat down, looking out over the pool. I tried to imagine this was a vacation at some luxurious five-star hotel; unfortunately, my imagination wasn't that good.

My thoughts kept returning to the photos and the blocked calls, so I went back inside, making sure to reactivate the security protocols. I pulled out my diagram of the MT offices and looked at the building. There were empty office spaces on almost every floor. I went back downstairs and retrieved my phone. Martin was nowhere to be seen. He was probably still in his office, so I headed upstairs, dialing the MT number and the extension. The phone rang. Once. Twice. Three times. I was ready to hang up when someone answered.

"Martin Technologies," a female voice responded. "How may I help you?"

"Can I speak to Mrs. Griffin, please?" I didn't know who I was talking to but figured I had to say something. Did MT have caller ID?

"This is she," the voice, which I hadn't recognized, replied.

Shit. My mind raced. To identify myself or to hang up, I had to decide now. "Hello, this is Alex Parker," I said, making my decision. "Mr. Denton said you moved offices." I had to buy some time to think of a good excuse for my call. "I just wanted to tell you my office was broken into over the weekend, and I was checking to see if anyone caught the vandal." Might as well reinforce the story Det. O'Connell used this morning.

"I'm sorry to hear that." She didn't sound sincere. "I

haven't heard anything about it. I can check and get back to you."

"That won't be necessary. I'm sure building security will notify me."

"Okay, if there is nothing else Mr. Martin needs." She wanted to get off the phone. Clearly, my needs and concerns were unimportant to her.

"No, that was it. Thanks."

Griffin was extension 325. Did the calls come from her or someone using her phone? I thought about the time frame. It was possible she could have called before and after her brief visit to the precinct, but it seemed unlikely. I could kick myself for tipping her off, or did she actually believe my bullshit story? I did have photographic proof I was with Denton today. How ironic? I went back down the stairs, deciding another admission to Martin might be the best course of action to demonstrate my trustworthiness and win back some lost brownie points.

"So," I began, walking into his office, but he wasn't there. "Great, now I'm talking to myself." I went into the living room to make sure I didn't miss him; then I checked the kitchen. "Martin," I called. Why did it feel like I was calling for a dog? The next question I'd be asking was if Timmy fell down the well. I checked the empty guest bedroom on the second floor, and then I went upstairs to the fourth floor. I knocked on his bedroom door and his office door. No response. "Where the hell are you?" I asked the empty rooms before going back downstairs. A noise came from the first floor, and I opened the door to the garage and went down the steps. "Martin," I tried again.

"What?" He was sitting in one of his convertibles with the speakers blaring rock music. He lowered the volume to a tolerable level, reminding me of a teenager anxious to get his first driving lesson.

"I called the extension, you know, from the blocked number." He didn't appear to be paying much attention as he played with the stereo controls.

"Get in."

"We aren't going anywhere."

"Why do you always have to argue? Just get in the damn

car."

I opened the door and got in. He didn't even have the remote to get out of the garage. Instead, it was as if we were sitting in a demonstration car in a dealership showroom. After he decided his stereo presets and bass levels were satisfactory, he turned off the stereo. I now had his full attention.

"I called the extension," I started again.

"I know. You said that already."

I tried to overlook the gruffness. "Griffin answered the phone." It was best to get straight to the point.

"So, she's been calling you all day?" He could be so aggravating sometimes.

"I don't know. Possibly. I just thought you'd want to know." I reached for the door handle, but he hit the locking mechanism, which was rather childish since I could easily unlock the door. And even if I were somehow unable to, we were sitting in a parked convertible. I could climb over the door. "Really?" I turned to him. His smirk was infuriating.

Once again, the madness that was James Martin surprised me. He folded his hands neatly over the steering wheel and gave me a sideways look. I wasn't sure what he was waiting for, but two could play at this game. I turned to him, leaning against the door, so I was facing him more directly.

"Now that I have your undivided attention, Miss Parker," I didn't like his sudden formality, "I think we need to clear the air, so to speak." I tried very hard not to glare at him. "First off, I don't particularly care for being interrogated. Second, if you are following a lead on my case, I would appreciate being informed before you rush out of here half-cocked. Third," he paused, and I wondered if he was making some perverted joke in his mind, "I do trust you. You saved my life, and that is something I won't easily forget." His entire tone changed, making me incredibly uncomfortable. "That being said," he swallowed and switched back to business professional, "there is now a target on your back. You can't continue being so reckless."

"I'm not reckless. It all comes down to a cost-benefit analysis." Business speak was something he'd more easily understand.

"You've given the reckless speech plenty of times by now." His tone was friendlier, almost teasing. "I thought you might want to hear what it sounds like."

"Sounds better when I'm the one saying it." I didn't like being told what to do or how to do it.

"At the office, things were easier. You did your job. You provided a daily report. It was just business. Here, it seems to be more than just business."

I brushed my hair out of my face. It was true. I wasn't sure if I'd recognize a boundary line even if it had customs agents and passport checkpoints all around it.

"I'm sorry, sir. It won't happen again." My training automatically kicked in, annoying the hell out of me, even as the words left my mouth. I reached for the door lock, but Martin grabbed my arm.

"Not quite the response I was hoping for, Alex."

I looked at him, completely puzzled. The way he switched from business to playful was astounding.

"Goddammit." I would need years of therapy after this job. Martin could make me spin in circles in a matter of seconds. "What do you want from me?" I watched his face carefully, and I realized he didn't know.

He hit the door unlock, letting go of my arm. "We're still fighting over who gets to lead." He sighed and leaned back against the headrest.

I slumped back in my seat, and we both stared at the garage wall. "You can't take anything I say or do personally," I spoke deliberately, trying to find the proper diplomatic terms. "If I have to dig into your private life and throw accusations at people you know and like, it's just my job." Maybe I could make some type of concession. "If you can understand that and respect it, I'll keep you informed of everything as it happens." Shifting in my seat, I was surprised to see him already turned toward me.

"I guess that's fair." The seriousness ebbed as he adopted a slightly devilish grin. "But when you say I can't take the things you do personally, is that supposed to mean you had to stage that bit of intimacy last night in the car and upstairs? Because I'm pretty sure there was no one snooping around my house that you needed to continue the charade for."

I rolled my eyes. "If you would prefer no physical contact whatsoever, that can be arranged." I couldn't believe he was bringing up yesterday.

"That's not what I'm saying at all."

He leaned closer and caught my chin between his thumb and forefinger. I was about to pull away and protest, but he was quicker than I expected. He kissed me. For a moment, nothing else existed, but then reality set in. I pulled back, pressing my lips firmly together.

"No. You're my boss." I opened the car door. "I have a job to do. We don't need any other complications." I got out of the car and headed for the steps.

"Alex, wait."

Pausing for a split second, I shut my eyes, resisting the urge to turn around or respond to him, before continuing up the stairs.

TWENTY-FOUR

I went back to the laundry room and busied myself with putting my clothes in the dryer. Things were already complicated enough. I let them get this way. I should have set down some ground rules from the first day. In all honesty, perhaps I hadn't wanted to, but I never expected things to spiral in this direction.

"I'm sorry." Martin stood in the doorway. I wasn't sure what to say, so I remained silent, hoping he'd just walk away. "I didn't mean to put you on the spot." He wasn't taking the hint.

"It's okay." Shoving my clothes in the dryer, I pulled a dryer sheet from the box and tossed it in, slamming the dryer door. When I turned around, he was blocking the exit.

"You have to push the button to turn it on." He pointed to the start button on the dryer.

"Oh." I was embarrassed. I hit the button and turned to leave. Either the room had just gotten smaller, or he had moved closer.

"I'm not used to having anyone around this much. Maybe I misinterpreted, and I shouldn't have. I'm sorry. Can we at least be friends?" he asked. He obviously had the mentality of a teenage boy when it came to relationships with the opposite sex. This surprised me, given how suave and calculating he always seemed.

"I didn't realize we were friends before," I joked. "But I

guess I can manage that."

Pleased, he left the room. Sighing, I collapsed against the washing machine and rubbed the bridge of my nose. I needed a break. I found my phone and called Mark, begging him to come by as soon as he got off work.

A couple of hours later, he arrived at Martin's compound with pizza in hand. The three of us sat around the kitchen table, eating and discussing everything that occurred today.

"Do you think Griffin's been calling?" Mark asked, pulling another slice of pizza from the box. I shrugged. "Come on, I know you. You've got instincts about this stuff."

"I don't think so." I had given this quite a bit of thought since I had stayed in my room until he arrived, trying to avoid the awkwardness with Martin. "Why would she have answered the phone?"

"Did she know it was you?" Mark asked.

"Not at first." I pondered this and cast a sideways glance at Martin. "Do the office phones have caller IDs?" I couldn't look at him.

"Not that I'm aware." Martin grabbed a beer from the fridge, and Mark gave me a strange look. I pretended not to notice.

"Maybe since she didn't know it was me, she answered," I backtracked, "and she was the blocked caller." It still didn't feel right, but I didn't know why.

"What was the point of calling?" Mark was playing devil's advocate.

"Hell if I know." That was basically my answer for everything.

"There has to be a reason." Mark leaned back in the chair. "Marty, any ideas?"

Martin took a long pull on his beer. He put the bottle down and thought for a moment. "Nope."

"Really insightful," I quipped, and Martin smirked. The cold war might just be coming to an end.

"Don't you know it," he teased.

I laughed, despite myself, and Mark looked at the two of us like we were lunatics.

"What the hell is wrong with both of you?" Mark asked, probably believing we needed to be committed.

"Not a thing," I replied, clearing the table. Mark was confused, but I was just glad the awkwardness had passed. Maybe now, things would return to normal. Well, normal as in more threats, mortal danger, and having no fucking idea where to even begin. "Any word on the plant footage?" I asked Mark.

"My tech guys are working on it. The earliest we'll know anything will be tomorrow, but it could take longer." Computers were great tools, but sometimes they were infuriatingly slow. Martin left the two of us in the kitchen, and Mark glanced into the living room. "What's going on?"

"Nothing. Why?" I dried the dishes.

"You begged me to come by and then that exchange at dinner." He scrutinized my expression.

"There was a moment," I admitted in a hushed tone. "It's over, thank god."

"A moment?" He could be such a guy sometimes.

"Let it go. It's been an incredibly long, stressful day." It was my turn to check to make sure Martin wasn't coming back. "Did you know he and Griffin had a one-night stand?"

"No shit. When?"

"Five years ago. The whole thing is a very sore subject. Needless to say, Martin wasn't pleased with my accusations against her."

"She must be at least twenty years older than he is. No wonder he doesn't want to talk about it. She sounds like one of those cougars." Mark's assessment was amusing. "Just do your job, and don't worry about the rest. Marty's a smart guy. He'll want this stopped regardless of personal feelings."

"I know." I heard Martin coming, so I changed the subject. "We know the blocked calls were from the MT building, and the photos were sent from a burner cell. Any way it could be the same person?"

Mark thought about it for a moment. "Anything's possible."

"What's possible?" Martin asked, entering the kitchen

with a stack of papers and a laptop.

"Maybe my mystery caller and your unidentified photographer are one and the same," I replied. It was just another theory, but it couldn't hurt. Plus, it made me feel better to think there might be one less psychopath trying to get to him or us.

"Could be." Martin opened the laptop and clicked a few keys.

Mark sat across from him. "What are we looking at, Marty?" he asked, turning the computer slightly so he could see the screen.

Martin clicked a few buttons and turned the screen completely around. "I have some new software I thought might come in handy." He clicked another button.

"Damn." Mark was practically speechless, so I went to see what was so impressive. On the screen were the photos, except Martin had modified them in some manner. There was an obvious reflection from the windows of the coffee shop. "I should have had my guys go over this, too."

"Don't worry about it. I just asked you to run a trace." Martin seemed proud of himself. "Plus, this is top of the line. I doubt any of your people have this software yet."

"Could you do anything about the grainy video footage with this?" I asked, recalling our earlier issues of the janitor, the mystery shoebox, and the plant saboteur, but Martin shook his head.

"Tried, but it didn't work. The images are too small and low-res. It only works with stills, and freezing the feed just made it worse," Martin tried to explain, but I dismissed his excuses as I realized what we were looking at.

"Would anyone like to explain why Todd Jackson is standing across the street from the coffee shop, holding up his phone like he's taking a picture?" I asked the room.

"Probably because he is," Martin surmised. I searched his face; he looked betrayed. The pieces were starting to fall into place.

"He's security. He has access to all the offices. He works the night shift. He knows what footage we've seen and what we haven't. He was working Saturday morning." I stopped and looked up at Martin. "He wasn't wearing a name badge. That's why I didn't know his name."

"What?" Mark and Martin asked simultaneously.

I shook my head, trying to make sense of the jumble of thoughts. "Remember, I asked what his name was. I didn't see his name badge."

"We can get him for more than breaking dress code," Mark retorted.

"No. I mean yes, but what if he didn't bother to put on the badge because he didn't want to be identified on camera." No one was following my thought process. I wasn't sure I was following it entirely either. "Just like the guy who broke into my office dressed like a janitor." I was trying to go from point A to point B. Luckily, Martin caught on.

"You think it was Todd, and that's why he didn't have the badge on. He didn't want to get caught on camera with the badge clipped to his collar because it might have been seen under the janitor's uniform."

"Hang on," Mark was catching on but was still unsure of my assumptions, "we have no proof."

"He had the keys to the offices which are kept in security." I tried to make the facts fit.

"Are you sure?" Mark wasn't buying it.

"I don't know. But the mystery man most likely had a key since the door wasn't picked."

Martin minimized the computer window and logged into the MT website. He accessed the employee schedules. "Todd Jackson worked Friday night into Saturday morning. He was scheduled to work two a.m. to two p.m. Saturday," Martin informed us.

This was the break we needed. Todd was in the building when the break-in occurred. He gave me access to the footage after he had the chance to view it and make sure it wasn't incriminating, and he was the mystery photographer.

"I'll give O'Connell a call." Mark stood up. "At the very least, we've got Todd for stalking."

"Why didn't you show me this sooner?" I asked Martin.

"I was just playing around with it before Jabber got here. The program was running while we were eating. It just finished when I brought it in here." Martin smiled. "Do you think this is almost over?" He was excited by the prospect.

"Too soon to tell."

I wasn't jumping on the optimism bandwagon just yet. There were too many unknowns and much too much speculation on my part. The only thing we could prove was Todd had been standing outside the coffee shop, looking suspicious. Maybe he was just making a phone call.

Mark returned. "I'm meeting O'Connell at the precinct. He's going to bring Mr. Jackson in as a potential witness and see if he can shake something more substantial loose." He looked at Martin. "I need your phone and printouts of the enhanced images. O'Connell might need you to come to the station, depending on how things go." Martin hit the print button and handed his phone to Mark. "I'll give you a call," Mark told me, "if we need Martin to answer some questions. O'Connell doesn't know what he has yet, but he might need a statement from you too. Stay by the phone until then."

"You got it." Martin put the printouts in a manila envelope and gave them to Mark. He was absolutely giddy.

TWENTY-FIVE

I paced the length of the living room. Mark had been gone for hours. It was already nine p.m., and we hadn't heard a word. I wondered if O'Connell had located Todd Jackson or if he was still maneuvering the bureaucratic red-tape in order to bring him in. Perhaps it was too much of a stretch to claim some paparazzi-esque photos were related to a hot dog cart bombing.

"How long are you going to do that?" Martin asked. He was in his office, still looking over the MT finances. I stopped, trying to figure out if he was on the phone or if he was talking to me.

"Do what?" I decided he was most likely speaking to me.

"Pace around the room. You're wearing holes in the carpeting." He exited the office and came down the hallway to the living room.

"I am not." I had too much anxious energy to sit still. "If I'm disturbing you, I can go upstairs." He shook his head and sat down. "Find the money, yet?" I asked, resuming my pacing.

"I'm fairly certain it's gone." He watched as I walked back and forth. "Where it went, I don't know."

"We'll find it. Just for my own clarification, it's not like the company is bankrupt now or anything, right?"

He chuckled. "No, Martin Tech is a multimillion dollar corporation." It sounded like he was reading the investment brochure.

"Just checking." I glanced out the back door. Everything appeared normal. "I'm going to give Mark a call." I headed to the coffee table to get my phone, but Martin grabbed it before I got there. I held out my hand, but he refused to surrender my phone.

"Jabber said he'd call when he knows something." Martin was being the reasonable one for once. "Calling now will be fruitless, and it'll just make you antsier. Quite frankly, I'm not sure I can deal with that. You're driving me crazy."

"You already are, so it won't make much of a difference." He had a sound argument, but I wasn't sure what to do until then. I circled back into the kitchen and randomly opened and closed some cabinets.

"Alex," he was trying his best to be patient, "come back in here. I'll distract you until we get word." I poked my head out and looked at him suspiciously. If his distraction was anything like what happened this afternoon in the garage, then I was most definitely not going back in there. "I'll behave, I promise," he said, reading my mind. Reluctantly, I went back into the living room. "You ever play chess?" He pulled a game board out from the small cabinet under the end table, and I looked at the board skeptically. "I can teach you."

"I know how to play." This was not a worthy distraction. "I just suck at it."

"Great, so do I." He set up the pieces. "C'mon, give it a shot. Worst case, you'll give the floor a rest for a few minutes." I sat across from him, the board in between us. My leg bounced up and down impatiently as we began the game. "I'm beginning to think I would know what an earthquake feels like."

"Sorry." I took a deep breath and tried to calm my nerves.

I captured two of his pawns. He took my bishop. The game went on until he finally captured my queen and forced me into a checkmate position.

"Round two?" he asked. I hated to admit it, but his distraction tactics were working well. We continued for another four games; the score was three to two, in his favor. I was setting up my pieces when the phone rang, causing me to practically jump out of my skin. "Alex Parker's phone," Martin answered. He frowned. "Uh-huh." My anxiety was back. Who was he speaking to? What were they saying? Why was he frowning? "Okay, sure. It makes sense. Just let us know as soon as you can." He hung up.

"Well?" He put my phone on the table and leaned back in the chair, deliberately taking his time. "You're a sadistic man, you know that?" He was drawing it out just to torture me.

"That was Mark." He paused, grinning, and I resisted the urge to throw the chessboard at him. "He sent you his best." I gave him my most powerful death glare. "They booked Todd Jackson, and he lawyered up immediately. Apparently, he's willing to cooperate for some kind of a plea bargain. The DA doesn't feel like dealing with any of this tonight. So tomorrow morning, they are going to talk to him, see what he has, and what kind of deal they can cut him. If they need anything from us, they'll call in the morning." I opened my mouth to speak, but he held up his hand before I could say a word. "This doesn't mean you are staying up all night, pacing back and forth. Just so we're on the same page, I will tie you down before that happens." He briefly raised an eyebrow, trying his hand at flirtation again.

"Fine." I was tempted to say something sarcastic or flirtatious but thought better of it. Midnight was fast approaching, and he followed my gaze to the clock.

"Want to get some shuteye?"

I shook my head. Now that Todd was arrested, how quickly would word get around? He worked the night shift, so they must have gotten someone to fill in for him. And at Martin Tech, gossip spread like wildfire. There was a very real possibility a second party could be involved in the conspiracy against Martin.

"Does Todd strike you as a mastermind who could rig a bomb, sabotage your plant, attempt to kidnap you, and send you all those threatening messages?" As I said this, the familiar cold chill traveled down my spine, making the hair stand up on the back of my neck.

Martin sighed and considered my question. "I don't know him very well." That wasn't an answer. "You don't think he's behind this, do you?" It was more a statement than a question.

"Maybe the kid will surprise me, but he doesn't seem like criminal genius material. If he wants to make a deal, maybe he'll roll on whoever is behind this." It was all we could hope for at this point.

We sat silently for a few minutes as I contemplated the other potential suspects worthy of consideration. The missing funds from the MT accounts pointed away from Todd and lent themselves to a much higher-level employee being involved. It was an established fact that most business types were sociopaths, so there wouldn't be a shortage of possibilities any time soon.

"I'm going to get some sleep," Martin announced. He rubbed his thumb across my cheek as he went by. I shut my eyes and sighed. "No more pacing," he whispered.

"No promises." I sat alone in the living room for a few minutes. A thought itched at the corners of my psyche. I was missing something, but what was it?

*   *   *

I heard ringing. At first, I thought it was part of my dream, but it kept getting louder. I rolled over and fell face first onto the floor.

"That was graceful." Martin's voice broke through my sleep.

"Screw you," I muttered, sitting up and rubbing my nose. At least it wasn't bleeding.

He grabbed the phone and took it into another room as I looked around bleary-eyed, trying to figure out why he was in my bedroom. He's not in your bedroom, dumbass; you fell asleep on the couch again. I got off the floor and stretched. My back was killing me. I really needed to stop acting like a narcoleptic. I was just getting ready to go upstairs when he returned.

"How's sleeping beauty this morning?" He seemed cheerful. Damn morning person.

"I apparently have an unnatural attachment to your couch. How long have you been up? Why didn't you wake me?" I ran my fingers through my knotted hair.

"I've been up for a few hours, but I was afraid to wake you. You might try to shoot me again." He gestured at the gun sitting on the end table, reminding me of the first morning I spent in his house.

"Makes sense." I stumbled toward the stairs. "Who was on the phone?"

"O'Connell. He wants us to stop by around noon." I continued upstairs. "I'll make you some coffee," he offered. I grunted my thanks and shut the bedroom door.

I took a nice long shower, letting the water beat down against my sore back. Finally, I emerged and dressed in semi-professional attire. I was now officially out of work clothes, not that I was going to the office. But in the event I needed to look a little more formal than jeans and t-shirts, I'd have to go back to my apartment. I dried my hair and put on makeup to hide the dark circles under my eyes. Looking almost human, I emerged and headed downstairs. Martin was sitting in the kitchen with two cups of coffee on the table.

"Thanks." I took a sip.

"Ms. Hartley called while you were in the shower," he said as I slowly sat in the chair. "She has some news on the missing finances and would prefer to discuss it in person. I told her we'd be in to see her after we finish at the precinct." He narrowed his eyes, assessing my appearance and posture. "Are you okay?"

"Yeah, why?"

He shrugged. "You're just quiet this morning."

"It happens, but we should probably get going. Where's Marcal?" I had grown accustomed to Martin's driver taking us everywhere.

"He has the day off. Don't worry. I know how to drive."

I internally debated whether to protest but decided it wasn't worth an argument and kept quiet. Maybe there really was something wrong with me today.

We made good time. Traffic seemed light; although, maybe it had more to do with Martin believing we were on the autobahn instead of the freeway. I kept an eye out for possible tails, but given his penchant for driving and the engine in his sports car, it didn't seem physically possible to be followed.

Once there, O'Connell escorted Martin upstairs to take his statement some place private. I was still sitting in front of the main desk when Thompson came to find me.

"Ms. Parker?" He seemed a little uncertain, and I tried not to judge his lack of facial recognition given his chosen profession. "Right this way, ma'am." The ma'am I couldn't overlook though.

"Please, it's Alex." I tried to be polite, honey and flies and all.

Thompson led the way to the interrogation room. He asked some fundamental questions concerning my connection with Mr. Martin and Mr. Denton, how well I knew Todd Jackson, if I had seen him following me at any other times, and if I noticed him at the coffee shop. All of these were baseline, matter-of-fact questions, and I answered easily. He excused himself and left the room.

Looking at my reflection in the mirror, I wondered if anyone was watching from the other side of the glass. I wasn't a suspect, and I wasn't being interrogated. They were just collecting information on their stalking case or whatever it was they now had against Todd.

"Ms. Parker, if you would be so kind as to write and sign a statement of events, it would be helpful in compiling our case," O'Connell said, entering the room with another person I assumed was an ADA.

"Not a problem."

He handed me a sheet of paper, and I wrote everything Thompson had just gone over, signing and dating the bottom.

"Thanks, that's all we need for now." O'Connell and the ADA headed for the door. "You can get out of here," he told me, but I waited for the ADA to leave before I stood up.

"Who'd he roll on?" I asked conspiratorially. O'Connell pressed his lips together and shook his head. "Come on, Detective. You and I both know someone's gunning for Martin, maybe me too. Isn't it part of your duty as a public servant to let me know who I need to watch out for?"

"It's still too soon to say, but rest assured, when we get some hard evidence, you won't have reason to watch your back anymore." He knew more than he was letting on, and I tried to stare him down. But he wouldn't budge. Giving up, I went past him and down the hallway. "Parker," he called after me, "you and Martin need to avoid the MT building for a while, okay?"

"Not a problem." I waved, continuing my retreat from the interrogation room. Well, on the bright side, I was right on two accounts. First, whoever was behind the conspiracy against Martin was an MT employee. Second, Todd Jackson wasn't the mastermind calling the shots.

TWENTY-SIX

Martin was waiting near the entrance to the precinct. He was having a conversation with someone dressed in a nice business suit. His lawyer, I guessed. When he saw me coming, he shook the man's hand.

"Finished?" he asked. I nodded, and we went outside. I gave him directions to the OIO building, despite the fact he didn't actually need them.

"So," I was curious if he had gotten any more information on the Todd situation, "how did things go? Who was that guy you were talking to?"

"My attorney." He shifted gears and switched lanes. "I asked him to meet me there. It's always good to have counsel present."

"Did you find out anything? Who Todd was working for? Anything?" The more time I spent working for Martin, the less patient I was becoming.

"Stay away from work and the employees. If they find anything else, they'll let us know." He mimicked what he'd been told, but there was more to the story. I watched his expression, but he kept his eyes on the road and wouldn't turn to look at me.

"You should probably slow down, unless you want to get arrested for reckless endangerment."

"I doubt they'd arrest me for that," he replied, but he decreased his speed, anyway. I waited him out. Finally, he glanced at me. "I'm not telling you this, but I'm going to see if I have any friends in the DA's office. Elections are coming up soon, so I might be able to get some information through unofficial channels."

Considering how aboveboard he was on most things, I was amazed he was talking about greasing palms with election funds in order to get answers. It wasn't a bad plan. It wasn't hurting anyone, I justified, but it seemed slightly uncharacteristic.

"Maybe you should wait and see if Mark has anything for us, first."

He shrugged, and I dropped the subject. Sometimes, it was best to have plausible deniability, just in case.

We pulled into the parking garage under the OIO building and took the elevator up. I called Kate to see if she could meet us. She said she'd be going on lunch in fifteen minutes and could talk then. I relayed the message, and Martin agreed to wait. With a few minutes to kill, we stopped to see Mark. Hopefully, Mark could talk some sense into Martin before he did something irrevocably stupid.

"Marty. Alex," Mark greeted. He appeared to be busy, but he pushed his work aside for a minute, confused by our presence. "Why are you here? Is everything okay?"

"Hartley's working on something for us," I told him. He was relieved we weren't in the middle of a crisis. "We just got back from giving statements to our favorite detective." Sarcasm dripped from my words.

"Uh-oh." Mark could tell I was displeased. "Let me guess, O'Connell doesn't want to play ball. He's keeping everything close to the vest."

"I'm working other avenues to see what I can find out," Martin offered. So much for keeping a secret.

Mark wasn't happy about this either. "Look, I'll see what I can dig up. In the meantime, the two of you better keep your noses clean, okay? Do you think you can handle that?"

"Eh," I shrugged, "I'll try."

Martin didn't comment, and Mark sighed, frustrated by being sent to do the dirty work again.

"Fine, go to your meeting. When you're finished, come back here. I'm calling O'Connell now to see what I can dig up. Worst case, his lieutenant owes me one, so I might call in a favor if need be." Mark understood how frustrating this was. He probably understood more than most since he had been working this case for Martin since the beginning.

"Thanks," Martin sounded relieved. Maybe he didn't want to use unofficial channels either.

When we reached Kate's office, I knocked on the open door. "Come in," she responded, not bothering to look up.

"Really, after all this time and all I get is a come in," I teased.

She looked up and grinned. "Parker, it's good to see you." She smiled at Martin who stood behind me, acting somewhat timid, at least timid for Martin. "Please have a seat." She gestured to the two chairs in front of her desk.

"This is James Martin," I introduced him. "Kate Hartley."

"Pleasure," he said, shaking her hand.

"I'm sorry it's not under different circumstances," she replied, pulling out a file folder and turning it around to face us. "I did some digging into the account numbers you gave me. It seems the missing funds were bounced around to a lot of different locations. They started out in the Caymans and then transferred out to another bank in the Bahamas. From there, they bounced to Argentina and then Zurich, and with each transfer, they fragmented."

I tried to keep up, but I needed a globe in front of me. Luckily, Martin understood the implications.

"How much was left after all that bouncing around?" he asked.

Kate glanced down at the folder. "Roughly a fourth. I don't know where the rest ended up. Each transfer was made so quickly and to countries with closed banking policies that I wouldn't be surprised if they fragmented further from the transferred accounts. I was only able to trace this part because it was the largest sum."

"Do you think the reason for the fragmenting and the decrease in funds was to make it more difficult to trace?" I asked, and she touched her nose and pointed at me. Surprisingly, I understood more than I thought.

"Who's primary on the accounts?" he asked.

"Dummy corporations, shell companies, each and every one is under a different name and heading. I bounced the names to the boys upstairs, figuring they might have better luck tracking it down." She frowned. "I'm sorry I couldn't be more helpful."

"It's okay. You did what you could," he said, but the wheels were already turning in his head.

"Who knows how to set something like this up?" I asked Martin. He was pondering something, and I wasn't sure if he even heard my question.

"I'd say there are only a handful of people, namely the members of the Board and maybe one or two people in accounting." He had some suspicions he wasn't sharing. The same small group of individuals who could have been responsible for the first accounting discrepancy was the same group with the wherewithal to fragment and bounce funds around the globe. "Did any of the money trace back to personal accounts?"

She thought about it for a moment. "No, but there was something odd that popped up. It might be a glitch or some crooked banker taking a payoff, but after the first move to the Cayman account, there was a cash withdrawal of twenty-five grand."

"Probably paying off the bank to look the other way," I surmised.

Martin leaned forward and rested his chin in his hand, thinking. "Can I get a copy of this?" he asked, staring at the file in front of her.

She shrugged and gave him the folder. "I don't need this. It's not an OIO case."

"Thanks," he told her sincerely. He seemed lost in his own world as he leaned back in the chair, holding the folder protectively against his chest. "We won't take up any more of your time, Ms. Hartley, but thank you again."

"No problem," she said. He got up and headed toward the door. I was about to follow, but Kate stopped me. "Parker, do you have a minute?"

I looked back at Martin, who was in the doorway. "Can you get to Mark's office on your own?" In a building full of federal agents, I wasn't too concerned someone would try to kill him.

"Yeah, I'll meet you up there." He disappeared down the hallway and out of sight.

"What's up?" I asked.

"You're working for the James Martin," she whispered, but it came out a high-pitched squeal.

"Yeah, so?" Why was she impressed?

"He's a genius." She sounded like a teenager with a crush. "His company is always on the *Forbes 500*. He's come up with all kinds of eco-friendly technology. He's rebuilt towns in the third world." I was pretty sure she was exaggerating.

"And he can be a total jackass."

"So the picture on *Page Six*, that was you." She pulled out the paper.

"Dear god." I hoped the flashing lights from Sunday night had been something I hallucinated.

"How is he?" She had always been a good friend. We had gone through Quantico together, but sometimes, she had the mentality of a thirteen-year-old girl.

"I don't know. He's rather pissed someone is stealing his money." I wasn't going to add fuel to the fire.

"You mean you aren't a couple?" She was absolutely astounded by this.

"Of course not." The implication perplexed me, but she gave me a questioning look.

"But he's your type."

"My type? I wasn't aware I had a type." I should have gone to Mark's office with Martin.

She stared knowingly at me. "Sexy with jackass tendencies, that's your type."

"That is not my type."

"Fine, but you owe me, so when you're done working," she made air quotes around the word working, "we are going out for drinks. And you are giving me the total dish."

"Okay, but there's nothing to tell," I maintained. Thanking her once again for the help, I went upstairs to find Martin and Mark.

The two men were sitting in the office, drinking coffee. I knocked on the door and walked inside, not waiting for an invitation. A quick glance was exchanged before Mark spoke.

"Mr. Jackson was paid to deliver a package to your office," Mark began. Before I could comment, he continued. "He claims he doesn't know what was in the box, but he was assured it wasn't dangerous and figured there was no harm. The thing is," he paused briefly, "he never got to deliver the box, so he was asked to take some pictures and send an anonymous e-mail. He turned over the burner phone to O'Connell."

"Who paid him?" I asked, resting my hips against the desk.

"You're going to love this." Mark paused for dramatic effect and plastered a fake grin on his face, like a clown. "Mr. Jackson doesn't know. He received an e-mail message originating from the office with the details of what he should do." The plot thickens.

"How much did he get paid?"

"Twenty-five grand," Martin chimed in. Coincidence, I think not.

"Before you ask, the cops are already working that angle. Evidently, Mr. Jackson didn't think taking a few photos or delivering a box would be considered a crime. He insists the anonymous e-mail said Griffin was leaving the box in her office to be delivered, so he assumed the whole thing was completely harmless."

The guy probably needed the money, I thought but kept it to myself. "What did he do with the box?" I asked.

"He tossed it, and when he went back later to retrieve it, guess what." Mark adopted the same fake clown smile. "It was gone." His eyes grew wide in mock astonishment.

"Dammit." I slammed my hand on the desk.

"My thoughts exactly," Mark muttered.

"So what was the point of bringing Todd in?" Martin asked cynically.

Mark shrugged. "Think of it as a piece of cloth with some loose strings. If you pull on the right string, the entire thing unravels."

"Todd just wasn't the right string," I deduced.

Martin was frustrated and walked out of the office. *I*

needed to keep him on a leash, I thought as I got up to follow, but Mark stopped me.

"Give him a few minutes."

I slumped into the now empty chair that Martin vacated. "Todd basically just rolled on Griffin for conspiring to plant a box in my office, and he alluded to some higher up conspiracy within the company. We're really making progress now." I rolled my eyes. "Is it me?" I asked. "I can't do anything right. I never signed on to be consultant and bodyguard, yet I'm doing both or at least trying to. I'm trying to investigate and work the angles, but I have no access to the databases or software. I have to stay at the compound and make sure he's safe, so I can't stakeout anything. I...I don't know what I'm doing."

Mark studied me, unprepared for my unexpected meltdown. "Easy there." He tried to sound soothing, but he might have been talking to a wild horse. "You're doing the best you can." He judged my face and overall appearance. "And on very little sleep, no doubt." I sighed. Obviously, death-warmed-over was the look I was achieving these days. "Plus, you're getting there. You know these things take time. How many investigations did we work that lasted for at least six months?"

"True. It just seems slow since every minute of the day I'm there, and he's there." I saw Martin coming back and shut my mouth.

Mark reached over and squeezed my shoulder. "You're doing just fine." He gave me a genuine smile.

"Ready to go?" Martin asked from the doorway, his demeanor once again completely neutral. I stood up, and Mark gave me a quick nod for encouragement.

"Hey, if you're going to be around tonight, I'll come over. Alex could use a break," Mark told Martin.

Martin looked at me, somewhat skeptically, or at least I interpreted it as skeptical. Maybe he knew I was whining about my own incompetence. "Sure."

TWENTY-SEVEN

The drive back had been quiet. Once we got to Martin's, he made himself scarce, holing up on the fourth floor. He was trying his damnedest to track the money and figure out who authorized the move. I was less than helpful on this front, so I figured I would just stay out of his way. My head was pounding from sleep deprivation and frustration over not being able to piece together the puzzle. I needed a new perspective and to catch up on some much missed sleep in a real bed. Changing out of my work attire and crawling under the covers, I checked the alarm near the French doors, making sure it was still active and working, before I fell asleep.

When I opened my eyes, my head still hurt, but I felt much more in control and capable of not melting down again. It was almost five. I threw on jeans and a t-shirt and ran a brush through my hair before stepping into the hallway. I had a feeling Martin hadn't moved from the fourth floor, and I was right. Trudging up the stairs, I found him in his office with the door open. Leaving him alone, I went to the second floor and rummaged through the guest bathroom for aspirin. Suddenly, he appeared behind me.

"Talk about unsociable," he quipped. "You came all the way upstairs, and you didn't even say hello."

"I didn't want to disturb you. You looked busy." I was having no luck locating the aspirin.

"I need a fresh set of eyes to double-check some things," he was being intentionally vague, "if you're up to it."

I shut the vanity drawers. "Sure. I'll trade you aspirin for assistance."

"Are you okay?" That was the second time today he asked this.

"I'm fine, just a headache." I brushed it off and followed him up the stairs. After his drunken night, he kept the aspirin bottle hostage in his bedroom. He handed me the bottle and went into the bathroom to get a cup of water. "Thanks." I popped two pills into my mouth and washed them down with the water.

"You know, you can look at this stuff later. It's not going anywhere."

"No, I can do it now. I'm okay, really." I followed him into the office where he had mapped out the money transfers, complete with account numbers and fragmentation amounts. "How the hell did you manage to do all of this?"

"I had some free time," he replied, and I graced him with a slight smile.

"So what am I looking at? Or for?" I was confused. I didn't know what he possibly needed me to assess.

He produced a stack of papers with account numbers, transfer authorization numbers, dates, and times. Maybe I should have taken him up on his offer to do this later.

"First, can you make sure I transcribed these numbers properly?" He sounded like a kid asking if I could check his homework. I rubbed my temples and double-checked the numbers. Everything looked accurate. "Good." He picked up the stack of paper. "That's enough for now."

"No, let's finish this. Now what do you want me to do?"

He stared, unyielding. "We'll get to it after dinner. It isn't going anywhere." I was going to protest, but he gave me a critical look. "You don't feel good. You're pale and in pain. You are not fine, and I don't want you to pass out on the papers and make a mess." He softened his accusation. "Why don't you go lie down or something?"

"I'm fine." A little headache wasn't a big deal. "I just got up from lying down. Just give the aspirin a few minutes to kick in, and I'll be raring to go."

"Well, in the meantime, I'll start on dinner." I was going to object, but he tried a different tactic this time. "I'm hungry, and it's my house. So I get to decide when I eat." He winked, and I rolled my eyes, which didn't help my head. "And you can watch me cook. I insist."

He ushered me into the kitchen and made me sit at the table. I rested my head in my hands and closed my eyes while he chopped and sautéed various ingredients. The aspirin began to take effect, and the pounding ebbed away. I got up and washed the dirty dishes in the sink.

"I'm fine now, honest."

He finished preparing dinner. With almost perfect timing, Mark buzzed the intercom and announced he was outside.

"I'll let him in," I offered and disarmed the security system.

"Hope I didn't miss dinner," Mark said, holding out a bottle of wine as we went into the kitchen.

"A nice red. Excellent." Martin took the bottle and found some glasses.

I stuck with water, and the three of us ate quickly. Martin was anxious to get back to the finances, and now, he was lucky enough to have two extra sets of eyes to help him out.

"Any new developments?" Mark inquired. I shrugged, but Martin launched into a summary of what he had already shown me upstairs. "Sounds like you've made some progress." Mark was impressed, and he looked at me.

"I can't take any of the credit." I put my hands up. "I'm lucky if I can balance my checkbook."

Martin tried to herd us upstairs for whatever it was he wanted help with earlier, but Mark cut in. "Why don't I look over this stuff with Marty and you can take a break?"

I felt better now, rested and refreshed, but Martin looked concerned. "Take a break. You've been working nonstop for almost a week. Get out of here." Martin jerked his head at the door. "We can manage for a few hours without you."

I remembered my lack of clothes and other necessities.

"If you're sure." I waited for a response, but none came. "Fine, I'm going." I looked at Mark. "You'll be here until I get back, right?"

"Yes, now go."

Grabbing my belongings, I went down the stairs to my car. Once I pulled onto the main highway, I felt free. Staying at Martin's had made me tense from constantly checking and double-checking to make sure there were no immediate threats. Until today, I didn't realize how worn out I was from only sleeping a few hours here or there and making myself crazy with the same few facts and limited surveillance footage. Mark was right; a break was exactly what I needed, even if it was only for a few hours.

I was practically giddy, pulling up to my apartment building and parking my car. It started to rain, but I barely even noticed. I was home. I walked up the six flights of stairs, not minding the smell of mildew or cabbage which permeated the building. Home sweet home. I was almost to my front door when I noticed something amiss. At first, I thought I was just imagining things, but as I got closer to my door, I could tell something was definitely wrong.

Pulling my handgun from my purse, I slowly approached my apartment. There were tool marks on the lock. When I gave the door a good push, it sprang open. Clasping the cold steel in both hands, I carefully entered my apartment. The place was trashed. I walked through my apartment, careful not to touch anything except the doorknobs. My gun was pointed in front of me, and I made sure no one was waiting inside or hiding some place, planning to strike. Once I cleared the apartment, I noticed the white mystery box from the surveillance feed opened and scattered on top of my dining room table.

From what I could tell, my résumé, address, and other personal information were laid out on the table, along with numerous photos of Martin from before we met. There were also more recent photos of the two of us in different public locations, both inside and out of the MT building. This was definitely a threat. Angry red Xs covered our faces, and I resisted touching the photos. There might be fingerprints or other forensic evidence I would contaminate. It was best to photograph as much as possible because once the police arrived, I might not get another opportunity to review the items. After using my camera phone to photograph everything visible, I dialed 911.

"I'd like to report a break-in." I gave the operator my address and information.

Next, I called O'Connell and told him what happened. It seemed like relevant information for his case. He reminded me not to touch anything, and he promised he'd take lead on the scene. Once that was complete, I decided to get out of my apartment. My sofa and mattress had been slashed. All of my drawers were dumped out and overturned, and my television and microwave were smashed. If I stayed here a moment longer, I would lose it. Leaning against the wall in the hallway, I dialed Mark's number.

"Hey." It sounded like they were having a good time. "What's up?"

"I'm not sure if I'll get back tonight. I need you to stay there and keep an eye out, okay?" My voice shook slightly, and I hoped he didn't notice.

"What's wrong?" Mark noticed.

"Just stay there." I hung up, trying to regain my composure, and slid down the wall until I was sitting on the floor. I took a few deep breaths. I was irate. Whoever did this would pay. My home had been violated. My house destroyed. I was going to nail the son of a bitch to the fucking wall. I was resolute in this decision, and now, I fully understood what Martin had been going through. My phone rang.

"What happened?" Mark asked patiently.

"Someone broke into my apartment." My voice was emotionless. "O'Connell's on the way. It might be a while."

"I can be there," he began, but I cut him off.

"Stay with Martin. Do not leave him alone. If they can get to me," I swallowed, making sure to remain detached, "who knows."

"Okay. I'll stay on the phone with you until they show up."

I chuckled. "Fine. Just as long as we don't have to watch

some romantic comedy together until one of us falls asleep, clutching the receiver." Sarcasm and bad jokes were my ingrained self-defense mechanisms.

"Describe the scene." He tried to keep me in a professional mindset, so I told him about the box, the photos, the documents, and the damage to my belongings as if I were speaking about a stranger's residence.

I could hear Martin in the background, and I wanted to insulate him from this, but that wouldn't help anyone. He had a right to know. After all, he was the one in the crosshairs. Luckily, I heard sirens and knew the cops had arrived.

"I gotta go. I'll be back when I can."

TWENTY-EIGHT

A couple of uniformed police officers came up the stairs and met me in the hallway. I waved them over and informed them of the situation. They entered my apartment to check for any intruders and put some crime scene tape around my door to secure the area until someone with more seniority could instruct them further. I paced the hallway in front of my apartment, waiting.

"Why does trouble follow you around everywhere?" O'Connell asked, emerging onto the sixth floor.

"Just lucky, I guess."

He glanced at the two uniforms. "I'll take it from here. When the crime scene guys get here, send them up." He signed off on the scene, and the two officers went downstairs. "Touch anything?" he asked.

"Just the doorknobs. The front door, bathroom, closets," I paused thinking, "that was it."

"Has anyone else been in your house lately? Friend, boyfriend, family member?"

"Just me."

He made some notes. "We'll need your prints for reference to cross out as scene contamination. It's your house, so they'll be all over the place anyway, just like your DNA." He was speaking more to himself than to me. "Shall we?" He held the yellow tape up, and I braced myself before re-entering my apartment.

"Box and the contents on the table might be of some

interest." I pointed to my dining room.

"I guess we know what was in the box. I assume this was left for you." I nodded. "Great." We continued walking through my apartment. "Anything else left behind?"

"Not that I noticed, but I was a bit preoccupied."

"I can see what you mean." He assessed my ruined furniture and stuffing covered floors, along with everything else that was discarded throughout my apartment. "Is anything missing?"

"I don't know." I tried to slow my breathing; my anger was edging toward full-blown rage.

"Anything James Martin related missing?" He tried again.

"No," I shook my head vehemently, "everything pertaining to that is elsewhere."

He considered my response. "Do you have insurance to cover the damages?"

"I don't know." I hadn't thought that far ahead. "Maybe."

"You should probably check into it. What time did you leave your residence?" he asked, back to business.

"I haven't been here since Friday night. I guess it was technically Saturday morning. It was around midnight."

He was surprised and made a note. "So you haven't been here in three or four days?"

"Correct." I stared at my overturned dresser and piles of clothing lying on the floor in messy heaps.

He noticed my gaze and escorted me into a more neutral environment. We went back into the hallway just as the crime scene guys arrived. He instructed them on the situation and what they needed to do.

"I'll get some officers to canvass the building, see if your neighbors have seen anything. You never know." He pulled out the radio and passed along the orders. "We'll see if anything turns up." After he instructed everyone on what to do and how to do it, he turned back to me. "Do you mind coming down to the station, again?"

"Why not? It's not like I have any place else to be."

"You got your car?" I nodded. "Okay, follow me in. We'll get this over with as quickly as possible." He was trying to be helpful, and I appreciated the effort. But I just wanted to put my fist through the wall or cry, probably both. I got into my car and followed him to the police station.

Once there, we went to his cubicle in the squad room. He pulled a chair up to his desk, and I sat down and began filling out the report. I was almost done when his desk phone rang.

"O'Connell," he answered. I leaned back in the chair, watching him animatedly talk on the phone. He frowned. "Where?" He waited briefly for a response. "Get the ME down there. Keep this quiet for now." He hung up and met my eyes. "A body was found in the dumpster of your apartment building, wrapped in plastic sheeting and duct tape. Thompson recognized the victim." He was watching for some sign of recognition perhaps, but I had no idea what he was talking about or how this even pertained to me. "No positive ID has been made yet, but he's reasonably certain it's Suzanne Griffin."

My hand flew to my mouth, and I stared at him. A million thoughts immediately came to my mind. I felt queasy and swallowed tentatively. "How?"

"Gunshot." He tapped his pen absently on the desk. He wasn't considering me a suspect for the shooting, was he? "Are you carrying?" I nodded. "Good. Keep it that way."

I snorted despite myself and rubbed my face. "What's going to happen now?"

"I have to get back, but I'll do my best to keep this out of the papers." We locked eyes. "Whoever gunned her down doesn't need to know we're aware of this." I concurred. Griffin's murderer might be coming for either Martin or me next. "I'll put a rush on your apartment. See if we can figure out who was inside. We might get lucky, and it'll be the shooter."

"Yeah." Everything was reaching a crescendo, and I needed to get ahead of the wave before it came crashing down on top of me. "What else do you need from me?"

He considered this for a moment. "I've done some checking. You're one of us, at least unofficially. Your prints are still on file, I assume, so I don't need anything from you. If anything else occurs, let me know."

"Thanks, Detective." I extended my hand.

"It's Nick." He shook my hand. "Stay safe."

"That's the plan." I gave him a slight smile and left the police station.

I thought about calling Mark to give him the heads up, but I didn't want to relay the news over the phone. It didn't seem right, not when Martin still had an attachment to the recently departed. I drove around the city in a haphazard fashion, watching for a tail or suspicious behavior. Maybe I was just avoiding giving Martin the bad news.

Once I was positive no one was following me, I drove to the compound and entered through the garage. I turned off the engine and sat in my car for a few moments. The rage I felt at my apartment had faded while filling out paperwork and hearing the news about Griffin, but now that I was back in a relatively safe environment, it was building again. I did my best to compartmentalize the evening's events. After all, not everything that happened tonight was about me.

Martin was standing in the doorway to the second floor. I closed my car door, pretending not to notice him, and kept my head down as I walked toward the stairs.

"Are you okay?" he asked softly.

I got to the top of the steps, and he reached for me. But I stepped past him and into the living room. "Yeah." I wasn't sure how long my emotionless resolve would last. "I'm okay."

Mark knew me well enough to keep his distance for fear that I might lash out. I caught his eye, and he could tell immediately I had bad news. "Do you want to sit?" Mark asked, but I shook my head, turning to Martin.

"James." I used his first name, and he knew instinctively something was wrong. "You might want to take a seat." I swallowed and avoided his gaze. He sat without question or protest. "Suzanne Griffin's dead. Fatal gunshot wound. They found her body in the dumpster outside my apartment building." Dragging my gaze from the floor, I looked up at him. His eyes were full of shock, concern, and pain.

"Are you sure you're okay?" he asked. Did he not just

hear what I said? His expression seemed sad and a little guilty.

"I'm okay," I said slowly, even though I was sick of him asking this inane question.

"I'm glad." He disappeared upstairs.

I looked at Mark, who shook his head slightly. I wasn't going to follow; I was barely holding myself together.

"Do you want to talk about it?" Mark asked, grabbing two beers from the fridge.

"What part? The part where everything I own is destroyed and the sanctity of my home no longer exists?" Pull it together, Parker. "Or the part where someone's gotten tired of this shit and is making sure there aren't any remaining loose ends left, which most likely means Martin and I are getting closer to the top of that hit list?" So much for being emotionless and compartmentalizing.

"Either," he said, taking a drink from the bottle.

"Why don't you tell me how your night went instead?" I needed something else to occupy my mind.

"Easier if I can show you," he replied, but I shook my head. I didn't want to risk seeing Martin. His sorrow and remorse would likely throw me over the edge. Mark realized what he implied and attempted to backtrack. "I'll just tell you about it for now."

"Did you get a name? Anything?" I didn't feel like dealing with elaborate explanations. I just wanted simple answers.

"The individual shell companies are set up so intricately we can't track them back to one person, but the cash withdrawal from the Caymans didn't go into a corporation. It was filtered back into a personal account which belongs to," he paused for dramatic effect while I stared, unenthused, "Todd Jackson."

"So? We already suspected that." I didn't see what the fuss was about.

"Yes, but Marty's figured out a way to follow it backwards to when the money was initially moved in order to identify who gave the authorization."

I wasn't entirely sure how that was even possible, but if Mr. Genius could figure it out, who was I to criticize. "You got a name or authorization or whatever?"

"We have the authorization number. Martin's checking with the corporate bank to get a name. He should have it by morning." One down, only a million more to go.

"Did you ever get word about the plant footage, and who the saboteur might be?" While he was here, I might as well get as much useful information out of him as possible.

"There weren't any good angles, and they couldn't get a clear enough view of his face." He went to his jacket and removed the disk from his pocket. "I was going to give this back to you earlier, but–" his voice trailed off.

"The shit hit the fan," I retorted, scowling.

"How bad is it?"

I slumped further into the couch, pulling my knees to my chest. "My place is trashed. Everything's destroyed. It's a fucking mess." I rubbed the corner of my eye.

"If there's anything," he began.

"I know, but I can't think about that right now. I have to be focused here. Griffin's dead," I whispered, afraid Martin, two floors above, would hear.

"Any leads?"

"They haven't even officially identified her, so I doubt it. I knew this would happen. I had a feeling on Saturday when we couldn't locate her. Things were fine yesterday, and now look." My volume increased, and I tried to calm down.

"It's not your fault."

"I never said it was." I practically jumped down his throat. "For all I know, that psychotic bitch was the one who broke into my apartment." I glanced at the stairs, hoping my voice didn't travel. "Those loose ends are being cut, but I don't know how a security guard being paid off and a secretary being murdered fit into anything. Who the hell cares about some photos? What? I'm supposed to be scared shitless because someone's been following me and taking pictures or because they know who I am and where I live? Get in fucking line," I growled. "We make enemies. That's the job."

Mark waited for my venting to stop. When I didn't say anything else, he decided it was safe to speak. "Jackson was paid to leave the box in your office, even though, technically, you weren't going into work, and then the box was left in your apartment, even though you haven't been there for days. Do they have bad intel, or are they just that stupid? Maybe the box and photos are meant to scare you away from Marty?"

"Unless they were staking out my apartment, they wouldn't know I haven't been there, and more importantly, I don't scare easily. The problem is whoever's behind this knows who I really am. They aren't fooled by the girlfriend act." When would the ME determine Griffin's time of death? "For all I know, the box could have been sitting in my apartment since Saturday after the attempt to leave it in my office failed."

"True," Mark said. We needed a way to narrow it down. "Looks like we're waiting for O'Connell and Thompson to come up with some better answers." I hated waiting. I really did. "I'm staying the night. Why don't you get some sleep? Marty's mentioned how you've been dozing on the couch, and given the current situation, you need to be alert and functioning at one hundred and ten percent. I'll keep an eye out."

I was going to protest since it wasn't likely I'd sleep much, if at all, but I could use the solace of isolation to get a grip on everything. "Are you sure?" I asked, and he nodded. "Okay."

I went to my room and shut the door. Stripping down, I stepped into the shower and tried to wash away the negative feelings and events from today. My tears mixed with the hot water before vanishing down the drain. Once my crying subsided, I dried off, put on an oversized t-shirt and pajama shorts, and crawled into bed. The noise on the stairs had to be Mark or Martin, and I resisted the urge to investigate. There was nothing for me to worry about with Mark on sentinel duty. I shut my eyes, hoping tomorrow would be better.

TWENTY-NINE

"Morning, sunshine," Mark greeted from the dining room table. I glared at him and sat down. It was early, and Martin wasn't up yet. "How'd you sleep?"

"Pretty good, considering." I had to admit not having to be on alert actually allowed a few restful hours of sleep.

Mark was reading the paper and drinking coffee. I decided to forgo the caffeine; I was jittery enough. Staring at the paper in front of his face, I sat quietly until he got tired of feeling my eyes on him.

"What?" he asked.

I honestly didn't have a clue. I wanted answers, and I wanted to make some heads roll. The question was how to go about making these things happen.

"I want this son of a bitch." I was determined, and he noticed the intensity in my eyes.

"You'll get him. We'll get him."

I picked up the plant surveillance disk and turned it over in my hands. The answers were here. I just had to get to them.

"Morning, sexy," Mark called.

Martin stumbled into the living room. His hair was wildly unkempt, and his eyes were red. He looked like hell. Was he drinking again last night? Either that or he wasn't a completely self-centered egotist. Cool it, Parker. I knew Martin better than that. The problem was me. I was angry at everyone, and although I knew intellectually my apartment being ransacked was not his fault, it was his problem I got dragged into. I did my best to push the resentment away.

"I get a sunshine, and he gets a sexy," I whined. "How exactly is that fair?"

Mark looked at me once again like I lost my mind, but he kept his mouth shut. I was used to getting those looks by now. Martin had yet to acknowledge either of us and instead rummaged through the couch cushions, looking for something.

"Shit," Martin growled, slamming his hand down.

Great, with the mood he was in, we were going to literally kill each other today. I looked at Mark, doing my best to convey I wasn't ready to deal with Martin. Mark got up to see if he could assist, and I went to the back door, entered the security code, and stepped outside.

Some distance from Martin and his drama might be just what I needed at the moment, so I sat on one of the chaises by the pool, watching as the wind blew the water across the surface. My reflection in the rippled water was only barely decipherable. The only thing I could definitively make out was the shiny reflection of my watch. The light bulb flashed inside my brain, and I jumped up and ran back to the house.

Grabbing the surveillance disk off the table, I went into the living room. Mark and Martin were discussing something, but I paid them no attention. I sat on the coffee table and inserted the disk. Hitting play and then fast forward, I waited until the suspect came on the screen and froze the footage.

"I got you," I exclaimed to the television. Mark and Martin stopped talking and turned to me. I pointed to the screen. "The watch." Still, no comprehension dawned on them. "Take this back and have the watch face enhanced." I ejected the disk and shoved it at Mark. "I will bet that isn't a run-of-the-mill watch. It's too large and too damn shiny." Denton's diamond encrusted watch face flashed through my mind, but I couldn't tell from the footage if they were one and the same. However, if I could find a bookie willing to take my bet, I would have put a few grand on that possibility.

"Get the watch, we get the guy." Mark smiled, catching on.

Martin seemed to see me for the first time since last night but didn't say anything. We cautiously studied each other for a few moments, sensing uncertainty and maybe some resentment boiling just beneath the surface. My resolve to be less angry seemed much easier now, given how utterly miserable he looked.

"I'm already out the door," Mark announced, grabbing his keys and jacket. He slipped the disk into his pocket. "Are you gonna be all right?" Martin nodded, and Mark went down the steps to the garage.

"Do you need anything?" I asked quietly. Perhaps extreme mood swings was a contagious disease. Martin shook his head. He wasn't himself. He lacked focus, drive, and everything that made him an infuriating, arrogant, and brilliant man. To coddle or not to coddle, that was my current dilemma. I didn't do emotions and feelings usually. At least I didn't do them well. "Go take a shower and make yourself presentable. God knows what's going to happen today."

He pressed his lips together, thinking. Then he headed back up the stairs without uttering a word.

After his door closed, I picked up my phone and called O'Connell. After two rings, he answered. We exchanged some basic pleasantries and got down to business.

"What have you got for me?" I asked, hoping he'd still be amenable to playing ball even in the light of day.

"Positive ID was made on Griffin. She was shot twice in the chest from close range with a small caliber handgun. No one's seen anything. TOD still needs to be narrowed down, but our best estimate is twelve to twenty-four hours from the time we found her remains."

My guess was Griffin was murdered Monday night after work, but I had no solid facts to substantiate my claim. Briefly, I considered the possibility Todd had done it, but O'Connell didn't think so. My gut tended to agree.

"What about the apartment?" I asked, no longer able to think of it as my apartment. It was simply the scene of a crime.

"Prints on the box matched Griffin and Jackson. We got a couple of partials on some of the photos, but they aren't in the database. And we don't have anyone else to run comparisons on." And then there were three. "The rest of the place was clean, despite the huge mess."

I ignored his attempt to joke. "I'm juggling on this end, working two separate angles. If either pans out, I'll give you a call."

"Is everything okay? I can spare a couple of guys to patrol if you want."

I thought about it but figured more attention would likely do more harm than good. "We can manage, but I'll be in touch." I hung up, trying to recall how many things were still in the works. The watch and the bank account authorization, was that it? Or was I forgetting about something?

I sat on the couch, pondering over the last few days, reminding myself it had only been six days since the hot dog cart explosion in front of the MT building. Everything was happening in overdrive, and whoever was behind this was escalating their attack strategy. Two conspirators had been removed from the picture. One was in custody, and the other was dead. We had partial prints for a third, but were there more?

Martin came down the stairs, freshly showered and his hair slightly wet. He went into the kitchen, retrieved a cup of coffee, and headed for the second floor office. I waited a beat before getting up and following him.

"You can't ignore me forever." Excellent use of melodrama, my internal voice chided.

He turned, cocking an eyebrow in confusion. "I wasn't aware I had been ignoring you." Obviously, the irritating Martin was still in there despite the ennui, but his words lacked their normal banter.

"Maybe I was embellishing just a bit." I gave him a tentative smile and took a breath. "Are you okay?" I asked sincerely.

"Funny, I thought that was my line that you didn't quite care for."

"Look, if you want to be angry or pissed off, that's fine. If you want to take it out on me because it will make you feel better, that's okay too. Hell, I'm pissed. I'm chasing my tail in circles, waiting for something to point me in the right direction. Meanwhile, shit keeps happening, and we're not getting anywhere fast."

He spun his chair around to face me. I wasn't sure what to expect, if it would be a verbal attack, a breakdown, or something else entirely, so I waited. He considered his words carefully. "I want my life back. I want my company back. I don't want to worry about answering the phone or opening an e-mail or walking outside."

His honesty floored me, and I took a step back as if I had been struck. That was exactly why I was here. "Okay." I felt the intensity of my newfound conviction. "Okay," I repeated as I left his office. I picked up my phone and called O'Connell back. "How do you feel about a civilian ride-along? Do you want to knock down some doors? I'm getting tired of waiting for the answers to come to me."

"I might be able to swing it. We'd be checking into some leads in an ongoing investigation." He wanted to make my request seem plausible.

"Great, I'll see you in a half hour." I found Martin standing in the living room.

"Where are you going?" he asked.

"To get your life back. I'm sorry it's taken so long." I put on my shoulder holster and tightened it, checking the magazine and making sure everything was in working order before snapping my gun into place. After zipping my jacket, I made sure my spare was close by in the event he needed it for anything.

"I didn't," he began, but I stopped him by placing my finger on his lips.

"You hired me to do this. Let me do my job." I was determined. I was pissed, and most of all, I was sick and tired of sitting on my ass while someone continued to destroy my small semblance of a life.

THIRTY

I arrived at the police station a little earlier than planned, so I used the extra few minutes to call Mark and tell him I was checking into things with O'Connell. Then I asked if he could keep an eye on Martin. I felt bad for sending him to the OIO only to ask him to return to Martin's, but he didn't argue. He just agreed. That was one of the things I liked about Mark; he would do what needed to be done. And he promised to call the moment the image enhancement was complete. Next, I called Martin and told him to expect Mark and asked for the banking information to be passed along as soon as he got it. He wasn't pleased by having a different babysitter, but he let it go. Finally, O'Connell met me at the front desk of the precinct.

"What did you want to look into?" O'Connell asked.

"I'm waiting on a couple of calls, but I thought we could go through what you've already gotten." Hopefully, he would see this as a fair trade. He had an open murder on his hands and wanted answers just as badly as I did.

We went up to his desk, and he handed me Todd Jackson's file and the coroner's report on Suzanne Griffin. I read through each one carefully, trying to make sure I didn't miss anything. Jackson agreed to provide corroborating evidence against the main conspirator, but he insisted he had no idea who it was. Griffin had been shot at close range with a small caliber handgun. There wasn't much to tell. Ballistics were running the slugs and trying to match them to a weapon now, but it was too soon to know anything definitive.

"Did you get any video footage from my building?" I asked after reading the reports.

"The cameras were busted, but a few of your neighbors remember seeing an unfamiliar man and woman lurking about."

"Did you get a description?"

"Nothing that stood out. Basically, average height, average build, and average looking. We passed around Griffin's photo, but no positive ID was made. You know how reliable eyewitnesses are."

I sighed and rubbed my neck. "Did you ever check into Griffin's B&B story?"

"Not yet."

"Want to take a drive? Maybe between now and then, I'll get something more concrete for you to run with."

"What the hell," he put on his jacket, "I need to go down there anyway before I can close the interview file."

*   *   *

I was sitting in the passenger seat of an unmarked police cruiser as Det. O'Connell drove down Route 9 toward the Cat's Cradle. What types of people actually enjoyed the B&B experience? B&Bs were never my thing. It was the equivalent of being subjected to staying in a room in a stranger's house, eating meals with even more strangers, and having to share a bathroom; it was like prison or college. My characterization was frighteningly similar to staying at Martin's residence. Maybe I was a closeted B&B enthusiast. I shuddered at the thought. Luckily, I was rescued from this chilling realization by my phone ringing. It was Martin.

"Hey, everything okay?" I asked.

"Yeah," he sounded preoccupied, "I got a call from the bank. The funds were authorized by Blake Denton."

"So he stole the money?"

"I don't know. It was his authorization code, but our banker doesn't know who made the transfer. It was done electronically. You know Denton. He likes to delegate duties all over the place."

Actually, I didn't know that, but I kept my mouth shut. "Is Mark there?" I asked, changing the subject.

"No, he got called away on some work thing." I could tell from his tone that Martin was reading something. "Rosemarie and Marcal are here. We're fine." Having extra people in the house was supposed to reassure me, but it didn't. Regardless, I was too far away to do anything about it.

"Okay. Stay safe. Call if you need anything." I hoped to get through to Martin, but I knew how he could be when he was focused on work.

He emitted a non-committal sound and hung up, leaving me to stare at the end call message on the screen.

"Good news?" O'Connell asked. I sensed a note of sarcasm.

"Do you think you might be able to subpoena someone's financial records on a little more than a whim?" I asked. He gave me a quizzical look, and I told him about the missing funds, the twenty-five thousand dollar withdrawal, and my suspicions on how the money withdrawal matching Todd's payoff seemed too coincidental.

"It's worth a shot. I'll pass it along and see if we can find a sympathetic judge to give us the go-ahead." He pulled out his phone and relayed everything to Thompson. We might as well get the ball rolling in the right direction.

We pulled up to the Cat's Cradle. It wasn't much to look at, but hopefully, the management would remember Mrs. Griffin and be able to give us some details concerning her stay. We got out of the car, and he looked at me.

"Let me do the talking," he warned. "I have the badge and the gun. You're just here to silently observe." I made a face but agreed to his terms.

We were greeted by a woman at the front desk who inquired if we would like a room. O'Connell flashed his badge and asked if she wouldn't mind answering a few questions about a recent guest. The woman seemed surprised but located the relevant guest information from last weekend. I was amazed it wasn't right on top, considering it had only been three or four days since Griffin's alleged stay. Maybe the B&B business was much more lucrative than I imagined.

"Suzanne Griffin," Ilene, the woman at the counter, repeated as she found the proper paperwork. "She stayed here Friday and Saturday night."

O'Connell and I exchanged a glance. "Would you mind taking a look at a photo, just to make sure it's the same Suzanne Griffin?"

Ilene looked at the picture. "That's her. They were a very pleasant couple. What's this all about?"

"Couple?" I blurted out, and O'Connell gave me a look. I shut my mouth and attempted to blend into the very busy wallpaper. A decent enough defense attorney could make a case for justified homicide based on the wallpaper pattern alone.

"She wasn't alone?" he asked, and I resisted the urge to roll my eyes since I just asked the same question.

"No, she was here with her husband. Well, I believe it was her husband. They checked in under Mr. and Mrs. Griffin." She flipped the page around to show O'Connell the information. He glanced back at me. *Sure, now you want my help*, I thought, but I remained silent.

"Can you give us a description of the man?"

"I'm not a good guesser at age, but I'd say forties, brown hair, pretty average. Sweet man, though." She was trying to think, or maybe she had gone into a trance from staring at the walls too long.

"Did anything stand out about him or their visit?" He was trying to cover all his bases, and she came slightly out of her trance.

"He left early Saturday before she did. He said something came up at work."

"Where does he work?" I inquired, expecting O'Connell to glare at me again, but he let it go.

"I don't know." Ilene went back into her trance-like state.

Who was Griffin's mystery man? The description was too old to be Todd; plus, he worked Saturday. But average described pretty much everyone.

"Thank you for your time. If we need anything else, is there a preferred number where we can reach you?" Ilene handed him a business card. He pocketed it and smiled at her. "Thanks. You have a lovely place. I might have to bring my wife for a romantic weekend." He was buttering her up, hoping compliments would lead to more useful information, but Ilene just smiled. I didn't think she knew anything else.

"Please tell me you really don't think that's a lovely place," I whispered as we went to the car.

"It is lovely. What's wrong with it?" he asked. My assessment actually confused him. I shook my head. The wallpaper violated the Geneva Convention's sanction prohibiting torture, but I kept that thought to myself. "Any idea who might be Mr. Griffin?"

I had a hunch, but I wasn't sure if it would pan out. "Give me a minute." I dialed Martin's number, and he answered on the second ring.

"What?" he greeted.

"Can you text me one of the photos you were e-mailed?" The light bulb clicked on for O'Connell, and he enthusiastically agreed this was a good idea.

"I guess. Why?" Martin asked, confused.

"Just following a trail of breadcrumbs. Everything still quiet?" I asked.

"Okay, it's sent." He didn't answer my second question.

"Thanks." I waited to see if he was going to say anything else.

"I'll see you later." He disconnected, causing me to involuntarily roll my eyes. How could he still be in workaholic mode right now? Maybe he was keeping himself busy in order to avoid thinking about everything else that was going on.

"You want to go back in there and ask if that's the guy?" O'Connell brought me out of my reverie.

"Yeah." I opened the car door, and we went back inside. Zooming in solely on Blake Denton, I handed O'Connell my phone.

"Can I help you?" Ilene asked from the counter. Had she forgotten us already? Luckily, I saw recognition on her face. "Oh. Is there something else? Did you want to make a reservation now?"

I hid my chuckle, and he gave her a bright smile. "Actually, I have to check with my wife first to see when she's free. But would you mind taking a look at this photo for us?" He held my phone out to Ilene, and she took it from him.

"That's Mr. Griffin," she said, proud of herself.

"Are you positive?"

"Absolutely."

We exchanged a triumphant look. He thanked Ilene again for her time, and we got back into the car.

"I'll bring Mr. Denton in for questioning. He might be a material witness in an ongoing homicide investigation."

I rubbed my palms together. We were making progress.

"What was the other call you were waiting on besides the bank information?" he asked as we headed back to the city.

"An image enhancement from the sabotage at Martin's plant." Full disclosure seemed fair at this point in the game. "But Agent Jablonsky got called away on something else," I relayed Martin's message, "so I don't know when I'll get it."

"You think it relates back to this Denton character?" He sounded like a television cop.

"I don't know. Martin isn't even sure the bank authorization traces back to him, and that seemed like solid proof." Martin knew Denton better than I did, so I was giving credence to Martin's opinion since mine was already so negatively biased.

O'Connell caught on to my displeasure. "Just between you and me, do you think Denton's involved?"

I mulled it over for a few moments. He was smart enough, capable, and in the right place at the right time, but he had also been one of the few people who opposed Martin relinquishing the company. Something just didn't sit right.

"Honestly, I don't know." Denton's drunken verbal assault at the charity banquet had thrown my instincts off. Whoever was behind this knew I wasn't an assistant. The proof was in the box left on my table. Was Denton that great of an actor? Had the entire night been staged just to force me to react? And if it was Denton, did he hope I would tip my hand? "I can't tell because even though I think it's him, the only reason I think that is because of my great loathing for him."

O'Connell seemed puzzled for a moment before replying, "It's a good thing I'm a detective. If not, I wouldn't have a clue what you just said."

We rode the rest of the way in silence. O'Connell dropped me off at the precinct, and I got in my car and went back to Martin's. I wasn't comfortable leaving him alone any longer, not when things were so precarious right now. O'Connell promised to keep me in the loop, and I just hoped we had overturned the right stones to get this investigation back on track.

THIRTY-ONE

When I arrived at Martin's house, I expected to see Marcal in the garage or Martin working in his second floor office. Instead, no one was to be found. I tried to keep my paranoia down to a minimum as I went up the stairs to the fourth floor. I knocked on the bedroom door.

"Martin?" I called through the door. I heard movement inside and waited, resisting the urge to pull out my gun. Martin opened the door, wearing nothing but a bath towel wrapped around his waist. "Sorry," I said, flustered. "I just wanted to let you know I was back."

"It's okay." He smirked, clearly amused by my embarrassment. "I just came in from a swim and was going to take a shower. If you want, you can join me to make sure it's safe." He cocked an eyebrow up and grinned wolfishly. He was going to be just fine.

Gracing him with my withering stare, I turned back to the stairs. "Maybe next time," I mocked serious.

"Tease," he called, shutting the door. Depressed Martin was bouncing back, even if it meant he was turning into womanizing Martin. In his case, having extreme mood swings was a beneficial thing.

I took the stairs down to my room to hang up my jacket and freshen up. Opening the closet, I noticed my dirty dry cleaning had been taken away and brand new clothing now stood in its place, tags still attached. I went into the bathroom. The towels had been changed, and everything had been tidied up. On my way out of the room, I noticed my sheets had also been changed and the carpeting had been vacuumed. At least Martin was on the level about Rosemarie being here earlier.

I rummaged around in the kitchen, still waiting for more calls to come in. The role I had initially adopted as Martin's assistant wasn't as much of an act as it was intended to be since a large portion of my job revolved around making calls or waiting on calls. Opening the refrigerator door, I made myself some lunch. The fridge had been restocked with freshly purchased items, and the pantry closet had been replenished. If Martin had gone out while I was gone, I was going to kill him. Taking my sandwich to the table, I sat down to eat. He came into the kitchen just as I was finishing my lunch.

"Food fairy brought all this stuff?" I asked around a mouthful of turkey and bread.

He sighed and sat across from me. "Marcal went grocery shopping. He does that, weekly even."

I swallowed. "I noticed the clothes. You didn't have to. It wasn't necessary." But he waved it off as if it were nothing.

"Thought you could use them. It's just a few things to tide you over until everything calms down. Consider it part of expenses and incidentals." The events of yesterday came crashing back to the forefront of my thoughts, and I shuddered, thinking about my apartment. "Are you cold?" he asked.

"No, it's not that." He understood and didn't push the issue. "So, I went with O'Connell to check on some leads." I hesitated, unsure what to tell him about Griffin and Denton. Maybe I needed to let things slide until something absolute surfaced. He sensed my trepidation and looked confused. "I don't know what I should tell you and what I shouldn't. Not anymore. It's your business and your case, but the people involved, or who might be involved, you have personal relationships with them. Perhaps I should only give you information once it's been corroborated."

"I want to know," he stared me down, "regardless."

"Okay." I filled him in on everything we learned today.

"Makes sense, I guess."

"I don't know. We'll see what O'Connell finds out. In the meantime, it'd be nice if Mark got back to us with that photo enhancement."

He let my comment go. Even though he wanted his life back, he probably wasn't in a rush to find out, or potentially find out, people he trusted betrayed him and conspired against him.

He was acting a little squirrely, and I eyed him suspiciously. "I'm getting a bit stir crazy," he admitted, and I stifled my laugh. "I know I haven't been cooped up that long, but I've run out of things to do."

"You must suck at vacations."

He considered my comment for a moment. "Guilty as charged."

"When this is over, I'll find you a W.A. meeting to go to," I promised, but he looked perplexed. "Workaholics anonymous."

Chuckling, he took my empty plate to the sink. "Couldn't you just take me along to your normal meeting?" he quipped.

"Ha. Ha. I am not that bad. I've successfully been unemployed for a few months. Well, before this job. Thank you very much." I stopped and considered my own words. Since when was unemployment a bragging right?

"Normally, I have projects and hobbies and other things I can work on, but now I'm stuck." He turned toward me, his eyes sparkling. "Maybe I'll take up painting. Do you want to model?" I narrowed my eyes. "Just a thought."

"So tell me something." I leaned back in the chair as he finished putting the dishes away. "Tell me something about you. Something real." I was attempting to have a genuine non-case related conversation. I'd been living at Martin's for almost a week, so maybe I should know something about my employer.

He sat down and thought for a moment. "Well, I'm a Libra, but most people figure I'm a Taurus." Why did I expect him to be serious about anything? "Okay, you want serious?" The way he said it sounded like a challenge.

"Go for it," I taunted.

"I inherited Martin Technologies from my father when I

was twenty-six years old. I had just completed my MBA from Harvard and had no idea what to do. I was a crazy kid, thinking I could build an empire." He was a little lost in thought. "I made a lot of mistakes starting out, bad investments and unreliable people. Dad's motto was if something doesn't work, then work harder. I guess you could say I'm still doing that today." He seemed sad.

"You have an empire," I replied. "You are allowed to stop working so damn hard." He shrugged it off. "I'm sure your dad would tell you the same thing."

He laughed cynically. "I doubt that. He loved one thing, and that was the company."

"What happened to him?" I regretted asking the moment the words left my mouth.

Martin frowned and barely shook his head, quickly changing the subject. "Let's see, what else?" He looked at the ceiling, contemplating what to say next. "I tend to favor smartass brunettes, especially ones who aren't afraid to call me out on my shit." He grinned and flipped a piece of my brown hair over my shoulder.

"Don't forget the part about how I could probably kick your ass fairly easily." I made a so-so gesture with my hand, and he laughed.

"You wish."

I got up from the table and stood in front of his chair. "You know what? I have an idea." I winked and went into the living room, surveying the area. Too much furniture. I opened the door to the garage and headed down the stairs. "Are you coming?"

Besides having a large garage/showroom, the first floor was divided into a few extra rooms I hadn't noticed. There was a small home gym, a bathroom and shower, what I assumed was Martin's work area, complete with power tools and things of that nature, a small lounge like area, and plenty of empty open spaces.

"What do you want to do? Inhale paint fumes or carbon monoxide?" he asked, heading down the stairs.

"We can do that later, when we get bored." I stretched my arms and back, enjoying the puzzled look he was giving me. "Limber up. I'm going to teach you some basic defenses. You never know when you might need them."

"Please," as if it were beneath him. I continued to stretch, and he gave in and played along. Luckily, he was wearing a t-shirt and jeans today instead of a suit. But his shirt alone cost more than everything I had on. "I don't want to hurt you," he patronized.

"As if you could," I trash talked in the hopes of getting him to go along with my plan. He seemed unperturbed by my challenge. "Fine. How's this sound? If you hurt me, you get to kiss it and make it better." I pursed my lips and blew a kiss. He laughed, and a mischievous glint quickly crossed his features. I was aware of my flirtation, but I was just happy he wasn't depressed. "So, let's say I'm unarmed," I said, circling around.

"Which you are," he pointed out. Thank you, Captain Obvious.

I wrapped my arm around his neck. "And I want to strangle you. What do you do?"

He attempted to shake my hold, but I tightened just slightly, unrelenting. He stopped, considered his next move, and to my surprise, tilted his body and flipped me over his shoulder. He knelt down to cushion my descent.

"Impressive."

He wasn't as clueless as I suspected. He gave me a smug, self-satisfied look. "Should we go find a can of paint now?" he asked, standing up, but I wasn't that easy to dissuade.

"Okay, let's say, I have a knife, and I lunge at you." I found a piece of window chalk to use as a prop. "Now what do you do?" I stabbed at him with the chalk. He stepped back, and I pursued.

"I don't want to hurt you," he insisted, continuing to step away.

"I'm trying to stab you to death, gut you like a fish and filet you, so do something."

He reached for my wrist, and I blocked his hand with my non-knife hand and stabbed him with the chalk in the chest repeatedly.

"You stabbed me." He clutched his chest.

"Be serious," I tried to overlook the theatrics, "if I'm

coming at you with a knife, more than likely, you're going to get cut by a few swings here and there. You need to protect all vital parts of your body."

We continued to go over defenses, ranging from knives to guns to means of escape and the best ways to incapacitate an attacker. My training at the OIO wasn't a complete waste after all. Martin was a quick learner; although, I suspected Mark must have given him a crash course, probably after the kidnapping attempt.

After a final takedown, Martin had me pinned on the floor. His once charcoal gray shirt was now mostly chalk white with a few streaks of charcoal that had somehow managed to remain unscathed. I was equally streaked with the chalk, and I slapped my palm against the ground.

"I give up," I exclaimed, laying my head back against the floor. He was too triumphant for my taste, so I waited for him to lean back before flipping him over and pinning him to the ground, using my body to keep him from moving. "Never underestimate your opponent," I whispered in his ear.

"But you gave up," he protested.

I leaned back, so I could look into his eyes. "Things are never that simple," I clarified. He attempted to roll me off, but I had strategically pinned his limbs. It would take more effort if he wanted to shake me loose. Luckily for him, I heard my phone ringing. "Lesson's over for today." I got up and ran up the steps.

"Parker," I answered, slightly out of breath.

"Denton admitted to being at the Cat's Cradle with Griffin," O'Connell informed me. "He says he left Saturday, just like Ilene told us. We have no hard evidence or valid reason to hold him, so we had to let him go about an hour ago."

"What about the money?" Martin came up the stairs. He had taken off his t-shirt and was assessing the chalk stains. "Sorry," I mouthed. He waved off my apology and continued to listen to my half of the conversation.

"I'm still working on getting a court order for the records. I'll let you know what happens. I did my best not to tip him off in case he is involved." O'Connell blew out a breath.

"But by bringing him in for questioning, he might be suspicious." I didn't like where this was heading.

"Keep your head down for a while, just to be on the safe side," O'Connell suggested.

"You got it." I hung up the phone. "Nothing conclusive, yet," I told Martin. "O'Connell brought Denton in as a potential witness in Griffin's murder, but he had to release him. We're still waiting for enough evidence to make him an actual suspect."

"Take off your shirt," he said seriously, but his eyes twinkled. I looked at him like he was insane. "You're full of chalk."

I looked down, noticing I was, in fact, full of chalk. "Fine." I went up the stairs to my room, and he followed close behind. Pulling my shirt over my head, I tossed it in his general direction. "Here," I said, walking into my room and shutting the door, so I could dress in private.

"Tease," he muttered, walking past my closed door toward the laundry room.

I chuckled and thought about those boundaries that were pretty much nonexistent and quickly dismissed the thought. After yesterday, there was nothing wrong with some harmless flirtation as long as it never went beyond that point.

THIRTY-TWO

After dinner, I tried to call Mark, but my call went straight to his out-of-office automated response. Deciding to leave a message, I asked when he had a positive identification on the make or model of the watch to pass it along to Det. O'Connell. I was sitting at the kitchen table, making a flow chart of the information I had. No matter how I listed it or categorized it, everything led back to Blake Denton. Was he really the mastermind behind the conspiracy? There were still too many unknown elements. I was positive Martin was targeted, but for what purpose, I was still unsure. The phone calls I received from the MT building, the photos taken of me with Denton, and the break-in at my office and apartment had all been designed to send me a message. We know who you are; stay out of this. Anyone with access to Griffin had access to my résumé and my hiring, which didn't help narrow down the suspect list. The stolen MT funds were another story altogether. Were the funds taken because Martin was away from the office, making them more easily accessible, or would they have been stolen anyway?

I leaned back in the chair and stared at the pile of papers, closing my eyes and trying to listen to my instincts. Denton's dirty was the only thought resonating throughout my body. My mind just needed to rationalize it.

"Maybe you should go to one of those sleep centers," Martin joked, retrieving a pear from the refrigerator. "I think you must be narcoleptic to fall asleep sitting up at a kitchen table."

"I don't have narcolepsy." I was frustrated, and he got caught by my bitchiness.

"Okay," he said, holding his hands up in surrender and leaning against the counter. "Touchy subject. Sorry."

I sighed. "It's me." I rubbed my face. "How brilliant would you say Blake Denton is? Because that bullshit move he pulled at the charity thing really fucked up my instincts about him."

"Well, on a scale of one to ten, where I'm," he tilted his head from side to side, "about an 851. I'd say he's maybe a seven."

I chuckled. "I'm glad you have a realistic self-image," I teased, picking at the corners of the paper. "Do you think he could be behind this?"

Martin frowned and thought for a few moments. "He has the capabilities and all the access he would need. I just don't know why he would do it. Then again, I didn't see him screwing Suzanne either."

I raised my eyebrows. Jealousy? Regret? Genuine surprise? What was his motivation for that particular assessment? I bit my bottom lip and stared, trying to get a read on him.

"How old is Denton?" I asked for lack of anything better to do.

"Five or ten years older than me, I'd say. Probably in his early to mid-forties." He threw out the pear rind and washed his hands.

Two theories were brewing in my mind simultaneously, except neither of them seemed solid. The first involved Griffin, so distraught over Martin she planned this entire thing. The problem was it had been half a decade, and while hell hath no fury, five years seemed a tad extreme. The second problem was she was dead. Dead didn't make a great endgame for a conspiracy, so I decided to nix this idea. My second theory involved a jealous man. Martin got everywhere faster than Denton. Martin was the CEO. He was brilliant. He ran the company. He bedded who knew how many personal assistants, the likes of which I didn't want to know about, and he was younger, in better shape, and definitely more personable.

"Does Denton strike you as jealous?" I asked once he turned the water off.

Martin didn't even blink before responding. "Definitely."

So my second theory had merit. Denton wouldn't have needed too much support since Griffin had access to a lot of information, personal and corporate. He could have swayed her easily and gotten whatever he needed. Todd Jackson was paid off anonymously, or so he claimed. If Denton hired outsiders to plant the bomb and attempt the kidnapping, he would have an alibi. The photos taken and sent to Martin might also cover his ass or force me to tip my hand.

"Do you think he's capable of killing someone?"

"I don't know." He had no basis for knowing this. Unfortunately, neither did I.

I thought about Griffin's body. From the report, it sounded like a professional hit, but there was no way to be sure. O'Connell needed to get access to Denton's financial records, and then maybe some of these dots could be legitimately connected. I had a feeling if Denton was responsible, he hired someone to do the wet work.

"If Denton is behind this, there has got to be some way to prove it," I mumbled to myself.

I put my elbow on the table and rested my head in my hand, thinking, but no good ideas came to me. Everything I thought of involved tipping Denton off, and we couldn't risk it. I tapped my nails against the table while Martin held my gaze.

"What if I go back to work?" He was serious. "If I'm back, I can confront him on the funds, and maybe something helpful will surface."

"No," I was adamant, "you are not bait."

"Are you sure? I'm living in a fucking fish bowl."

"We don't have any hard evidence yet, and if you go back, I don't know what he'd do." I swallowed. "Griffin was murdered. My guess is he paid someone to take care of that loose end. He could pay someone to take care of you, too, and I can't be everywhere at once. And I really don't like those odds." He crossed his arms, trying to come up with a better solution. "O'Connell is working on getting a court order for Denton's financial records. Maybe when he does, we can track the spending." The only problem, which I didn't mention to Martin, was O'Connell didn't have enough evidence to get access to the records.

"Wouldn't it be nice if the plant saboteur's watch and Blake's watch matched?"

"Yeah, except Mark isn't around at the moment." Would the partial prints on the box match Blake Denton? "Hang on." I called O'Connell. He was off duty, but I left a message for him to call me back.

"What is it?" Martin asked, taking a seat.

"There was a third set of prints in the box or on the box. Whatever. The semantics aren't important. They didn't match anyone in the databases."

"Maybe they were Blake's."

"Maybe." If we can tie him to the break-in at my apartment, it should be enough for O'Connell to get a warrant. Then we could take things from there. Could all the pieces really be coming together this easily? "We'll have to wait it out. Just give me a couple of days before you decide to do something insane."

"I'm impressed, Alex. You left the house this morning and said you were going to get my life back. I didn't really think you'd put things together this quickly. Had I known, I would have said something sooner."

"It's a working theory. For all I know, it was Mrs. White with the rubber hose in the garden."

"I don't think that's how the game is played." He smirked.

*   *   *

The next morning, O'Connell called back. Amazingly enough, I was already awake, wracking my brain for a more plausible alternative theory.

"What have you got, Parker?" He got straight to the point, and I filled him in on my theory and reasoning. He didn't think it was completely sound, but it was more than he had before. "So you think Denton's fingerprints might be a match to the unknowns?"

"I do." I was optimistic.

"The only problem is I don't have enough to get them. I'm not sure I can call him back for a follow-up either. He seems the litigious, harassment type."

I thought about it. "I can get them. It'd be easy enough for me to go into the office. If you want, you can come with me to ensure chain of custody." I knew when I told Martin the plan he wouldn't be pleased, especially since I forbade him from going back to the MT building.

"It might just work. When do you want to do this?"

"The sooner, the better. Let's say around noon."

I updated Martin on the situation. As I suspected, he was less than pleased but agreed to stay away from the office and let me do my job. Now I just needed to figure out a plausible excuse for meeting with Denton.

"Why don't you take this?" Martin rummaged through his office and found a stainless steel clipboard. "Have him sign something." He clicked a few keys on the computer until some employee forms popped up. "Tell him I forgot to renew the contract for the vending machine operators, and since he's acting CEO, he should sign it."

I gave him a skeptical look. "You think he'll buy that?" It sounded like a load of bull.

"Of course, it's a legitimate thing."

"So, I get him to hold the clipboard, we get his prints, and that's that. Easy as pie." This was starting to sound like a ridiculous plan.

"It was your idea," he pointed out. Plus, I was resigned to at least try it.

"Okay, I'll be back soon." I didn't bother to give him my usual stay put speech since I was sure he had it memorized by now.

"Good luck," he called.

*　　*　　*

On my way to the MT building, I called Denton. His

assistant transferred the call, and by the third ring, he answered the phone.

"Alexis, it's so lovely to hear from you today. Is everything okay?"

"James just happened to find some paperwork in his home office, and he thinks you probably need it. It's some kind of contract for the vendors or vending machines. I'm not really sure. You know James's philosophy on work," I tried to sound annoyed by the whole ordeal.

"If you give me the address, I'll send a courier," he offered. The suspicious part of my brain wondered if this was his way of getting easy access to Martin's home.

"I'm actually on my way now. The detective who is investigating the break-in at my office wanted another chance to look around, so I figured two birds, one stone." I tried to sound nonchalant, but I didn't know if it was coming across that way. The news had made no mention of Griffin, so hopefully, O'Connell's appearance at the MT building wouldn't spook the guilty party.

"Oh, I remember hearing about that vaguely. Any suspects?" He seemed interested.

"Not that I'm aware. It didn't seem like a big deal to me, but we know how cops are." I downplayed the situation as much as possible.

"Okay, come find me when you get here. I should be in my office most of the day."

Game, set, match, I thought.

By the time I arrived, O'Connell was loitering out front. I pulled out my MT ID card, and we entered the building. He flashed his badge at the security guards working the desk, and we went to the back of the lobby and took the elevator to the fifteenth floor. During our ascent, I filled O'Connell in on the cover story.

"Mr. Denton," I called, knocking on his slightly open door.

"Alexis, do come in." He waved me into the room. His office was much smaller than Martin's but absolutely exquisite in décor. I walked over, carrying the clipboard and a pen. I had wiped my prints off the clipboard and carefully touched only the sides. I wanted to wear gloves, but considering the warm weather, it would seem too suspicious, especially if he was already on to me.

"Here's that form."

"Great, thanks." He took the clipboard, read the form Martin had printed out, signed his name, and started to hand the clipboard back but stopped. I looked at him confused. *Just give me the damn clipboard*, I wanted to scream. "I can mail it for you," he offered.

"Oh, you don't have to go through any more trouble." I was trying to be gracious and not rip it out of his hands and run for the exit.

"It's no trouble, really." He placed it on top of his desk.

"Great, thank you so much." I headed for the door. "Oh, actually," I spun on my heel, "can I get the clipboard back? James is driving me absolutely crazy. We've already searched the entire house for the damn television remote. If he blames me for misplacing one more thing, I'm going to kill him." I feigned annoyance at Martin, and Denton laughed, handing back the clipboard after unclipping the form.

"Here, it sounds like you might need to give him a good slap. Maybe the clipboard will come in handy."

I did my best to appear contrite. "I really am sorry about that." I tried to sound sincere and embarrassed.

"I deserved it. It's fine. Have a good day." He stood, briefly embracing me while I tried not to gag.

"Thanks, you too."

I headed straight for the elevator with O'Connell at my heels. Once the doors shut, he took out an evidence bag, and I dropped the clipboard inside. He tucked it into his jacket, out of sight.

"Do you think this will pan out?" O'Connell asked as we rode down to the lobby.

"It needs to."

THIRTY-THREE

It had been two days since I had gotten Denton's prints for O'Connell. The lab was backed up, and I wasn't sure when or if the identification was going to be made. Mark was still out of the office. He was working something undercover or was out of town for some other work related reason. Either way, I was irritated by the waiting. Martin was another story altogether. He was itching to get back to work and had decided, since I was the one preventing his return, he was going to hold me responsible for his constant entertainment and amusement.

"Join me." He was swimming laps in the pool and stopped to take a break.

I sat on a lounge chair, my nine millimeter and cell phone next to me. "I don't have a swimsuit."

His eyes danced with mischievous glee. "I keep them stocked just in case I have an unprepared guest. Guest bathroom, top drawer in the vanity." I couldn't tell if he was kidding. "Go get changed," he insisted.

I hedged, but he kept staring expectantly at me. "Fine." I marched into the house. After changing into the least skimpy two-piece I could find, I went back outside. "Happy?"

"Ecstatic," he replied. I descended the steps into the pool, so I was halfway submerged. "The blue brings out your eyes." He attempted to charm me by mentioning the shiny blue swimsuit I had selected.

"How would you know? You've been staring at my tits the whole time."

"I have not. Well," he paused, giving me an admiring grin, "not the entire time."

"So you were staring at my tits?" I smirked at him, teasing.

"You just think you're so smart."

"I am actually." Smiling demurely, I suddenly stopped, horrified. "Oh dear god, you're rubbing off on me." I cringed, and he laughed before going back to swimming laps.

I watched him swim, glad to be in the cooler water instead of sitting on the lounge chair in the scorching sun; although, I'd never willingly admit that. When I turned to make sure my phone and gun were still on the chair and I didn't accidentally take them back inside, he used the distraction as the perfect opportunity to reach for my leg and pull me through the water towards him.

"I thought you said you were joining me?" he asked innocently, having dragged me into the middle of the pool.

"I'm in the water. What more do you want?" As I tried to edge my way back to my perch on the steps, he grinned seductively, so I splashed him. And that was it. The stress of the last few weeks was temporarily forgotten as we swam and splashed about. "Stop." I cocked my head to the side, listening. There had been a sound.

"What?"

I put my finger to his lips and frowned, straining to hear. "I thought I heard something." Extracting myself from his grasp, I headed toward the pool steps, still listening intensely.

I went to the chair, grabbed my gun, pulled the slide back to chamber a round, slipped on my shoes, and carefully walked around the side of the house as I checked for intruders. There was no one to be seen, out front or anywhere else. When I returned to the pool area, Martin was toweling off.

"What did you hear?" he asked, watching as I put the safety back on and took the offered towel.

"I don't know. I must be losing it. It sounded like a car

door or something." I squinted into the distance just to be sure I didn't miss anything. "Let's head inside, anyway. It's better to err on the side of caution."

He knew my serious mode and didn't question it. After he deactivated and reactivated the alarm system, he went to shower and change while I checked, then double and triple checked the security system and the monitors Mark and Martin had set up, making sure no unwanted visitors were around.

"You're cracking up, Parker," I said to myself.

I activated the exterior motion sensors and physically checked the four floors of Martin's compound, making sure no one was lurking in the shadows. Once I was reasonably satisfied we were alone, I rinsed off and dressed quickly. Something had spooked me, and I couldn't shake the feeling something horrible was about to happen. The entire time, the noise kept replaying in my head.

I put my wet hair in a ponytail and was back downstairs in less than three minutes. Watching the surveillance feed as the cameras rotated throughout the grounds and house, I searched for a vehicle. I was positive I heard a car door, the characteristic thump of the metal against the foam-like waterproof sealant, but there were no cars and no intruders. Before I could go outside to check for tire tracks, my phone rang, and I nearly jumped out of my skin.

"Goddamn," I cursed, trying to calm my heart which was now pounding loudly in my ears. I fumbled for the phone and hit answer. "Hello?" I took a few deep breaths.

"Parker?" O'Connell's voice sounded over the thumping in my ears.

"Yeah, what's up?"

"We got a match. We're waiting for the arrest warrant, and then we're bringing in Denton."

"That's great." I guess my excitement seemed anti-climactic.

"Is everything okay? Are you okay?"

"Sorry, something just spooked me earlier, and the phone nearly gave me a heart attack," I admitted. "But that is excellent news. What are the charges?"

"For now, just the B&E, but it will place him close

enough to our murder scene. It should be enough to gain access to his financial records, and hopefully, we can get him on conspiracy. Maybe even murder."

"Okay, keep me updated."

As I paced in front of the screen, my eyes never left the video feed. I struggled to be rational. There was no sign of anything amiss outside. Maybe I hadn't heard a thing with all the splashing and tomfoolery. Running scenarios through my mind, I couldn't decide if leaving the house would be worse in the long run. Maybe I should call O'Connell back and ask if some uniforms would drive by, just to be on the safe side. I had just decided to check outside once more before phoning for backup when Martin came down the stairs.

"You look like you've seen a ghost." He scrutinized my face.

"I don't know." I double-checked the magazine in my gun and put on my shoulder holster out of habit.

"Are you going out?"

"No," I came out of my focused mode, "um, O'Connell called. Denton's prints match the partials on the box. They're bringing him in." I gestured oddly with one hand as I clipped the gun into the holster with the other.

"Are you going with them?" He was confused by my unusual behavior.

"No," I repeated, leaning against the back of the couch. I felt a little shaky. The ringing from the phone had thrown my nervous system into fight or flight mode. "I'm going to call O'Connell back and see if he can spare someone to drive a patrol car by, just to make sure I'm clinically insane and having auditory hallucinations."

"I think that's called paracusia."

"Thank you, Mr. Word-of-the-day," I snapped, and he raised his eyebrows but kept his mouth shut. I called O'Connell, and he promised someone would pass the house as soon as they could. I thanked him and hung up. "You really didn't hear anything outside?" I asked Martin.

Either I heard something, or I had gone mad. Maybe my erratic sleep habits had made me a little crazy and put me far enough on edge to intensify the unshakeable feeling of impending doom.

"Not a thing." He watched me cautiously as if I were a rabid animal.

"Great," I said sarcastically. I slid down to the floor from my position against the couch and shut my eyes, hoping to clear my head and force my brain to think rationally.

"Hey." Martin knelt on the ground next to me and touched my cheek. "You're okay. Stress and heat and all this can mess with anyone, but you're fine. Everything's fine."

I opened my eyes and looked at him. Things did not feel fine.

"Shit." My eyes got wide.

If there was a vehicle on the private road, I wouldn't be able to see it because the road winds up to the house and is surrounded by trees. He seemed even more worried by my outburst, but I ignored him as I frantically flipped through the cameras, trying to determine if any of them covered the road that far from the compound. Could I have even heard a car door from that distance? Maybe I was spiraling into some kind of nervous breakdown.

"Call O'Connell and tell him to get some guys here ASAP." I stood up and went to the closet, pulling out the flak jackets Mark had left. I tossed one to Martin and fastened the other around my torso. "Put that on and keep away from the windows." He was still watching me nervously. "Do it. I might be crazy, but honestly, that's a much better option than what I'm thinking."

I carefully peered out the front window, but I didn't see anything. I needed to know what was coming in order to devise a feasible plan. "I'm going out the back. Make sure you lock the door behind me and keep the security system armed." I deactivated the exterior motion sensors to avoid tripping the alarm, but I wanted the house to remain as impenetrable as possible.

He seemed frightened by my outburst and even more so by my barking orders. "Alex," he said my name forcefully, and I caught his eye. But he decided it was best to do what I asked. "Be careful."

"Always."

Slipping out the back door and staying against the house as I circled around to the side, I listened for the sounds of cars, voices, or pretty much anything else. I didn't hear a thing. Avoiding the driveway, I went through the yard, remaining hidden within the shrubbery. As I approached the treed private road, I saw it. A black SUV, tinted windows, brush guards — the works, parked just far enough up the private road to avoid being seen by drivers on the main thoroughfare but still far enough away to avoid detection from the house.

I flattened myself against the ground. What to do? How many people were in the SUV? It was definitely large enough to hold an entire assault team. Backup was on the way. I just had to keep the situation under control until then. Slowly, I edged away from the tree line and went back to the house, keeping myself as invisible as possible. When I got to the back door, I entered the security code, went in, shut the door, and re-engaged the security system. *Some good that would do*, I thought bitterly. Martin was where I left him. Luckily, he put on the bulletproof vest.

"Okay, you made the call?" I asked from the kitchen as I retrieved the shotgun and loaded it with shells.

"Yes, they're on their way." He came into the kitchen, and I handed it to him.

"Do you know how to use one of these?" I was serious, and he knew we had a problem. He nodded. "Good." I opened my mouth to speak, but no words came out. I tried again. "There's an SUV parked on the road, black, looks like what the paramilitary types drive. My guess would be they're mercenaries. I don't know how many guys are in there, but it could be an entire assault team. Best to prepare for the worst. I need you to get to the safest location possible."

"We should call 911."

The entire situation was surreal, and I wasn't sure if calling for a squad of police cars was a good idea. The flashing lights and sirens could mean a death sentence, or it could scare them away. It was a coin toss decision, and O'Connell already had guys en route.

"I don't know if that's a good idea," I cautioned, but

Martin picked up the phone.

"It's dead." He looked confused, and the blood drained from my face.

"Move now!"

I shoved him from the room and to the staircase. Up or down? My mind raced. The front window shattered as a small metal canister hit the ground, and simultaneously, the home security system began to wail. The flashbang went off disorienting me with the bright light and sound. I pushed Martin up the steps. They'd be closing in any second.

THIRTY-FOUR

The back door blew open, and two guys in full tactical gear entered the house. I took cover in the stairwell while Martin headed up the steps. They were professional killers as indicated by their gear and assault rifles. I couldn't afford to be in a shootout since I was outgunned and without the proper body armor. Taking the stairs sideways, I prepared to provide as much cover fire as possible. Martin stopped on the third floor, and I motioned for him to go up another level.

Quickly, I went into my room and got my backup pistol, stowing it in the now empty slot on my shoulder holster. Pressing my back against the wall next to the stairway, I cast a brief glance up the steps. Martin disappeared on the top floor, and I hoped he would be safe.

The men were downstairs, methodically clearing all of the rooms on the second floor. After which, they would either go down to the first floor, or they'd come up to the third, unless more guys had already breached on another level. I pushed the thought out of my head. Focus on one problem at a time. I held my position, waiting and listening. Somehow, I managed to ignore the wail of the security system and focus solely on the two mercenaries.

I heard them at the bottom of the steps, and I took a breath and waited. If these bastards were going to kill me, I would take as many of them with me as possible. The door to the first floor opened, and I risked a quick peek to see if more of their friends had joined the party. Amazingly, the two men headed down the stairs to clear the first level. One waited near the top of the steps, only barely in the garage, while the other went to check the area.

I crept down the stairs as quickly and silently as possible; my window of opportunity was closing by the second. *Why the hell didn't I have a taser*, I thought angrily as I got behind the man. I couldn't fire a shot. It was too loud, and his partner would turn me into Swiss cheese in a split second. Grabbing the man in a firm chokehold, I held on tight as he grabbed at my arms and tried to buck me forward, but his footing on the narrow steps limited his movements. *This is an incredibly stupid idea*, my internal voice screamed. Thankfully, he went limp, and I did my best to set him down quietly. I didn't know how long he would be out or how quickly his partner would finish checking the ground floor.

Taking the assault rifle from around his neck, I slung it across my body and noticed a few zip ties stuck in his back pocket. At least one of us came prepared. I debated dragging him up the steps and away from his teammate. Divide and conquer. I grabbed the man's arm and dragged him up the two steps. He was heavy, and I strained to pull his bulk and combat gear just a few inches. Once I managed to get him onto the second floor, I zip tied his hands and ankles and glanced down the stairs.

The footsteps of the second mercenary were getting closer. I grabbed the downed gunman by the ankles and dragged him into the living room. My back screamed out in protest, but I ignored it. It was only a couple of feet, but it was enough. I just needed to be able to shut the door, but the second mercenary was already at the bottom of the stairs, looking up at me.

I swung the assault rifle forward and fired wildly, spraying the area with bullets. The man took cover, and I shut and locked the door. Shoving the side table in front of the door like a barricade, I knew it wouldn't hold him for long, but it was the best I could do. I needed to buy time. As I ran up the stairs, gunfire erupted from below, splintering the wood door and the table. I needed to find someplace secure to hide.

Martin, I thought frantically. Hopefully, he was holed up on the fourth floor somewhere safe. I couldn't risk leading the gunmen straight to him, so I took refuge on the third floor. Create a distraction. My mind circled through possibilities, dismissing the unfeasible ones faster than any supercomputer. I ran down the hallway to the laundry room, looking for something to use as a makeshift Molotov cocktail. Too bad laundry detergent and bleach weren't flammable. I sprinted back to my room. By now, the door to the first floor had been broken down, and I had only seconds before the mercenary came up the stairs.

I ran into the bathroom and found the mouthwash and hairspray. Would the alcohol content be enough to ignite? It was my only option. I popped the top off the hairspray and poured it into the mouthwash and stuffed some rolled up toilet paper into the mouth of the bottle. The bathroom drawer contained a matchbook, and I lit the corner of the paper. I didn't need to hurt him with this. I just needed to create a diversion. Throwing open the French doors, I set the slowly burning bottle on the terrace, just out of sight. I got into the closet, cracking the door open slightly and waiting.

Heavy footsteps sounded outside the room. *Please check the terrace first*, I silently prayed. The armor-clad man entered the room slowly, glancing around cautiously. I held my breath. He circled toward the terrace and the bathroom, his gun poised, ready to decimate any and everything. He checked the bathroom first before going out the French doors. He was barely outside when the mouthwash concoction flared up, not quite the explosion I hoped for but enough to make him turn and shield himself.

Emerging from the closet, I rolled for cover and crouched against the bed. I aimed and fired, unrelenting. The bullets made contact but didn't penetrate his armor. The mercenary returned fire, and I ducked down as feathers and stuffing exploded around me. I fired blindly, hoping to get lucky.

This was a really bad idea, the voice in my head criticized. I was pinned down. We continued to return fire until I squeezed the trigger and heard a click. Empty. I grabbed my nine millimeter from my waistband and took a breath. The sound of the return fire was so loud the room echoed as white fluff and feathers flew through the air like macabre confetti indicating the death of hundreds of birds. The moment the bullets stopped flying I knew I had only a second while the man reloaded. Leveling my gun at him, I used what was left of the mattress to steady my shot and pulled the trigger. I fired twice, initially missing. The second shot made contact with his neck, and the impact sent him tumbling over the balcony to the ground below.

Unsteadily, I made my way to the balcony. The mercenary lay on the ground, not moving. The pool of blood around his head spread across the concrete walkway that led to Martin's Infinity pool. *One down*, I thought. If there were only two guys, one was dead and the other may still be unconscious on the second floor. I was going to check on the first guy when I heard a sound from above. Racing up the stairs, I had to get to Martin before it was too late.

I took the stairs two at a time until I emerged onto the fourth floor. Ducking against the wall, I peered around the corner. No one was in sight. I crouched down and checked again before crossing the hallway to his bedroom. I opened the door and looked around, but I didn't see anyone inside.

"Martin," I hissed. I needed to make sure he wasn't here before I continued down the hallway. There was no response, so I carefully made my way back into the hallway and down to the next room, which was his office.

Pressing my body against the wall, I turned the doorknob and crossed to the other side of the doorway before nudging it open with my foot. My gun was leveled in front of me. As I entered, I came face to face with the business end of a shotgun. Martin and I were frozen momentarily, guns raised, as the realization dawned on us.

"Thank god." He sighed, lowering the shotgun as I lowered my handgun. "I heard all those shots."

Checking the room, I wondered what caused the noise I heard. "I got one of them, and I have one tied up downstairs. But I don't know if he's still there." I approached the window, intent on looking to see if reinforcements were preparing to storm the castle. Where the hell were the cops? "There could be more, I heard–"

Something threw me full force into the wall. My head swam for a minute, and I blinked away the blackness that crept into my vision. My gun was already out and aimed at a third mercenary, who was firing into the office from the hallway.

I knocked the desk over in one quick move to provide cover. Had I been shot? Where was Martin? I returned fire and looked around. The mercenary had taken refuge in an alcove.

"Oh my god." The words escaped my lips without my permission.

Martin lay on the ground, and blood soaked through his shirt alarmingly fast. I shoved the sideways desk over to provide as much cover for him as possible. More shots were fired into the room, and I ducked my head as they whizzed past. I had no vantage point.

The blood pumped out of his body with every beat of his heart. My only desire was to help him, to try to stop the bleeding. But right now, I had to prioritize. If I didn't take down this mercenary, we'd both be dead in a matter of minutes. I saw the shotgun laying discarded on the floor just beyond the desk.

"Hang on," I told the unconscious Martin as I crawled over him toward the edge of the desk.

Rolling from my cover position, I picked up the shotgun and pressed myself against the wall, out of sight of the mercenary who was still firing at the desk. Edging toward the doorway, I waited for the burst of bullets to stop, and then I broke cover and fired both barrels. The shotgun bucked, but I held my position. The blast knocked the mercenary back, and I reloaded as quickly as possible, firing again.

During his return fire, bullets hit my vest, and I landed on my back hard, knocking the wind from my lungs. I reached for my holstered handgun as I lay on the ground, unsure if the shots punctured my vest. The man emerged from the alcove and walked over to me. I gasped for air, and with each breath I took, my ribcage threatened to explode. He stood over me with his gun raised.

"Nothing personal," he said coldly, aiming his weapon.

I lifted my head and without a moment's hesitation brought my handgun up and fired. The bullet impacted between his eyes, and he went down. I lay back against the ground, unable to move.

Get up, Parker, the voice in my head screamed. The pain was intense, almost unbearable, as I pulled the Velcro loose and got the vest off. Carefully, I felt around my chest and abdomen. No blood. I forced myself into a seated position. Despite having the vest on, it felt like I had been hit by a speeding car. Even the smallest movement sent shooting, agonizing pain throughout my body. My breathing was ragged, but at least my lungs were semi-functional again. I crawled slowly back into the office. I had to get to Martin.

"Martin." I leaned over him, ripping at the Velcro straps, so I could assess the damage. "Martin." I kept repeating his name, hoping he'd open his eyes.

After getting his vest off, it was apparent he had been shot at an angle. The bullet didn't go through the vest; it had gone underneath it and sliced diagonally from his shoulder toward his clavicle and downward. I didn't see an exit wound.

The point of entry was on his right side, just below the clavicle and shoulder joint. Blood poured out, and I feared the damage was too extensive. My first responder training was limited, but an artery or worse must have been hit. If he had any chance of surviving, I needed to slow the bleeding.

I reached down and grabbed his belt buckle, undoing it as quickly as I could. "Martin... James. Open your eyes. Look at me, dammit!"

I got his belt off and glanced around the room, searching for a shirt or towel, anything to press against the gaping hole to try to staunch the bleeding. There was a small pile of microfiber towels folded on the corner of another desk, likely meant for cleaning the electronic equipment and monitors. I grabbed the towels and folded one, pushing it against the wound. Then I looped his belt around it and tightened it as best I could to hold it in place.

"Martin." My hands were covered in his blood, and tears formed in my eyes. "Martin." I grabbed another towel and placed it under his head. He grunted. "Open your eyes," I pleaded. I saw the telltale green irises flash in front of me.

"Alex?" He tried to move, but his eyes weren't focusing.

"Stay still. I'm right here. You're going to be okay. Just stay awake." My voice shook. I didn't know what else to do.

"Are you okay?" He sounded distant.

"Yeah, I'm okay."

There was gunfire in the distance, but I had no fight left. He tried to smile, but it looked more like a grimace.

"Good." His eyes closed, and my palms pressed more urgently against the blood-soaked towel.

I expected to be taken out by a bullet at any moment, but it didn't matter. Nothing mattered anymore as I stared at the lifeless James Martin.

"Parker." Someone called my name, and I looked up. O'Connell and two tactical support guys stood in the doorway.

"Help," I implored as they entered the room.

O'Connell radioed for the paramedics. They must have been right outside because instantly they were up the stairs. The paramedics pushed me out of the way, and O'Connell grabbed my shoulders and hauled me to my feet. I didn't think I could stand on my own, and he seemed to sense this because he lifted me into his arms and carried me from the room and down the steps.

"You're in shock," O'Connell stated, attempting to calm me down. "You'll be fine. Just relax."

I sat in the back of an ambulance while the paramedics assessed my bruises. But I couldn't stop shaking as I stared at my hands, caked in Martin's blood.

"Looks like some bruised, maybe fractured ribs," the EMT said, "but other than that, there are no other obvious injuries. She needs more extensive tests to rule out internal bleeding and soft tissue damage." He shined a flashlight in my eyes and continued to check my pulse. "We should take her to the ER, just to be on the safe side."

"No," my breathing was erratic, "I'm fine." The EMT
protested, but O'Connell waved him off.

"Not yet," he told the guy.

"Martin?" I was afraid of the answer.

"They're getting him stabilized, so they can move him.
We'll do our best." I swallowed uneasily. He sat next to me,
picking up a blanket and wrapping it tightly around my
body to minimize my trembling. "It looks like you had your
hands full," O'Connell commented, and I forced the lump
down my throat as the gurney came down the stairs and
out the front door.

"I want to go with him." I was determined not to leave
Martin.

"Okay." O'Connell helped me into the ambulance.
"Jerry, let's get this show on the road," he called to the
EMT.

Despite protocol, the EMT left me on one of the benches
while O'Connell sat quietly beside me, and we followed
Martin's ambulance to the hospital.

THIRTY-FIVE

Through sheer willpower, I managed to stand up and walk out of the ambulance and down the hall, following the gurney to a trauma room in the ER. The nurses blocked my way, and I was left waiting in the hallway. O'Connell followed me and stood close enough so our shoulders touched.

"Ma'am, are you okay?" a nurse asked, and I wondered how long she had been there.

"I'm fine." I wanted to see what was going on in the trauma room. The door opened, and a group of nurses, doctors, and whoever else whisked the gurney with Martin quickly down the hallway. I wanted to follow, but a woman emerged and approached us. "What's going on?" I asked, watching as the group disappeared down the corridor. O'Connell flashed a badge, and the woman decided she could answer the question.

"He's going into surgery now. We won't know how extensive the damage is until we get him opened up." I swayed slightly but remained standing as she continued after them.

"Ma'am, are you sure you're okay?" The original nurse remained in front of me. I didn't even notice she was still there. She examined my appearance, and I looked down. My hands and shirt were covered in Martin's blood, and I felt nauseous.

"It's not my blood." I swallowed.

O'Connell looked from the nurse to me and made a decision. "Where can she get cleaned up?" he asked. The nurse led us to a restroom, and O'Connell thanked her. "Wash up. I'll get you something else to wear, so stay here."

I was grateful to have someone tell me what to do since I was lost and swimming through a sea of numbness and confusion. Scrubbing my hands in the sink, I watched as the clear water turned bright red before it ran down the drain. So much blood. How could anyone survive that? I finished washing my hands and bent to splash some water on my face. My ribs protested, and I grabbed the sink to steel myself against the onslaught. There was a knock on the door, and O'Connell came in. He had a police t-shirt in his hands that he must have taken from one of the cruisers outside.

"Here, let me help." He gently peeled the blood-soaked shirt off my body and over my head. Three large blue and red colored welts covered my torso.

Assessing them in the mirror, I reached out and gingerly touched one. "Shit," I grunted, taking only shallow breaths to keep from aggravating my ribs further.

He helped me dress and watched me carefully. "You need to get checked out." He was prepared for my protest. "Martin's in surgery. It's going to take a while. The only thing you'll be doing is sitting in the waiting room, so go get a CT or x-ray or whatever, and then you can sit in the waiting room." I didn't have any fight left, and I quietly agreed. Apparently, O'Connell had conspired with the nurse from earlier, who waited outside the restroom with a wheelchair. "Is there anyone I should call for Martin or for you?" he asked as the nurse wheeled me back to the ER.

I didn't know. Even though I spent weeks with this man, I didn't know anything about his family or who to contact in an emergency. "Call Mark, or try to call Mark. He's somewhere working, but he'd know who to contact." My voice shook again. I really wasn't stable.

"I'll be waiting for you, once you're cleared," he promised.

Over the course of the next hour and a half, I was poked, prodded, and scanned. I refused all drugs; my mind was already jumbled enough. The doctors were insistent on keeping me for overnight observation, but I was adamantly opposed to their recommendation. Finally, after being released against medical advice, I made my way out of the room and into the hallway. O'Connell was outside, waiting as promised.

"Any news?" I asked as he led the way to the waiting room.

"Nothing so far. How are you holding up?"

"A little worse for wear, but nothing that'll kill me anytime soon." It was a callous remark, but I didn't care. We sat in a couple of chairs, far away from everyone else.

"I've ordered a protection detail for you and Martin. Thompson brought in Denton, but until we're certain he ordered the hit, I don't want to take any more chances." Neither did I. "You're both safe here."

"Unless he doesn't make it," I numbly replied. I couldn't do this anymore. All emotion was turned off for the time being.

"We don't have to do this now, but do you want to tell me what happened?"

I shut my eyes and leaned back in the chair. "Do you have a tape recorder?" I asked. "Because I don't think I can do this more than once."

He pulled out the device and turned it on, giving the relevant information, and then I told him everything that happened from the time we were swimming in the pool until I was carried down the stairs. The pool seemed so far away. It had only been a couple of hours, but it felt like a lifetime ago. Or maybe it was only a story I once heard.

During my recitation, it dawned on me what happened in the office. Martin had thrown me into the wall. Once I was finished and the tape recorder was shut off, I turned to the side and buried my head in my hand. Martin had shoved me out of the way of the bullet. He was in surgery, possibly dying, because of me. Not only did I fail to do my job and stop things from escalating to this point, but he saved me from taking a bullet to the brain.

"Parker?" O'Connell asked anxiously. He touched my shoulder, and I forced the guilt, the fear, and the tears away. *No emotions*, I reminded myself.

"I'm okay," I lied, not making eye contact. He sat quietly. No more questions needed to be asked right now. "I heard gunfire. How many were there in total?" I had to be practical.

"The two you got and three more. One guy was in the vehicle, and another was outside the house. The third was unconscious in the living room, so I assume you took care of him too." I nodded. "We're trying to get one of them to talk. Two are currently in custody. The third didn't quite make it." Before I could comment, his radio went off. He answered, and the next thing I knew, Mark was escorted in by a couple of patrolmen.

"Alex." I rarely saw Mark move with such purpose. He hurried over, kneeling on the ground in front of me. "Are you okay? Where's Martin?"

O'Connell excused himself and went to speak to the patrolmen.

"He's in surgery. I don't know. I just don't know." I didn't have any answers.

Mark got up and sat in the vacant chair. "Are you okay?" he asked again. I was about to say I was fine, but he knew me better than that. "You don't always have to be fine, you know." I let out a derisive snort as I tried to find a more comfortable position. "I'm sorry I wasn't there."

"Me, too." I thought for a moment. "O'Connell wanted to know who to call for Martin. I figured you would know."

Mark looked sadly at me. "You're here. I'm here. He'll be okay. He's too damn stubborn not to be." He squeezed my hand.

Over the next few hours, O'Connell and Mark took turns pacing the waiting room while I sat uncomfortably in the chair. The longer I remained still, the worse I felt as my muscles stiffened. My back ached from dragging the mercenary up the stairs, and my ribs fought to hold my attention with every breath I took. Some patrolman brought coffee and sodas, but I didn't feel like anything. Finally, a surgeon came to speak to us.

"James Martin's family?" he asked. I was sure he knew we weren't family, but he sat down and gave us an update anyway. "We've moved him to the ICU. He's lost a lot of blood, but we've transfused him and removed the bullet. There is some muscle and nerve damage to his right arm. We won't know the full extent until the swelling goes down, and we run more tests. He's very lucky. The projectile didn't hit any organs and only nicked one of his arteries which we've repaired."

"Thank god," Mark exclaimed, clasping his hands together. "When can we see him?"

"Once we move him into recovery. We need to monitor him for the next few hours to make sure there are no complications. In the meantime, you might want to head home or get something to eat." The doctor looked at me, probably afraid I'd be next on his table. "I'll send someone to get you when you can go up."

Once the doctor left, O'Connell returned. "Good news?" he asked.

I nodded, and he smiled.

"Want to get out of here for a bit?" Mark asked me, but I shook my head. "At least get something to eat, you look like you're about to drop dead."

I glared at him for the bad choice of words. "I'm not hungry."

O'Connell and Mark exchanged glances. Obviously, they thought I needed a constant babysitter.

"I'll get some burgers in case you change your mind," Mark offered. "I'll be back in a few minutes." He stood and rubbed my shoulder gently, and O'Connell sat in the chair Mark vacated. Apparently, we were in the midst of playing a very twisted version of musical chairs.

"I don't need a babysitter," I told O'Connell.

"Probably not. But maybe a priest, a doctor, and a pharmacist," he said. I lifted an eyebrow. "Okay, maybe that's the beginning of a bad joke." He spoke just for the hell of it, and I sighed, regretting it immediately.

"I'm going to share something with you, but you aren't going to hold it against me. Okay?" He tentatively agreed. "I can't move." He seemed confused by my statement. I winced, and he understood.

"Oh." He got up and wrapped his arm around my

shoulders, lifting me out of the chair. I felt like a ninety-year-old woman. Once I was standing, things didn't seem as bad. Movement helped reduce the stiffness in my back, and pacing was always a great go-to for stress relief. "You should probably take some of those meds they prescribed," he suggested, eyeing the bottles of muscle relaxants and prescription grade ibuprofen the medical staff thrust upon me during my escape from the exam room.

"We'll see how things go," I replied.

Mark returned with the sandwiches, and I nibbled on one. Relenting, I popped two ibuprofen, feeling a little more in control and less frazzled. The initial shock was wearing off. Martin was out of surgery, so the worry was ebbing away. The only thing left was the desire for revenge on whoever was responsible.

Hours later, a nurse came downstairs to tell us Martin was moved to another room. O'Connell helped me out of the chair, and Mark scrutinized the exchange.

"Go on up," O'Connell said. "I'll talk to the hospital staff and get the details on the room, so I can have some guys posted outside his door."

Mark and I followed the nurse to the elevator and down a corridor to his room. Despite the IVs and various other tubes running to and from his body, Martin looked a million times better than when I last saw him.

"Has he woken up?" Mark asked, even though Martin was asleep or still under anesthesia.

"Yes, he was awake and coherent when we moved him in here. He kept asking about someone named Alex, but his body's still recovering. He's feeling the effects of the sedation, so he'll probably be in and out of consciousness for the next day or two. But that's normal." She waited to see if we had any questions before leaving the room to give us some privacy. I sat in the chair next to the bed, grateful that he was going to be okay.

Mark found a chair in the corner of the room and pulled it over next to mine. "What happened?" he asked, and I gave him the Cliff notes version of the day. "And the reason you can't get out of the chair is?"

"I took three hits to the vest." I grimaced, and he lifted

my shirt to check my bruises. "I'll be fine. I just wish they lined the insides of those stupid vests with packing peanuts or fluffy cotton. Hell, even gelatin would be better than this," I joked.

We sat in Martin's room for a few hours. Mark kept trying to chitchat but finally gave up and flipped through the TV channels. It was getting late, but given the circumstances and the police presence outside the room, no one told us visiting hours were over, which I appreciated. I saw Mark glance at the time.

"You can get out of here," I said. It had been a long day. "Martin's going to be fine. At least that's what the doctors keep saying."

"Can I give you a ride?" he asked, even though he knew I wasn't leaving.

"I'm working. Can't you tell?" Somewhere during the long hours spent waiting, I had crossed over into blaming myself for Martin being shot.

"Don't do this, Parker. Not again," he cautioned. "You saved his life. And to be honest, it's a fucking miracle either one of you are still breathing right now. Those bullets should have shredded the flak, and Marty could have easily bled to death if it wasn't for you."

I pressed my lips into a thin line and shut my eyes, trying to shut out the harsh reality. "You're not helping me here, Mark." My vision blurred as tears threatened to fall, and I rubbed them away and blew out a silent breath.

"Try to take it easy." He hesitated, considering camping out in Martin's room with me. "If you need anything, or if anything else happens, call me." He stood up, kissed the top of my head, and walked out of the room, stopping in the hallway to talk to the protection detail.

"Looks like it's just you and me," I said to the unconscious Martin. I tried to make myself more comfortable in the chair. "You know, getting yourself shot for your bodyguard is completely ass backwards. Don't you ever do anything that stupid again."

Sitting in the silence, I alternated between staring at him and the walls of the room. My only companion was the constant aching that ran up the length of my back and down the front of my ribcage. Opening the ibuprofen, I took another one and settled into the chair. A while later, a nurse came in to check on Martin.

"Husband?" she asked.

"Not quite." I wasn't sure if I was supposed to continue this whole related thing or not, but with the police officers outside and me dressed in cop attire, it probably didn't matter. "Just a pain in my ass."

"Aren't they all?" She went to the closet and handed me a pillow and blanket. "I'm guessing you're staying the night."

I thanked her and tried to get more comfortable. When I couldn't take it any longer, I relented and took a few of the muscle relaxants. I was exhausted, but every time I shut my eyes, I'd see the gunman standing over me ready to fire or Martin bleeding on the floor. I turned the TV back on and found some wholesome, classic, black and white programming. It droned on throughout the night. At some point, the medication kicked in, and I fell into oblivion.

THIRTY-SIX

I opened my eyes. The sun was up, and it was morning. It was the beginning of a new day, but that fact provided little relief or consolation. Martin was still asleep, but the steady beeping of the monitors eased any concern I might have. Slowly, I got out of the chair, thankful I was able to do that much, and went into the hallway. Thompson was outside, talking to the officers.

"Hey," I greeted him, "what's going on?"

"There's a man, Marcal," he looked slightly embarrassed, "I can't pronounce his last name. He's at Martin's compound. The uniforms grabbed him, but he's insisting he works for Martin."

"He does." I completely forgot about Marcal. He must have come to work today and freaked out, but at least Thompson seemed relieved.

"Okay, I'll pass it along and let the man go about his business." Thompson picked up his radio.

I stumbled down the hallway toward the restroom to freshen up. A nice hot shower would have been preferable to washing up in a bathroom sink. Unfortunately, I had no other options. With my apartment trashed and Martin's house turned into the O.K. Corral, there was nowhere for me to go. I finished up in the bathroom and went back down the hallway.

"Detective," I called to Thompson, "if you can tell Marcal where we are, I think he'd like to know."

Thompson narrowed his eyes. It wasn't procedure, especially since Martin had an assigned protection detail outside his room, but Thompson agreed anyway.

I went back into the room and shut the door. Taking a seat, I stared impatiently at him. "You know, I'm getting tired of talking to myself."

He ignored me and continued to sleep. A doctor came in to check the monitors and Martin's vitals. He offered a friendly smile as he left the room. It was around noon when Martin finally opened his eyes.

"Alex," his voice sounded thick and scratchy.

"Hey." I smiled and carefully leaned closer to the bed, even though leaning wasn't a good idea. "How are you feeling?" He seemed disoriented. "You're in the hospital. You were shot, but you're okay." I thought about running into the hallway to get a doctor, but he clumsily reached for me with his left hand. He brushed a wayward tear from my cheek, and I clasped his hand against my face.

"You were worried." He smirked. Even drugged up after almost dying, he still had the strength to smirk. "I guess that means you really do care."

"Not in the least. I'm just allergic to hospitals." We stayed like that for a moment. He was doing his best to remain awake, but it was a losing battle. "I'm going to find a doctor, but I'll be right back," I promised, letting go of his hand and gritting my teeth as I got up from the chair.

A nurse passed by, and I told her he was awake. She didn't seem surprised by the news, but she followed me back to his room, performed some perfunctory tests, and asked some basic questions while I waited in the hallway.

"He's asking for you," she said on her way out of the room, and I went back inside.

His eyes were closed, and I figured he had fallen asleep. But when I sat down, he opened his eyes.

"Listen," he sounded serious, "tell Marcal to get everything set up. He'll know what to do." I had no earthly idea what Martin was talking about, but I agreed anyway. His eyelids drooped, but his expression conveyed his satisfaction with my response. "Are you staying here?"

"Of course. I am still working, right?"

He gave my hand a light squeeze before falling back to sleep.

Leaving the room, I needed to get in touch with Marcal. Amazingly, he had shown up at the hospital once he heard the news, and the uniformed officers told me he was in the lobby. When I got downstairs, Marcal was waiting with an overnight bag. After hearing Martin was in the hospital, he had picked up a few necessities he thought Martin would need. I really needed to hire someone who would do that for me. Yesterday had been a horrendous ordeal I wasn't ready to revisit, so I only gave Marcal a brief rundown of Martin's medical condition and the instructions I was told to pass along.

"Mr. Martin has a lot of contingency plans, and his credit card is kept on file in quite a few places around the city. Don't worry. I'll take care of everything. When will he be released from the hospital?" Marcal asked.

"I don't know. In a few days, maybe." I wasn't sure about anything.

"Okay, I'll have lodging and necessities waiting for him. What can I get for you?"

"Everything." I laughed. "No, I'm just kidding. I'll manage. Don't worry about me, but make sure you coordinate with Detective O'Connell. The police are trying to keep Martin safe, so before you do anything, confer with them."

He agreed and went to enact whatever doomsday scheme Martin had devised.

*　　*　　*

Over the course of the next two days, I spent most of my time sitting in a very uncomfortable chair at Martin's bedside. The doctors were impressed with the rate of his recovery and hinted he would be going home soon. Finally, on the third day, Martin was discharged from the hospital. I was instructed on how often to change his bandages and when he should take his antibiotics and pain medications. My new job was to play nursemaid. I couldn't complain. It was a much better position than eulogy writer. O'Connell and Marcal retrieved my phone and car from Martin's compound and set up a room reservation at a five-star hotel.

We arrived at the hotel and were given the entire top floor for security purposes. Martin and I were splitting the presidential suite, and our constant police presence was given the room across the hall in order to keep a watchful eye on things. As promised, Marcal had stocked the closets and bathrooms with all the necessities — clothing, shoes, and toiletries. I wouldn't have been surprised to find the fridge chockfull of food, but I resisted the urge to look.

"Home sweet home," Martin declared, entering the lavish suite with his arm in a sling. Despite his weakened state, he was back to being full-on Martin.

"It'll do for now," I grumbled, looking around the room.

There was a master bedroom suite with a private bathroom, a common living room, kitchenette, dining area, bathroom, and a smaller bedroom. I was dying to take a nice hot shower and lie in a real bed after the last three days of washing up in a hospital bathroom and sleeping in a chair.

"Do you want me to order room service?" he asked. "After eating nothing but green gelatin and some slop they insisted was food, but most definitely could not be considered food by anyone still in possession of their taste buds, I could go for some actual food. Maybe a steak or a lamb chop, something solid and tasty. Hell, a shoe with the proper seasoning and cooked to a decent texture would be preferable to hospital food."

"Before you call down to the kitchen and order a shoe medium-rare, hang on." He was being particularly absurd in order to shake me out of my foul mood. I gave him a fleeting smile before going across the hall and knocking on the door. "Check out the room service menu," I told the uniformed officers, "whatever you want. We're ordering dinner." They happily placed their orders, and I relayed the message to Martin.

"Anything in particular you would like?" he asked.

"Steak, chops, whatever you're having. Just no shoe. And you can take theirs out of my paycheck too." I knew what it was like to be stuck on a stakeout, and while this was a protection detail, it was still the same monotonous waiting around.

He waved my offer away and picked up the phone. "Hi, I'd like to order some room service," he said into the phone, but they put him on hold or were transferring the call.

"The cops are out front to keep an eye on things, so I'm going to take a shower." I retreated into my bedroom and found some clothes hanging in the closet. The tags were still attached, and I wondered if they had been taken from the closet at Martin's or if they were brand new. Either way, I was grateful. Thank you, Marcal.

Entering the bathroom, I took off my shirt and checked my reflection in the mirror. The blue and red bruises were now a deep purple, almost black, tinged with green. *Just beautiful*, I thought sarcastically. Stepping into the shower, I let the hot water work its way through my sore body. When it ran cold, I got out and dressed, wrapped my hair in a towel and returned to the living room. The only things left to do today were eat and sleep. Not necessarily even in that order. The last three days had been hell.

Martin lay on the couch with his eyes closed. Following my new routine, I sat down in an overstuffed chair next to him, not wanting to disturb his rest.

"Thanks for staying," he said without opening his eyes.

"Just doing my job," I replied automatically. I didn't want to think about the firefight or him bleeding, but I couldn't hold my tongue any longer. "You know, what you did back at the house, pushing me out of the way, I wish you hadn't." I wasn't being very expressive, but he was smart enough to get my point.

"I had to." He opened his eyes and stared with a fierce intensity. "You were my best chance of survival. Plus, I wouldn't have been able to live with myself if I didn't do something."

I dropped the subject, but he continued to stare with those soulful green eyes. Thankfully, there was a knock at the door, and I got up and glanced through the peephole. I opened the door, and the uniformed officers wheeled in the dining cart.

"Dinner is served," one of them said, and I thanked them.

Martin ordered steak and potatoes for both of us. He wasn't kidding when he said he wanted solid food. We ate in silence, and when we were finished, I tried to get up from the chair. Unfortunately, the plush factor worked against me, and I didn't quite make it. I slumped down, wincing. Shutting my eyes, I tried again. *Success*, I thought as I pushed the cart to the door and left it in the hallway outside our room.

"What's wrong?" he asked, concerned.

"Nothing."

"Liar." He scrutinized my face before shifting his gaze to my arms wrapped tightly against my aching sides. "What happened?"

"Just some bruises. It's no big deal." I went into the kitchenette and retrieved his pills. I brought the bottle over and tried to hand him the pill. "Take this."

He refused to give me his palm, deciding instead to use his stubbornness for his own personal gain. "I'll trade you." He was back to being insufferable. At least he was feeling better. "I'll take my pill if you tell me what's wrong." His gaze moved pointedly to my torso.

"You are a piece of work, you know that?" I couldn't help but grin. Despite everything, he was okay.

He saw my grin. "What?"

"Nothing." I shook my head, trying not to laugh. The novelty of him being alive would wear off quickly if he kept this up. "I'm just bruised." He didn't believe me, so I raised my shirt.

"Jesus." He was shocked by my multi-colored midriff and ribcage. "How?" I didn't have to say anything because the light bulb went on inside his head. "Alexis, I am so sorry."

"Don't be. Things could have been worse. After all, you saved my life, almost at the cost of your own." I picked up his hand and put the pill in his palm. "Now if you don't mind, I am going to get some sleep in an actual bed."

Without waiting for a response, I went into the bedroom

and climbed into bed, still wearing my clothes, but I left the door open in case he needed anything. The TV played for a little while, and then he went into his room. It had been a long three days.

The next morning, I woke up actually feeling rested and less achy than I had been. I took a leisurely shower and put on some comfortable clothes and dried my hair. I made coffee in the hotel-provided coffeepot and went across the hallway to see if the boys in blue wanted anything for breakfast. They politely declined, and I went back to the suite and sat in the chair, flipping through channels. I heard the water running in Martin's bathroom and hoped he remembered the instructions the doctors had given him. After some cursing, he emerged, dressed from the waist down. A button up shirt hung from his good arm, and he held a bandage in his hand.

"Need help?" I asked.

He reluctantly sat on the couch, and I took the bandage and changed the dressing on his shoulder. Once it was secured in place, I helped him slide his shirt on and buttoned it for him.

"I've never had a woman dress me before. Usually, it happens in reverse."

"First time for everything." I brought him some coffee and his pills. Alex Parker, R.N., it definitely didn't have the right ring to it.

After ordering breakfast, he spent most of the day asleep on the couch. The blood loss and surgery had taken a lot out of him. I spent the day playing phone tag with Mark, who was still working but had called for an update on Martin's condition. O'Connell hadn't checked in, but I dismissed the thought as irrelevant. Hopefully, he was putting the final nails in Blake Denton's coffin.

After realizing there wasn't anything else to do, I decided to take a nap too. If you can't beat them, join them, but closing my eyes brought images to my mind that I didn't want to focus on. I tossed and turned until I heard Martin moving around in the living room. Getting out of bed, I went to see if he needed anything.

"You know, those child safety caps were designed to

keep intoxicated people from taking medication," I remarked as he unsuccessfully attempted to open his pill bottle using only one hand.

"Really? I thought they were meant to torture people with only one good arm." He obviously wasn't feeling too great. Being shot could do that to a person. I opened the bottle for him. "I hate feeling like an invalid," he commented, swallowing his pill.

"Join the club. Unfortunately, we're stuck here for the time being, which means you're stuck with me pretending to be your nursemaid."

"Does that include sponge baths and a sexy outfit? Maybe some white stockings and a garter belt?" He raised an eyebrow.

"Sorry, but no," I mocked regret. "I'd hate to make you feel any more like an invalid than you already are."

"Me and my big mouth."

I laughed and winced. Even though I felt better, I wasn't back to one hundred percent. Maybe in another two or three days I'd be able to laugh and get out of chairs just like before. Damn, I really was turning into an old woman.

THIRTY-SEVEN

The next morning, O'Connell showed up at a rather ungodly hour. "Do you really have to knock so loudly?" I asked, opening the door.

"That's the point of a knock, to be loud and get attention."

"Martin's asleep, so can you please just shh." I went to the coffeepot and measured out the coffee and added water before turning on the machine. I flipped over two of the upside-down mugs. "Just give me a minute." I went back to my room, found some clothes to change into, and hurried to make myself presentable. When I came out, O'Connell was sitting on the couch, drinking a cup of coffee.

"You should be a quick change artist," he commented as I poured my own cup and joined him.

"What's going on?" He didn't come all this way for a lousy cup of coffee.

"How are you doing? Are you feeling any better?"

I took as deep a breath as I could, testing the waters. "Eh, getting there." I looked at him suspiciously. "What do you want, Nick?" I asked, using his first name for the first time. It sounded strange.

"Forensics has been working on Martin's house. We got the video footage off his home security feed and everything, but," he paused, "I hate to ask."

"What?" Either I was still half asleep, or I didn't want this to be going where I thought it was going.

"If you're up to it, can you take me through the house and give me a play-by-play? Who shot where, what weapons, all of it."

"How badly do you need this?" I asked. "I thought you had two of the shooters in custody. Can't they do it?"

He gave me an uncompromising look. Clearly, asking the bad guys, who were looking for a plea deal, to give a walkthrough would be a ridiculous notion. "It would make my life easier."

I sighed. "Okay, fine." We sat in silence, drinking our coffee for a few minutes. "Since I'm helping you out, you have to tell me something. Is this as simple as Denton, Griffin, Jackson, and some hired guns?"

"It looks that way. Denton's financials are the real kicker. There are so many transfers in and out that it's taking our guys a long time to track it all down. We don't want to miss anything. That's why we're keeping the detail across the hallway, in case more than one team was hired to do the job."

"You know what else I'd like, Detective?" I earned the right to be somewhat demanding this morning. "A piece."

"Everything's in evidence right now. There's nothing I can do."

"Worst case scenario, I'm still the last line of defense. What do you want me to do? Offer any would-be attacker some ghastly coffee?"

"I'll see what I can arrange, but honestly, the coffee's not half bad."

I made O'Connell wait since I wasn't willing to leave until Martin was awake and I got the chance to tell him what was going on. Since his surgery, I hadn't been more than a few dozen feet away from him, and I was still paranoid. Also, I felt extremely guilty and grateful, and I couldn't disappear without a word. O'Connell understood, and we spent the rest of the morning discussing the case.

The majority of my assumptions turned out to be pretty accurate. Denton was locked up without bail due to his monetary means and ample travel opportunities. All information relating to the shooting at Martin's compound and his injuries had miraculously been kept secret. I was amazed there weren't any leaks at the station house or hospital. This would be headline news if the press got wind of it.

When I heard the water running in Martin's bathroom, I knew my departure time was fast approaching. I looked at O'Connell, hoping he had changed his mind. So much for wishful thinking. Once Martin was dressed, properly medicated, and bandaged, I told him what was going on. He didn't seem particularly pleased by the prospect either, but he was lucky enough to be legitimately injured so he didn't have to come along.

O'Connell drove to Martin's compound, and we entered the house, ducking under the crime scene tape. We began in the living room and slowly made our way up the stairs, going from room to room and shadowing my actions from the day of the shooting. I moved methodically through the house. O'Connell took notes, and a ballistics guy followed us around, noting weapons and trajectories as friendly or unfriendly fire.

We were on the fourth floor, near the office or, more accurately, the room that once resembled Martin's private office. The bloodstain from my second kill of the day left a discolored, damaged place on the wood floor, but it was nothing compared to the blood-soaked carpeting inside the office. My stomach twisted violently, and I covered my mouth and ran down the hallway to Martin's bathroom, getting there just in time to throw-up repeatedly in the toilet. By the time O'Connell found me, I was dry heaving. He gently rubbed my back until my body gave up the fight to physically purge the memories from my system.

"I've got a pretty clear picture. We don't need anything more. I'm sorry I brought you here," he said quietly.

I made sure my stomach had settled before standing up and rinsing my mouth in the sink. My chest and ribs were on fire, and I wrapped my arms protectively around my body, hoping to ease the agony.

He drove back to the hotel and escorted me up to the presidential suite. I used the hotel key to get inside, and he followed me in.

"Are you going to be okay?" he asked, and I gave him a

disgusted look.

"I'm fine," I growled.

After brushing my teeth, I found my pill bottles and brought them to the kitchen. Martin, who had been in his room, came out to see what was going on.

"Get everything settled?" Martin asked.

"Yeah. Parker's help will be instrumental in finalizing our reports," O'Connell replied. My back was turned, but I could feel eyes staring as I headed for the mini-bar, looking for some ginger ale. "Can I get you anything?" He cut me off halfway to the mini-bar.

"Ginger ale." I glared daggers at his back.

He pulled out the soda, opened it, and handed it to me. Reading the directions on my two pill bottles, I popped one of each and washed them down with the canned drink. I took a seat in the chair and leaned back, shutting my eyes and hoping to make everything disappear with the power of my mind. Martin remained on the couch, watching the entire exchange.

"Detective, if there's nothing else." Martin's tone sounded off, perhaps even slightly threatening. I had heard that same tone the day he'd gotten the photos in his e-mail. At least I wasn't on the receiving end of it this time.

"Okay," O'Connell took the hint, "thanks for doing this, Ms. Parker." He gave my shoulder a supportive squeeze. "If you need anything, call." It wasn't his fault. He was just doing his job, and now I felt guilty for my invidiousness.

"I'm fine. It's just...difficult." It took a moment to find the right word, but he understood, wished Martin a speedy recovery, and left.

"You look green." Martin eyed the ginger ale suspiciously. He reached over with his left hand and picked up my pill bottles. "If you want some of the good stuff, feel free." He jerked his head at the kitchen counter.

"I'm part Martian," I replied, "and no, I don't even like taking these." I knew what his next question would be. "I got a little queasy at your house, and it didn't agree with the ribs."

He picked up the phone and ordered toast, soup, and more ginger ale. "What?" He smirked. "I suddenly had this insane desire for chicken soup and toast points."

We ate our lunch, and I changed the dressing on his wound and brought him his pills. He was lying on the couch, dozing, so I grabbed a pillow from my room and sat in the chair. The next thing I knew, the room was dark, except for the flickering light from the television. Cautiously, I stretched and got out of the chair, just to make sure I could. It was almost eight o'clock. I looked at Martin to make sure he was still breathing, which he was. *Paranoid much*, I thought as I sat back down, not wanting to wake him. Curling up on my side, I watched him sleep until I could no longer hold my eyes open.

When I finally opened my eyes again, the room was brightly lit, and he was flipping through the morning news channels. For a moment, I thought this last week had been a bad dream, and I was still at the compound. But I saw the sling on his arm and realized my nightmare was our reality. Carefully, I sat up. My neck was stiff, but my ribs didn't protest as much. Maybe all I needed was some sleep.

"No narcolepsy jokes today?" I asked, yawning. Maybe I was high, but he even looked better. More color was in his face, and his green eyes seemed brighter than they had been in days.

"It didn't seem fair since I started the trend yesterday."

"You probably caught it from me."

We went about our new daily routine, except he was much more awake and active than he had been since the surgery. He still napped, but he was getting antsy. He read the paper and caught up on the business world. He even suggested a game of strip poker, but I declined on account of my now greenish-brown torso and his inability to take off his own shirt.

O'Connell called and said the report was finalized, and Martin could start the process of repairing his residence sometime next week. Life was getting back on track. The forensic accountant was almost finished tracing Denton's transactions, and hopefully, in a few more days, our need for the boys in blue would be nonexistent.

I went to sleep in my bedroom that night feeling as if matters were resolved. Unfortunately, my subconscious didn't share my positive sentiments. I was back in Martin's office. The mercenary stood above me, and Martin was to my right, unconscious and bleeding. The gun was poised, and the man's trigger finger twitched. As I was looking at his face, the mercenary morphed into Blake Denton, and he fired.

"No!" I cried, jolting upright and gasping for breath.

Two men burst into the room, handguns raised. I screamed and reached for my own gun, which wasn't next to me. My lungs weren't getting enough air. I was hyperventilating. One hand wrapped around my battered ribcage, and the other clutched the side of the mattress. This was how I was going to die.

"It's okay. It's okay." Martin's voice mixed with my terrified confusion. I spun my head to the right. He wasn't lying on the ground, and I wasn't in his office. Where was I? The men lowered their guns. "She was dreaming. Leave before you give her a heart attack." His words didn't make sense, but I heard mumbled apologies as the armed men retreated from the bedroom.

Martin appeared in the doorway, but I couldn't speak. I was still struggling to catch my breath, and my heart pounded so forcefully my entire body moved with every beat.

"Alex," he said softly, probably afraid to spook me further, "it was just a dream. You were having a nightmare."

I swallowed but couldn't find my voice. I was still fighting to regain control of my breathing. I was fairly certain I was in the midst of a panic attack. Without a word, he climbed into my bed and wrapped his left arm around me, pulling me gently against his side.

"You're okay. Just breathe. Slow, deep breaths," he instructed.

I wrapped both of my arms around his waist and buried my head in the crook of his neck, trying to slow my gasps to match the steady rise and fall of his chest. He tried to move his right arm but realized it was still immobilized and cursed quietly.

Once my heart rate slowed and I managed to catch my

breath, he carefully leaned back, bringing me with him, so we were lying against the pillows. "I thought they were here to kill me," I squeaked, feeling the need to explain my hysterics, but he shushed me.

"No one is going to kill you. I'm right here, and I'm not going anywhere. The cops are outside, where they will stay if they know what's good for them."

"I'm sorry," I apologized again, but he cut me off.

"Try to get some sleep." He kissed my forehead. "It's late."

I shut my eyes and snuggled against him. I couldn't argue, not tonight, not when I needed to know he was safe and I wasn't alone.

THIRTY-EIGHT

The next morning, I woke up to find Martin holding me securely against his chest. Embarrassment flooded over me as I saw things in a much more rational light. It had all been a nightmare, likely brought about by my recent trip through Martin's decimated residence. The armed men, who I thought wanted to kill me, had been the protection detail responding to my screams.

"Oh god," I muttered, rolling onto my back and covering my face in my hands. This did not need to be happening.

"You know, it's a lot more common to hear those words screamed out in ecstasy when I'm in bed with a woman. Not to mention, there is always a lot less clothing involved." He rolled onto his side to face me.

"Oh my god," I repeated. My face flushed, and I was certain I was bright red.

"It's still missing a certain oomph," he teased, "but we can work on it another time, when I can use both of my arms."

"Shut up." I slowly pulled my hands away from my face. "I am so sorry about last night. I just. I don't. I..." Words were not cooperating. I climbed out of bed, trying to distance myself and regain some semblance of professionalism.

"Hey. Calm down." He tried soothing since joking had clearly led to my currently frenzied state. "You had a nightmare. It's not a big deal." He gauged my reaction as I hastily flipped through the clothes hanging in my closet, just for something to do. "Plus, now we know the protection detail is actually doing more than watching football and eating pizza."

"Oh god," I repeated again. I'd have to apologize to them for the commotion last night too.

Martin laughed. At least someone found this whole thing amusing. "I'll leave you alone now." He unsuccessfully tried to hide his laughter as he got out of bed.

Once he was gone, I slumped onto the bed. "Shit. Shit. Shit. Shit," I muttered. Get a grip, Parker. Nothing horrible happened, and given the nightmare, waking up in his arms completely embarrassed was definitely preferable to my subconscious alternative. Perhaps I was overreacting. It wasn't like we *slept* together.

Selecting the most dignified outfit I could find, I spent as much time in the bathroom as possible, showering and dressing, just to avoid the situation a little longer. When I emerged perfectly coifed and looking the part of security consultant, he raised a questioning eyebrow.

"Job interview?" He gestured to an empty seat at the table. He had ordered breakfast and was already halfway through his.

"No," I replied cautiously, "just hoping to keep the one I currently have."

He shrugged away my comment with a wave of his fork. "I wouldn't worry about it. The guy you're working for isn't too unreasonable." He referred to himself in the third person. "It makes him feel better to know he's not the only human in the room." He dropped the joking. "Are you handling this okay?" he asked sincerely.

"Nightmares come with the territory, but usually, I'm in the privacy of my own home."

He looked thoughtful. "I'm glad you weren't this time."

I didn't know what to make of the comment, so I chose to ignore it and dove into my breakfast. Before I even made a sizable dent, there was a knock at the door. I checked the peephole. It was Thompson and O'Connell.

"Just in time for breakfast," I said, opening the door and

gesturing them inside.

Thompson glanced at his watch. "It's almost lunchtime."

"No breakfast for you then." I went back to the table, and O'Connell helped himself to a cup of coffee. As I resumed eating, the two detectives sat down.

"What brings you here this fine morning, or should I say afternoon?" Martin asked. Despite his last conversation with O'Connell, he was trying to be friendlier.

"Was everything okay here last night?" O'Connell asked. "We got a call about a disturbance, which was promptly followed by another call saying it was a false alarm." My cheeks heated up, and I ducked my head, staring intently at my plate as I continued eating.

"Just peachy." Martin's friendly tone turned venomous. "I'd prefer if, in the future, you didn't traumatize my security."

I sighed and put my fork down.

"Are you okay, Parker?" O'Connell asked.

"Nothing I can't handle," I interjected. I didn't need Martin fighting for me, especially when I had willingly agreed to go back to the house.

"It paid off though," Thompson remarked, defusing the tension. "The information you provided was enough to encourage the two paramilitary types to concede on a few of the finer details. Needless to say, if you shake the tree hard enough, you might get more than a couple of coconuts."

Intrigued, I alternated my glances from Thompson to O'Connell, waiting for one of them to elaborate.

"This is strictly need to know. We can't discuss an ongoing investigation, which I'm sure you're both well aware of," O'Connell provided his disclaimer. "So I can't tell you these freelance mercenaries were hired, not only for the hit at Martin's, but also for the kidnapping, bombing, and subsequently, the not so accidental murder of Denton's ex-girlfriend." Martin looked shocked while I searched my memory for the missing puzzle pieces.

"Jill?" I asked, dumbfounded by the revelation.

"Jillian Monroe, the bombing casualty," Thompson chimed in. "Obviously, not so casual. We ran a background on her. She used to strip under a different name, so we did some digging and found the connection between the two. Apparently, Denton had been a frequent visitor to the club where she worked. We ran with some photo IDs and verified she was Denton's one and only. Her phone records indicated she received a text message from a burner cell earlier that morning asking her to meet Denton out front. Financials and corroborating testimony from our favorite paramilitary mercenary group and—"

"You got him on multiple counts of conspiracy and murder." I stole the big reveal.

"It looks that way, but we can't really say. It's all official police business," O'Connell continued. "So I'm not telling you we have Denton for a laundry list of crimes from murder to conspiracy to B&E. The state plans to throw the book at him."

"Then it's over?" Martin asked, his posture becoming more relaxed in the chair. I was sure he was already planning on going back to work the moment O'Connell gave him the all clear.

"It looks that way. Give us some time to verify he has no other private accounts we haven't uncovered and no one else has been paid to make your life miserable," Thompson told him.

"What about Griffin?" I asked. Not all the loose ends were explained yet. "Was she a professional hit?"

O'Connell and Thompson exchanged a look. "We're still working on it. The mercs deny they were hired to do it. Maybe Denton did it himself, but we haven't been able to identify or locate the murder weapon," O'Connell admitted.

I tried to think. Denton's prints, along with Griffin's and Jackson's, were on the box. "Any prints at my place?" I asked, but O'Connell shook his head. "If there's a secondary contract killer, that might be who carried out the hit on Griffin."

"Do you think Blake will talk?" Martin asked. The cops looked at him as if he were mentally impaired.

"Not much incentive. We've already got too much on him. If he's half as smart as he seems to be, he'll keep his mouth shut and deny everything," O'Connell replied. Thompson and O'Connell got up to leave, and Martin thanked them for their time and hard work. I walked them to the door.

"After hearing about last night, I don't think you need a gun right now," O'Connell quietly said. He reached into his jacket pocket and removed a small object. "Just promise me you won't electrocute my guys."

"I'll do my best." I shut the door and looked at the taser. It wasn't much, but it'd work in a pinch.

Again, Martin was fighting with his pill bottle. Opening it, I handed him back the container. "It seems like things are coming to a close." He swallowed his pill, looking positively ecstatic.

"It's getting there," I said noncommittally. "They need to solve Griffin's murder before you go traipsing back to work. So I would suggest you use this time to recover. It's only been about a week since you had surgery." My heart leapt into my throat, and I swallowed. "Just give it some more time."

He agreed, acknowledging his own limitations.

* * *

I spent most of the day contemplating the murder of Suzanne Griffin. Griffin had been a part of Denton's plan. She had left the MT building before the explosion with various means of transportation away from the city and away from the scene of the crime. Denton had been with her at the B&B, and both of their prints were on the box recovered from my apartment. It seemed reasonable to assume Griffin had informed Denton who I was and why I was working for Martin, which led to him paying Jackson to take the photos.

All of the pieces fit nicely, but why kill her? Maybe it was because she knew too much and her loyalties seemed fickle. My guess would be if Martin had batted his green eyes at her, she would have caved and confessed to everything. Did Denton kill her himself? I thought about my nightmare with Denton holding the assault rifle. Real-life Denton would be just as willing to pull the trigger, especially given his predilection for hiring people to do it for him. The only problem was finding the weapon.

I was pacing the length of our hotel room, from my bedroom to the kitchen, when I noticed Martin was asleep on the couch. He had tired himself out by spending the bulk of the day calling Marcal and lining up contractors and architects to meet with him in the next week. He hoped to begin repairs on his compound as soon as possible. The fact that he was asleep now was just another indication he was not ready to go back to work, and he still needed more time to properly recover. Hopefully, he realized this and wouldn't overdo it too soon.

In desperate need of an escape from my thoughts and the confines of the room, I opened the door and slipped into the hallway. Now was as good a time as any to apologize to our protection detail. I knocked on their door, and one of the guys answered, grinning.

"If it isn't sleeping beauty," he joked.

"I just wanted to thank you for the prompt response last night." I stared at the floor. "I um...it's...." I looked up at the cop.

"We get it," his partner said from inside the room.

"Okay." I turned on my heel, ready to retreat.

"Just for clarification, if we hear screams, but no one entered the room, should we still come busting in?"

"Might as well, just to be on the safe side."

The guys were willing to obey my request, and hopefully, they wouldn't be inadvertently tazed for their trouble.

After last night, Martin deserved a chance to get some sleep without me disturbing him, so I stayed outside our room, pacing the length of the hallway. In the middle of my pacing, the elevator dinged and a maid exited. The protection detail emerged and checked her and the cart to make sure everything was kosher. She cleaned their room and asked if we needed anything. We were okay, so she headed back to the elevator.

The entire exchange reminded me of the surveillance footage of my office being broken into. A thought gnawed at the corners of my brain. I went back into my shared hotel room and slumped in the chair. Martin was still sound asleep, but my brainstorming wouldn't wake him up unless he was telepathic.

The break-in at my office occurred at least three days before Griffin was murdered. So why was I convinced the janitor's cart and the missing murder weapon were linked? *My brain must not be working properly*, I thought as I stared at the upholstery and picked at a stray thread. Going into my room, I shut the door and phoned O'Connell.

"Did you check Denton's office?" I asked.

"Yeah, we didn't find anything."

"Did you check Griffin's office?"

He was getting agitated. "You know, they don't hand out detective's badges based on good looks alone," he remarked.

"Did you check her other office?"

"What other office?"

"The one on the fifteenth floor, next to Denton's." With extension 325, but I kept that to myself.

"We'll check it out," he promised, but before he could hang up, I continued with my last few remaining thoughts.

"Maybe you could lean on Jackson. Martin had the metal detectors rigged to allow security and the like to enter without tripping the alarm. Depending on her TOD, maybe he carried the gun back into the building for Denton. He wouldn't have tripped any alarms." It was a stretch because Todd Jackson had been in custody before I found my apartment ransacked, but Griffin could have been murdered Monday night prior to his arrest. It was worth investigating since I didn't know exactly how long Griffin had been out in the dumpster.

"It couldn't hurt," O'Connell mused. "Any other brilliant ideas?"

"Did Agent Jablonsky ever give you the photo enhancement from the day of the manufacturing sabotage?" I still had no idea where Mark was or what he was doing. It was work related because, given the circumstances, he would have checked in if he could.

"Actually, yeah. I received an e-mail attachment two

days ago. The watch in the picture might be a match to Denton's, but the quality of the image makes it a crapshoot. It's not conclusive when compared to everything else we already have on him."

I nodded, even though he couldn't see it. "Okay. Well, that's my two cents."

THIRTY-NINE

A few days later, Thompson and O'Connell came to deliver the good news in person. The murder weapon used on Suzanne Griffin was found in the MT building in the desk of her fifteenth floor office. Todd Jackson insisted he had no idea how it got there, but twenty-five grand should buy more than a few photos and moving a box from one room to another. The gun had been wiped clean, and the serial number was filed off. But a partial print had been found on a bullet casing in the magazine. The partial print was a three-point match to Denton's fingerprints, and given its location, it wasn't too much of a stretch to assume Blake Denton had used it in the commission of Griffin's murder.

Most likely, Denton intended to set Jackson up as a scapegoat. Jackson had broken into my office. He had access to the box left in my ransacked apartment. The stolen funds from MT had filtered back into his private account, or at least twenty-five grand had. Then the blocked phone calls, followed by the stalker-like photos that were e-mailed to Martin, all culminated with Griffin's murder weapon being taken back into the MT building by Todd Jackson. This would have made a very nice frame-up job had the mercenaries been successful and Denton hadn't pulled that bullshit act at the banquet, making it onto my radar. Luckily for us, Denton's own paranoia and trigger-happy escapades worked in our favor instead of his.

"We just need to make sure the 'I's are dotted and the

'T's are crossed," Thompson said, but Martin didn't hear a word. He had a faraway look and was experiencing his own euphoria by finally being divested of this mess. "The DA's office is finalizing the case now. You'll have testimonies and depositions to deal with, but it's a small price to pay, given the outcome."

To my surprise, Martin nodded. Maybe he actually was listening.

"Just between us," O'Connell turned to me, "how'd you know?"

"How'd I know what?"

"You had it pieced together, or mostly pieced together, without any hard evidence. And the gun, how'd you know it would be in the office?"

"It was the only thing that made any sense." I couldn't rationalize or explain my gut feelings. "What I still don't understand is why he didn't dump the gun. Why keep it around?"

"We've speculated on that too. The only thing we could come up with is maybe he was hoping it would add to the frame-up. Denton clearly wanted to pin the murder on Jackson, but the whole thing fell apart before he got the chance," Thompson interjected.

"We'll let you get back to whatever you were doing," O'Connell said, standing up, and Thompson followed suit. "We'll be in touch." They let themselves out of the room.

Martin let out the breath he'd been holding for the last month and a half, and I could visibly see the weight lift from his shoulders. "You did a damn good job," he said, flashing his brightest smile. I didn't quite agree with his assessment, but I kept my mouth shut. Now was not the time to argue. He noted my lack of cheering. "What?" He knew he didn't want to hear whatever I had to say.

"I think..." I wanted to be diplomatic, but I couldn't come up with the proper terms.

"I know what you're going to say." He held up his hand. "Don't worry. The doctors won't clear me to work for another couple of weeks. My house is...well, I don't really have any place to live, and the media circus surrounding this will be a bitch." I raised an eyebrow in confusion. "The point I'm trying to make is I'd like you to stay on as my private security for the next two weeks, maybe a month, until everything gets straightened out."

"No one else is gunning for you, but you have me for as long as you need."

He offered a crooked smile. "I might always need you, Alex."

"What you need is to hire an actual full-time bodyguard. Mark can recommend someone trustworthy," I suggested, and he looked thoughtful. "Are you going to live at your house after the repairs are completed?"

"Of course. It's getting renovated. I'll change some things around, but it's home."

"Then might I suggest having a safe room installed." I was just full of great ideas today.

"I'll take it under advisement." He winked.

*   *   *

The next two weeks flew by at light speed. Martin met with contractors and architects, who started on the repairs and restructuring his compound. Marcal was given the task of supervising and making sure everything shaped up properly. Martin kept himself busy by coordinating press releases through the public relations department at Martin Technologies. The other board members, the ones who didn't try to kill him, had been instrumental in reassuring shareholders the company remained in good working order, despite the homicidal maniac who had been vice president. The stocks declined slightly but stabilized, much to Martin's relief.

After Mark completed his undercover assignment for the OIO, he spent quite a bit of time holed up in the presidential suite with us, searching for an appropriate bodyguard for Martin. I was adamant the man be named Bruiser, but unfortunately, Mark didn't know any Bruisers. I wasn't completely unreasonable, and as long as whoever was offered the job was willing to legally change his name, that would be acceptable.

While Martin was busy dealing with meetings and press

releases, I called my insurance company to have the damages in my apartment assessed. A check was in the mail. Once again, I was facing unemployment, but things weren't quite so bleak this time. Martin paid me handsomely, even though I felt partially incompetent and one hundred percent responsible for him being shot. Despite my obvious flaws, I decided rather spur of the moment to start my own investigation and consulting firm and filed the paperwork for a private investigator's license. The only rule was absolutely no more bodyguard work ever.

There was a small office space for rent at a strip mall, and I called the real estate office and expressed my interest. All I needed to do was sign the paperwork. Things were shaping up for everyone. Life was returning to normal, and I was beginning to dread that notion. Normal could be a lonely existence. I had lived with James Martin for over a month. Solitude would be an adjustment.

"I ordered champagne," Martin declared as we sat at the table, eating dinner. Tomorrow, he was going back to work, and I was going home. "I thought we should celebrate the excellent job you did."

I smiled sadly. "Martin, you almost died. That is not an excellent job. In fact, I'm pretty sure that's the opposite of excellent."

"I lived because of you." He took my hand in his. "You figured this whole thing out. You stopped Denton. You found the gun. You did everything I hired you to do. You got my life back."

"No, I'm alive because of you," I corrected, borrowing from his own declaration.

"We are not arguing about this." He dropped the subject. "Plus," he adopted a wolfish grin, and his eyes sparkled, "I'm no longer your employer."

I laughed. "You are unbelievable."

"So I've been told." There was a swagger to his voice, and I was beginning to feel a bit uncomfortable when the knock at the door provided a wonderful interruption.

"I'll get it since I still work for you," I said pointedly, and the room service guy rolled in a cart with champagne and strawberries. I sighed audibly at the cliché.

"Can't blame a guy for trying." He poured the champagne, and he clinked his glass with mine. "To you," he toasted.

I took a sip. I would miss Martin, even his irritating, drive-me-up-the-wall expressions and habits.

The next morning, he dressed and left for the office, his arm still in a sling. He said I could stay as long as I liked, but it was time to go home. I retrieved my car and left the posh hotel. On the way, I stopped and signed the lease for my new office which had been in the works for the last couple of weeks.

Pulling into the parking lot outside my apartment, I reminded myself the place was an utter disaster. I checked my mailbox and carried an insane amount of mail up the six flights of stairs. Thankfully, I had automatic bill pays for all of my expenses.

Unlocking my door, I was confronted by the destruction and the remnants of the crime tech's investigative tools. "I came home, why?" I asked my empty apartment.

Setting the mail down on the only empty counter space I could find, I pulled out a huge garbage bag. Beginning in the kitchen, I methodically discarded anything that was destroyed. Everything else was tossed into the sink to be cleaned at a later point. I called a haul-away service to get rid of my couch, bed, and other ruined furniture. I needed to go shopping and replace a lot of things.

Almost seven hours passed. I was getting ready to start on the bedroom when the phone rang. "Want to get dinner?" Martin asked, and I smiled.

"You miss me already?" I teased, looking around my room.

"Of course. Bruiser just isn't as sarcastic. He doesn't keep me on my toes the way you did. Plus, he can't pull off a dress very well." I couldn't help but laugh. "Come on, meet me. You have to eat. I have to eat." How could I argue with that kind of reasoning?

"Fine, but I swear to god, if gunmen try to rob the joint, I will hold you personally responsible." I flashed back to my interview.

"No gunmen. You can even pick the place."

I looked around my apartment. I had no furniture and very few nice things left. "How do you feel about a diner?" Eating cheaply would be a priority until everything was replaced.

He agreed to meet at the place around the corner from my building. I changed out of my clothes and into one of the clean, new outfits Marcal had supplied. Then I headed down the street to wait for him.

We sat in a booth and ate cheeseburgers and fries. It wasn't an elegant dinner, but he didn't complain. "What did you do today?" he asked, and I explained the attempt to clean my apartment. He listened intently, and when I was finished, he looked thoughtful. After paying the check, he asked Marcal to bring the car around, and I noticed Bruiser in the passenger seat.

"You took my advice." I was astounded.

"I had to. You're a damn good security consultant," he complimented. "Now get in the car."

"I'm just a couple of blocks from here. I don't need a ride."

"Come back to the hotel. Your room's empty, and you left half the clothes in the closet. You can't stay at your place with no furniture." He was being the voice of reason, but it seemed strange to return to the hotel when we said our good-byes yesterday. "It's what friends do," he insisted. "I even promise to be a perfect gentleman, if that's what you want."

"Fine, but only tonight. My new furniture is getting delivered tomorrow."

*   *   *

The next day, a new mattress and box spring were delivered, along with a sofa and love seat. I was sitting on the floor in my bedroom with Kate, and we were sorting through the piles of clothes strewn about the room. If it was ripped, it was tossed into the large black trash bag, and if it wasn't, it was tossed into the large white trash bag for sorting before being washed in the laundry or sent to the dry cleaner. Kate had agreed to help if I supplied the pizza and wine.

"You mean to tell me you never slept with him?" she asked, tossing another blouse into the garbage bag.

"Kate," I said patiently, "I worked for him. We weren't like that."

"I would have been." She grinned evilly. "Did you see those eyes and that body? Grr-rowl."

I rolled my eyes and grabbed another slice of pizza from the box. As if on cue, my phone rang.

"Hello?" It was Martin calling, but I didn't want to give her another reason to tease me.

"Did the furniture arrive?" he asked.

"Yeah, it's here, all nice and assembled. Kate's here too, helping to clean up."

"That's good," he sounded distracted. "I just wanted to make sure you didn't need a place to stay."

"I appreciate it." We stayed on the phone for a moment, not saying a word. "I'll let you get back to work."

"Okay. Dinner next week, pencil me in." He hung up before I could reply.

"Who was that?" she asked, suspecting it was him.

"Just a friend," I responded, trying not to let my expression betray me.

We finished eating and cleaning my apartment. I had a large pile of clothes to bring to the dry cleaner in the morning and about ten loads of laundry to do tonight. After she left, I got started on the laundry and looked around my residence. Maybe it was because I hadn't been here in so long or that the sanctity of my apartment had been violated, but either way, it no longer felt like home.

FORTY

Martin and I were having our ritual weekly dinner. This had been going on ever since we closed the case. We were discussing our upcoming court appearances and testimonies.

"Sounds like the fun is just beginning," he surmised, but he didn't seem to mind all the legal appearances. He had gotten his life back. He was working like a man possessed and loving every minute of it.

"How's the arm?" I asked.

It was still in a sling, but he was going to physical therapy. There had been some talk of a follow-up surgery, but things were still uncertain at this point.

"It's getting there, little by little. The nerve damage will take the longest to repair, if it can be," he said. *Great way to put a damper on the evening, Parker*, I berated myself. "I'm going out of town next week, so I'll have to take a rain check on dinner. It's a business trip. I have to finalize an overseas acquisition since I'm still looking for Denton's replacement."

"I'd suggest you don't hire anyone who wants to kill you."

"That was really insightful," he replied sarcastically, and I shrugged.

"And I got paid the big bucks, how stupid do you feel now?"

We finished eating and left the restaurant. He gave me a hug before getting into his town car and driving away.

* * *

I was standing in my new office, trying to hang some pictures on the wall. I only moved into the building a few days ago, but I wanted to get things up and running as soon as possible. It would probably be a couple of months before I was hired, considering the economy and my unknown status in the world of private eyes and security consultants. The only bright star was being able to name-drop Martin if I needed a reference.

The bell above my door dinged, and I turned, expecting to find someone asking about a public restroom or directions to the donut shop that used to occupy my office space. To my surprise, it was Martin, dressed in his signature business attire.

"What are you doing here?" I asked, astonished.

He surveyed the small office space and my cheap press-wood furniture. "Sparse," he commented.

"It's enough to get started."

He looked around, assessing the rest of the room, and I sat down in my rolling office chair, waiting for him to explain his presence. He reached into his jacket pocket and pulled out a folded stack of papers. He sat in my client chair across from me and carefully unfolded the paper.

"Alex," he looked up, very serious, "I'd like to keep you on retainer for consulting and investigation." I looked down at the pile of papers. It was a retainer contract for Martin Technologies. "Obviously, it wouldn't be a full-time gig, but we'd pay you a monthly stipend. And as issues arise, you can address them. I've added a clause allowing for expenses and incidentals." I stared at the contract. After everything that happened, I couldn't believe he was serious. "Oh, and absolutely no bodyguard work necessary." He flashed a smile.

I rubbed my neck, considering the offer. "I don't know what to say."

"Think about it." He stood up. "Like I said, I'm gone for the week, but when I get back, we can discuss it some more. You know how much I like negotiations." He walked around to my side of the desk and leaned against it. "Just so we're clear, you won't be working for me. You'll be working for the company."

"You are the company. Or the company is you. Whatever."

He tilted his head back and forth in a so-so fashion. "The company is much greater than just me. In fact, it's not even like I'd be your employer. Martin Tech would be your employer." He smirked, but I was smart enough to realize he simply found another way to rephrase his previous statement.

"I think you're splitting hairs."

He ran his left hand through my hair, grasping the back of my neck and gently kissing me on the mouth. *Why not?* I thought. I shut my eyes and returned the kiss. He pulled away finally, a self-satisfied grin on his face, but he seemed a bit surprised by my reaction. He turned and went to the door.

"Just remember, I don't date my employer," I retorted, and he spun around.

"We'll see, especially since I won't really be your employer." His eyes danced.

"This is not a unilateral decision you get to make," I responded as he walked out the door, waving good-bye. I watched him get into the car and drive away. "What the hell." I picked up the pen and signed the contract. Things couldn't be any more harrowing than they were the first time around.

DON'T MISS THE NEXT INSTALLMENT IN
THE ALEXIS PARKER SERIES.

THE WARHOL INCIDENT IS NOW
AVAILABLE IN PRINT AND AS AN E-BOOK

ABOUT THE AUTHOR

G.K. Parks is the author of the Alexis Parker series. The first novel, *Likely Suspects,* tells the story of Alexis' first foray into the private sector.

G.K. Parks received a Bachelor of Arts in Political Science and History. After spending some time in law school, G.K. changed paths and earned a Master of Arts in Criminology/Criminal Justice. Now all that education is being put to use creating a fictional world based upon years of study and research.

You can find additional information on G.K. Parks and the Alexis Parker series by visiting our website at
www.alexisparkerseries.com

Made in the USA
Columbia, SC
02 July 2023

19674916R00176